The Last Road Trip

by

Megan Zalkan

The Last Road Trip

Cover Art by *Tina Lynn Stout*

The Wild Rose Press, Inc.
PO Box 708
Adams Basin, NY 14410-0708
Visit us at www.thewildrosepress.com

Publishing History
First Edition, 2024
Trade Paperback ISBN: 978-1-5092-5852-9
Digital ISBN 978-1-5092-5853-6

Published in the United States of America

Dedication

To Sofie and Brett, who make the stories come alive.

Part One: Davenport, Iowa

Chapter One

August 15, 2024
Dear Em,
The world is ending in eight short weeks, and I can't decide which I'm more afraid of—dying when the comet hits, or never getting a chance to apologize for ruining your life.

God, I wish you were here. Nothing has made sense since you left, but it's even worse now. Everyone here in Iowa is losing their minds. People are rioting, neighbors leave in the middle of the night. At least school is permanently over. Just imagine if I had to spend the last eight weeks of my life in trigonometry, using tangents and cosines to figure out the comet's distance from Earth. I'd be praying for it to hit sooner.

Mom and Dad are staying put on the farm, which is good, because I'm hoping maybe you're on your way back. It's the literal end, Em—if not now, when? You were eighteen the last time I saw you, and I was only eleven. Six years later, and we're all about to die.

None of the coping skills I've tried have helped. Not denial, crying, binge eating. Not even screaming at the night sky till my throat goes hoarse. I thought curling up in the fetal position under my duvet might do the trick, but no. None of it helps.

I counted today and I've written you over a hundred letters since you left. Never sent any of them because I've never known where to send them to. They just sit here in these notebooks. I guess you can count on a few more before time runs out. Writing to you makes me feel a little better, calmer. Maggie says I live in a fantasy world, and I guess she's probably right. But it's a lot nicer in there than it is out here in reality.

So that's the plan. I'll keep writing.

I'm so sorry, Em, for the hundredth time. I'll be sorry until the day I die. Which will be in exactly eight weeks, so that's nice and tidy.

I love you. I wish you'd come home before the end.

Love, Lou

****

I found out about the comet at the worst possible moment—gripping the steering wheel with sweaty palms as I tried not to fail my driver's test. There I sat, cracking stupid, nervous jokes, doggedly coming to a full stop at every white line and corner. The driving examiner, a stern-looking little man in gold-rimmed glasses, sat beside me with a clipboard, making noises like "hrm" and "ahem" and sometimes "oh my" when I did something especially alarming. The scent of my panic sweat slowly filled the car; neither of us acknowledged it.

Like most farm kids, I'd been driving in one form or another for years. I could drive the tractor across a field at thirteen, and I knew how to drive the old scooter that lived in the barn. But driving on a street with lights, and signs, and other cars? Totally different.

The test wasn't going very well, which is why it was almost a relief when my instructor's cell phone suddenly blared out one of those emergency alert tones. Like when a kid or an old person goes missing. We both jumped. I stomped on the brake in traffic and nearly got rear-ended. The man quickly directed me to pull over until the ungodly shrieking noise stopped.

I swerved toward the curb, accidentally taking up half of two different spots, and then looked over at my instructor, ready to apologize for my parking skills. But he was staring at the phone, face gray, eyes wide. He poked at it a few times, clearly opening some kind of link, and I once again cursed the fact that I was the only kid in my grade not allowed to have a phone.

"What? What is it?" I asked. The test wasn't over, was it? Had I failed? I really wanted this license.

He cleared his throat and straightened up. "It's—there's been—well, I think we better switch seats. I'll take you back to the office. Things might get a little crazy out here."

I hopped out, mystified, and we swapped. He eased his ancient Buick out, nosing around cars randomly abandoned in the street, double parked with no thought to safety. People on the sidewalk were acting strange, clustered in groups on the sidewalks, most of them looking at their phones, some gesticulating wildly. I couldn't tell for sure from the quick glimpse I got, but it looked like some of them were crying.

"Can I see?" I asked. "I mean, it's an automatic fail if I touch a phone during the test, but you're driving now, right?"

He waved a hand, the ultimate study in distraction as he carefully maneuvered around one stopped car after another, heading back across town to where my mother was waiting. "Go ahead. You pass. It doesn't matter."

He passed me the phone, and I skimmed through the first few paragraphs.

Comet. Large one. Icy with a huge rocky iron core. Officially called Comet C/2024 N1; unofficially called Comet Lucinda in honor of the scientist who held the dubious honor of identifying it. Previously deemed not a threat. Sudden inexplicable change of course. Heading straight for Earth. Exploring options. Potential extinction level event. Do not panic.

I shut my eyes as a wave of dizziness rode over me, and almost without meaning to, a prayer started spilling out of me. God, make this not be real. Please, let this be a joke or something. Maybe some radio station or movie studio was behind it? It could be a promotion gimmick, right?

Please, please, please. Make this not be real.

****

A week later, none of us held any further illusions about this being a prank.

I closed the notebook I'd been writing to Emmett in, then pried up the cover on the air conditioning shaft in my bedroom to add the notebook to the small pile I'd been hiding there for years. Five composition books, one for each year, their covers battered and their spines destroyed, pages half loose and wavy from frequent handling. I slid the newest one on top by rote and numbly put the vent cover back in place, using my thumbnail to turn the screws enough so that nothing would jar it out of place.

I'd barely returned to my bed and was contemplating whether it was too early for a nap when my mother swung the door open without knocking or waiting for permission.

That was close. I knew better than to let her find the letters. Emmett was beyond a sore subject around our house; he was a nonentity. Mentioning his name once was a sure way to shut down any conversation. Mention it twice and I'd get sent to my room. If she knew I'd filled notebooks with letters to him, who knows what would happen?

"You're still in bed?" She cast a critical eye over me, then smiled and leaned over to tug gently at one of my feet beneath the worn quilt her mother had made. "Come on, you know church starts in twenty minutes. Get up and get moving."

I sighed. "Mom, you know I don't want to go. What does it matter?"

I was doing my best to believe none of this was actually happening. The government would find some way to prevent the impact. The world couldn't really end, could it? Not when I was just seventeen? Something, someone, had to be preparing to save us. Or maybe my powers of hiding away in a fantasy world, honed by hundreds of hours spent with my nose in a book, were stronger than I had ever realized.

Sympathy flashed across her face before she shuttered it down again. "Church matters more than ever right now. Please get dressed, and I'll see you downstairs in a few minutes."

She shut the door behind her, and I listened to her footsteps thump down the creaking old staircase before I gave up and stood. Some things were not worth fighting. Mom found peace in the church right now; it was the only time she didn't look like she was about to cry. I couldn't make her understand it was different for me.

Scowling, I dug around in my closet for something clean that wasn't farm-wear. Our church, which had grown increasingly conservative over the years, believed girls should wear dresses, which made me want to punch someone. Reluctantly, I dragged on my one decent skirt—shapeless denim, cut unfashionably below the knees—and a striped, short sleeve top that met the letter of the church's rules without looking the least bit feminine. I dragged my frizzy, rust-colored hair back into its usual braid.

"Lou, come on!" My mother sounded on the verge of angry, so I gave up and clomped as loudly as I could down the stairs, wishing I was anywhere else, to where she was waiting for me by the front door.

Time to go.

****

Our church was one of those small country ones with a charismatic leader and a congregation with enthusiastic opinions on education, critical race theory, and whether the devil was hiding in Harry Potter novels. Collectively, we championed traditional heterosexual families with strong, silent men waiting for a heart attack and wives with their arms full of pies and babies, dreaming of Valium. We believed Jesus was coming back, and the Rapture was a wondrous event awaiting the faithful.

I'd believed all this once, too. It's hard not to when you're raised on it, attending services every week on Sunday and sometimes Wednesdays too, spending your summers at bible camp, and showing up for the occasional weeknight at youth group. It sinks in. I never really questioned most of it.

At least, not before Emmett left.

Since then? I'd slowly realized that my church was highly suspect. There were so many contradictions. Love your neighbor, honor your parents, care for your

6

children, but kick them out if they decide they like someone of the same gender? The church supported my parents and viewed them as having made a heroic sacrifice by doing what they'd done to my brother. The congregation prayed that he'd overcome his sinful ways and return to the fold. It was complete and utter bullshit. Emmett wasn't sinning. He was better than all of them.

As I followed my parents into our usual pew near the front of the church, I studied the faces around me. Things had gotten strange here since the comet announcement. A few people looked appropriately shell-shocked, but mostly, the congregation seemed oddly jubilant.

I stared down at the gold-colored carpeting as the reverend rambled on about the Rapture, this idea that Lord Jesus himself was riding in on the comet like some kind of space cowboy, ready to gather us all up like a herd of wandering sheep with his holy lasso. How we'd all been waiting for this day! Seven weeks from now, we'd be sucked up into Heaven, leaving our clothes behind for the disbelievers to puzzle over, to spend eternity being rewarded for being so, so good.

Personally, I didn't believe it for one second. I'd learned enough about good and evil in the last few years to know we weren't any better than anyone else. If Cowboy Jesus was truly riding in on the comet, he was in for some disappointment when he got to my town.

Still, the congregation doubled down in a weird, fatalistic celebration. Services that used to be a half hour were now an hour long, and daily. The women of the church were serving communal meals in the church basement every evening. Some of the most devout were even sleeping in pop-up tents in the churchyard, like they couldn't bear to leave. So far, we'd stayed put on the farm, but my father had been eyeing the tents with interest.

"Lou!" Mom nudged me as the congregation rose for the first hymn. I stood and accepted the red hymnal she stuffed into my hands but didn't really sing along. I mumbled enough to make it look like I was taking part, but mostly I stared at the stained-glass window at the front of the church, all purple and blue. It sat behind the organ and the small pew for the choir, just behind the preacher. He wore a long, white robe with a tasseled stole around his neck, and as the singing stopped, he started up again. His eyes bulged as he went on in his powerful voice about how lucky we were to be alive at such a wondrous time when God would gather us closer.

Lucky? Wondrous?

I was done. A wave of nausea rolled over me as I stared at my fellow church-goers. I didn't know how I wanted to spend the short time I had left, but it wasn't here, listening to this nonsense and pretending to agree.

Mom turned to me as I stirred, giving me a quick glare.

"I'll see you at home," I whispered.

She looked shocked, but I slid out the side of the pew and was gone before either of them could stop me.

The sun seemed brighter as I stood on the front steps of the church, alone. I flung my arms out and sucked in a deep breath of late summer air, smelling dust and dry grass and a faint scent, somewhere, of cow. Then I grabbed a bicycle from the rack out front and headed for home. No one locked their bicycles here, and stealing didn't seem like a big deal right now. What did it matter who it belonged to at this point? The world was ending.

People had bigger things to worry about.

****

I dropped the stolen bike around the back of the tool shed—no need to advertise my thievery to the world, however immune I might feel—and headed straight for the big red barn where the animals lived.

We hadn't talked much about what was going to happen to the farm when the end came. The Compton Petting Zoo was well populated, if sparsely attended these days by actual living customers. Goats, chickens, rabbits, even alpacas. You name it, we had it. The stars of the show, though, were the four tired horses who gave pony rides to the kids, and the three goats, who were extra good at learning tricks. My job had always been to feed all these creatures. Over time, I'd taken on the job of training those that could learn to perform in ways that would make customers laugh and leave good tips.

But now? I still fed and brushed and tended to them because they were members of the family. They weren't in any danger of becoming food. We had a meat locker and plenty of produce laid in from the summer garden, more than enough to get us through the next two months. But I was torn. Should they die captives here in the barn? Was it kind or cruel to set them free before impact day?

"Maybe I should let you all go," I murmured, nuzzling the head of Mitch the donkey. "Would you be okay if I let you loose in the world?"

"Probably not," a strange voice behind me said. "You know he's as dumb as a goblin."

I whirled around and saw… no one. Just the clucking chickens scratching in the dirt and Bazooka the goose, who flapped his wings out in a display of random aggression directed at no one. This was pretty much normal behavior for him.

"Who said that?" I called, the hair on my arms standing up as I eyed the dark corners of the barn. I walked toward the open door, expecting to find someone from the church who'd followed me home to bring me back lingering outside. But there was no one in sight.

"Oh, come on, I know you're smarter than that," the voice said behind me again.

When I turned, Bazooka stood front and center, fixing me with his beady gaze.

A cold sheen of sweat broke out on the back of my neck. I took a step forward. "Did... did you..."

Bazooka bobbed his neck. "Yes, I did. Oh now, don't faint on me. I'm not sure I can keep the goats from eating you if you do."

My legs crumpled, and I sat in the dirt, cross-legged. "Bazooka?"

"Yes. And also, no."

I shook my head. "What does that mean? What's happening? You can't talk, you're a goose. You... you bite me all the time."

Bazooka made a dry, rattling sound that sounded almost like a laugh. "Your goose friend here is quite the comedian. I'm almost enjoying being stuck inside of him."

"Stuck inside of him?"

Awkwardly, like a marionette driven by a puppeteer unfamiliar with where all the strings were, the goose I knew as Bazooka stepped forward and stretched one wingtip toward me in a gesture reminiscent of a handshake. "Nice to meet you, Lou, is it?" it said. "I'm Falthaom the Repulsive, son of Lamech, but you can call me Bazooka if it's easier. I'm from the ethereal realms, and I'm temporarily stuck inside your goose. Perhaps we can help each other?"

I stopped breathing entirely as time stretched out and folded back in on itself. I suddenly understood what dissociation might mean, as part of myself stepped back and watched in shock as I, ever the good Midwestern girl raised to have manners, reached out and took careful hold of the offered wing tip.

"Nice to meet you," I said, shaking hand to wing.

Bazooka, or Falthaom the Repulsive, or whoever he was cackled again and let out a spectacular honk.

And then I fainted.

Chapter Two

August 20, 2024
Dear Em,
Forty-nine days until impact, and as you might expect, things are getting weird. Pastor Freeland has founded a tent city in the back of the church. He says we need to move in and meet the end together as a community of faith. What's crazy is that people are actually doing it! Two of our neighbors already abandoned their houses and farms, let their animals loose and moved there. Half of their chickens and horses wandered onto our property, and now I'm feeding them. Which is fine—you can always fold a few new chickens into a flock even if our goose seems kind of pissed off about it.

Our goose... well, that's a whole other story, and I'm still not sure I'm not hallucinating it. I'll save that for another time.

Anyway, the scary thing is, I think Mom and Dad are thinking about joining them in the tents. There's a lot of praying and whispering going on at home, the kind that stops the second I walk into a room. And the other day after church, one lady took Mom out to the tent city to "show her around." Then the praying and whispering at home kicked into overdrive.

I'm worried. I don't want to die, but I especially don't want to die in a refugee camp, away from the only home I've ever known. I want to be here, surrounded by my memories and all my stuff. Taking care of the animals and sleeping in my bed.

No one's said anything to me yet, but when they do, I'm going to refuse to go. They can go if they want—I'll stay here alone if I have to. If they make me go, I'll leave. I'll keep leaving, keep coming back here.

I mean... what if you do come back and we're gone?

I dream about it sometimes—that I wake up and look out the window and you're standing in the yard, backpack in hand. I pound down the stairs and fly out the front door to land on top of you in a heap, all hugs and tears. You tell me you forgive me and, of course, you're going to be here for the end. How could you not be?

I know it's unlikely. But the slim chance of seeing you again is better than nothing. And I'm not going to miss it to go sleep on a cot.

More soon.

Love, Lou

****

When I opened my eyes, Bazooka was still there, sitting near me, clucking quietly to himself. He looked like... a goose. He wasn't talking or giggling or doing anything strange. A wash of relief swept over me. Maybe I wasn't losing my sanity. Maybe everything was normal.

"Did I imagine that?" I asked.

"Nope," the goose said. "Wow, you're a dramatic one, aren't you? I didn't know people fainted anymore."

Oh, man. Apparently, my grasp on reality was weaker than I thought. I sat up and brushed the hay off my shirt and hair and considered my next move.

"So, you're what, a demon?" My voice remained

calm enough to smooth over my low-level panic.

This was the wrong opener. Bazooka stepped closer and hissed, his black tongue vibrating shrilly.

I skittered backward. "All right, all right! Calm down! Geez, what did I say?"

Bazooka settled, turning one beady eye on me. "I am NOT a demon, and if you ever say anything like that again, I'll kick you in the head."

I believed him. Even unpossessed, Bazooka could be aggressive. You had to approach him carefully, remind him you were a friend, before he would warm up and be his usual sweet self. If I did it wrong, he'd run at me with his wings out, ready to rumble.

"Okay, I didn't know," I said, making a conciliatory gesture. "So, uh, what are you, then? If you don't mind me asking."

"I'm an imp." Bazooka ruffled out his wings and shook his tail, smoothing everything into place and somehow striking a posture that looked proud.

I could tell I was supposed to be impressed, so I nodded wisely and lied through my teeth. "Ah, an imp. I, uh, thought maybe that was it."

He wasn't fooled. He gave off a rattly sigh and bobbed his head down low. "An imp," he repeated. "You know what an imp is, don't you?"

"Something like a gargoyle? Little guy? On roofs?"

Bazooka appeared too insulted to even attack me. "No, I'm not a *gargoyle*," he shrieked. "I'm a primordial nature spirit. One of the oldest in the world. I was here before humans were even planned. I'll be here after every one of you dies a fiery death! How dare you call me a—" He broke off, suddenly noticing the look on my face. "What?"

My reaction to his casual mention of death was immediate and brutal. My throat closed, and it was like all the feelings I'd been shoving under since I'd heard about the comet exploded out of me, all at once. Before I could blink, I was curled up with my knees pressed against my chest and the barn wall at my back. I squeezed my eyes shut, trying to stop the tears from emerging.

Crying wouldn't help. I knew. I'd tried.

"Oh, for fuck's—" his scratchy voice cut through. "Is this because—what in the seven Hells—?"

I swiped at my eyes with the back of one hand. "Sorry. I… You aren't going to have to wait long for that. The 'I'll be here after you're long gone' part."

The goose scratched at the dirt uncomfortably. "Well, I didn't mean that. It's a… what do you call it? A figure of speech. Oh, now come on, this is too much. Fainting, and now this?"

I took a deep breath. "I'm not usually this much of a hot mess. But, you know, the world is ending, and I'm stuck here on this farm, and I've never done anything, or seen anything, or kissed anyone, or g-gone to college, or—"

Bazooka carefully stepped next to me and then into my lap, the way the goose I loved had done a hundred times in the past. As much as he could be touchy, at the heart of him he was a sweet, sappy love bug when he felt safe. He loved to cuddle.

"What is this body doing?" he gasped. "I didn't agree to this."

The goose continued to ignore him, pressing himself against my torso and curling his head up over my shoulder in our favorite snuggling posture. Despite the discomfort of his uninvited passenger, I lifted a hand to scratch his neck the way I knew my Bazooka loved. And despite himself, the imp seemed to relax.

"I don't understand," he muttered. "Why are we doing this?"

"Shut up. This is what we do." I pulled out the big guns and reached for Bazooka's favorite spot, just in the center of his chest, and smoothed out the feathers there.

"Oh hell," Bazooka muttered, all but dissolving against me like a pile of gelatinous goo. "Why does that feel so good? This is so humiliating. I have standards, you know—"

"Shhhh," I whispered. "Just go with it."

The feeling of his warm body in my arms convinced me I wasn't imagining this. Something was really happening here in the barn. I tried to ignore the chorus of "this-can't-be-reals" that whirled like moths inside my head. It was the end of the world. All bets about what did and didn't make sense were probably off.

His chin settled in on my shoulder, and together we rocked.

****

"And please, Lord, forgive our daughter Lou for walking out of services this morning," Dad said, as we held hands and bowed our heads over our supper plates. He squeezed my hand meaningfully, and I tried not to sigh or roll my eyes. "Bless this food and help us hold firm to our faith in these trying times. Amen."

"Amen," Mom repeated.

I said nothing. It seemed like the wrong time to tell them we might have a possessed goose living in the barn. I kept that nugget of info to myself, since the possibility that my brain had snapped was equally likely. I didn't need their over-zealous concern.

"So," Dad said, helping himself to a prime slice of flank steak before passing the platter to my mother. "I know it's a difficult subject to think about, but we have some planning to do."

I looked up. "What kind of planning?"

He heaped potatoes on his plate and then spoke without looking at me. "The next two months. I think we should join the community at the church before all the other families take the remaining spaces."

"I knew it," I muttered, plopping a spoonful of steamed spinach onto my plate and considered. How could I get out of this? And if I couldn't, how many animals could I bring along? Could I bring Bazooka as my emotional support animal?

"You mean living there? Oh hon, I don't know," Mom said. Her nose wrinkled the tiniest bit. She wasn't much for camping. My parents had always joked that her idea of roughing it was sleeping on a pullout couch instead of a regular mattress.

My father leaned back. "I know neither of you loves the idea, but we'd be wise to take Pastor Freeland seriously. I like the idea of being as close to the church as possible."

I swirled my fork around, building a replica of Comet Lucinda out of a ball of potatoes and smearing a long tail of gravy behind it. I admired my artistic rendering, then used the same fork to swipe it into oblivion. When I looked up, both of my parents were watching me with looks of deep concern on their faces. I blinked and set my expression to the neutral blandness that usually kept me out of trouble.

"I know this is hard for you, Lou," Dad said, his

voice gentle. "It can't be easy to find yourself in the End Times when you're seventeen."

"End Times" was one of those phrases that my father somehow capitalized, even in speech.

I swallowed hard and pivoted away from the swimmy, disconnected feeling I was busy stuffing down. "What if it's not the end, though? Why are we all accepting this? What if someone blows it up, and it doesn't hit the Earth after all, and we've given up our house and lost all the animals and moved into a tent when we didn't have to?"

My mother reached for the tiny gold cross she always wore. "Then we come home. I'm sorry to say it, Lou, but your father might be right. And we can always replace the animals. And the house will still stand in seven weeks if we're wrong."

"I don't care, I'm not going to go live in a tent, even if the world does end," I continued, my eyes burning with either fury or imminent tears; I honestly couldn't tell. "Can't we just build a shelter in the basement or something?"

My parents looked at each other and that wordless communication that grownups are always doing passed between them, lightning speed.

I tried to stop. I really did. The struggle was immense. But the words built up in intensity, taking control of my mouth, so that all I could do was sit back and watch as they burst out of me.

"And what if Emmett comes back?"

Dead silence.

"We'd want him to find us, right? How will he do that if we aren't here?"

My mother stared helplessly at her plate. "Of course

we would, Lou. If he repents and comes back to join the fold before the end—and I pray every day that he does—you know we'd welcome him with open arms."

"And if he doesn't?" My voice sounded nasty, even to me. "Repent, I mean? Do we all just die without ever speaking to him again?"

My mother covered her face with her hands and my father put down his fork and faced me directly. "Lou. We did what we thought was right with your brother. It's a complex situation. Please don't make this harder for your mother."

"It should be hard!" I said. "We're pretending he doesn't exist, and that's screwed up on so many levels. We need to find him!"

The silence all but crackled with gathering lightning. I'd never gone so far before.

My father's voice took on a tone of finality. "I don't expect you to understand at this age. Please drop it."

I curled my hands into fists, fingernails biting into my palms, then pushed back my chair with a loud screech of wood on wood and ran up the stairs.

****

Of course, as a farm kid, having a snit didn't mean you got out of evening chores, so later that night I threw on my dirtiest overalls and my rubber boots and headed back out to the barn to feed and water everyone, lock in the chickens, and do everything else that had to be done to put the farm to bed.

I stopped outside the back door, looking around. It was one of those sweltering late August nights, the heat so oppressive it wrapped around me like a blanket. The cicadas sang with a deafening hum from a million hidden spots, and as I looked out across the fields of ripe corn, their golden stalks swayed in a breeze that was nowhere near strong enough to make a difference to anyone's comfort. I could hear the animals shifting around inside as I walked down the path to the barn.

Bazooka was waiting near the door, and followed me through my rounds, as I checked food and water bins, laid down fresh bedding, and gathered up droppings. He ran a nearly nonstop commentary on the animals as we visited them. The chickens were gossip mavens, he told me as I locked the coops against predators for the night. The alpacas—dumber than rocks and liked heavy metal music—they greeted my arrival with headbutts and affection. Apparently, the goats had a nickname for me he didn't want to tell me. Mitch, the donkey, was ever so slightly in love with me.

At least someone was. It's not like I'd had much of a romantic life, being the girl who always smelled like hay or something worse. The lack of interest went both ways, though. I hadn't found any of the boys at school appealing enough to raise my heart rate. My only real friend, Maggie, told me I was waiting for one of the characters from my books to come to life and sweep me off my feet. Mr. Darcy, striding over the Iowa cornfields, come to infuriate me into a heretofore unknown level of passion.

She might be right. I found the idea pretty appealing.

"Are you even listening to me?" Bazooka squawked, ramming his body into the side of my knee hard enough to wake me from my reverie.

I stepped aside to prevent a second attack. "Sorry, thinking. So, have you got powers?"

Bazooka ruffled his feathers and stood proud. "Of course I have powers."

"Like what?"

He tried to shrug the goose's shoulders. It sort of worked. "We get our powers from the element we were born from. I came from rock. Makes me strong, lets me change forms, and a bunch of other stuff you'd never understand."

I frowned. "So, then, how did you end up stuck in a goose?"

He made a sound like a sigh. "Good question. It's certainly not what I would've chosen. If I had to pick an animal to be crammed inside, I'd have chosen a stag or a snow leopard. Something worthy, you know?"

"I don't think geese are so bad."

He scoffed. "They're a total pain. I mean, I admire their fighting skills. But good gods, they're sentimental and clannish and driven to protect every living thing around them. Did you know this moron thinks it's the mother of all your chickens? It keeps making me gather them up!"

I laughed. "But you didn't tell me how this happened."

Bazooka craned his neck and started preening something in his right wing. I let the silence grow, determined to wait him out. Eventually, he peeked and saw me still staring at him.

"It was an accident. I didn't really know what had happened until I woke up here," he muttered, then he went off on another tangent, seemingly unable to stop himself. "And let me tell you, it was downright horrifying waking up inside a meat sack. Its vision is all weird, and before I got the hang of its musculature, I walked it right into a wall. Knocked us both out for an hour. And there's all these ropey bits, moving things around. And everything is moist."

I made a sympathetic face but didn't let him distract me. "How did you accidentally get stuck in my goose? Did you just trip?"

"Nooo.... It's more like someone who was kind of mad at me put me in here, and I can't get out for a while."

I snorted. "Who was mad at you?"

"An actual demon."

I put my bucket down with a thump, my breath suddenly speeding up. "This can't be good. You're telling me you have a literal demon who's after you? Are they going to come back here and mess with you? Are they going to hurt the other animals? I can't have some pissed off demon burning down my barn—"

He squawked and swung his wings wide in a display I was now recognizing as the goose/imp version of "please shut up".

"No," he said. "You don't need to worry about that anymore. She's gone. The demon."

"Where did she—" Then it hit me. The comet. "Oh. She's getting away before it hits, isn't she?"

He bobbed his head. "Yeah. Coward. Off for greener pastures. Of course, she'll probably come back eventually, depending on how many of you survive and whether there's enough of a planet left to offer her decent entertainment. They don't love the planet enough to stay if all the humans are gone."

I took that one in with a shudder. "Do you know anything about the comet, then? I mean, is it really going to hit? Is it as bad as they say?"

Bazooka fluttered his wings and soothed a few feathers back into place before answering. "It's definitely going to hit," he said. "Directly on course.

Beyond that, I can't tell you very much, except that it's very large, and it's not going to be a great experience for any of you here on the ground."

I sat on the dirt floor next to him. "And you don't have the power to, like, stop it… do you?"

He turned a beady eye toward me, opening and closing his bill several times before he answered. "I'm not powerful enough to stop that rock. Don't you think I would have told you if I could? I don't have many powers while I'm…" he flapped his wings irritably, "a damn waterfowl."

I sighed. "Okay, I had to ask."

He poked me with his bill. "This stupid body wants corn. Got any?"

I heaved myself back up and headed over to the feed bins to find some.

****

True to my word, I went along to church without a fuss two days later to keep my end of the bargain with my father—go to church, stay in the house. It turned out to be a good thing when my friend Maggie grabbed me as soon as we entered, and I got permission to go sit with her and her family. Maggie's family was staunchly religious, too. I'm sure Mom thought I couldn't get into too much trouble if I was with them.

We scooted as far away from her parents as we could get and huddled up before the service began. The organist was playing the prelude, missing the occasional note here and there, giving us enough cover to allow a private conversation.

"You okay?" Maggie said, sliding her hand into mine. Her eyes were red, like she'd been crying. But even with that, she looked pretty in ways I would never be, with her pale blond hair and gray eyes. She was small and willowy and all the things I wasn't, but somehow, I never felt jealous of her. She was too important to me for that to matter. "I haven't seen you since school didn't start."

I nodded. "My parents are being intense. Dad wants to move into the tents out back. I made a deal with them that if I stopped walking out of church, we could stay at home."

Maggie swiped a piece of hair out of her face and tucked it behind an ear. "Yeah, that's what I was going to tell you. We're moving in over the weekend."

I looked down at her hand in mine and tried to think.

"Do you want to come stay at my place instead?" I couldn't imagine her parents would allow it, but we'd try to make it work, somehow.

She shook her head. "No, I have to stay with them. I just…" Her voice wobbled. "I can't believe this is all happening. Do you really think we're all going to—" She cut herself off, unable to say it.

I squeezed her hand as the preacher stepped into the pulpit and the organ quieted down.

"Dunno," I whispered. "I'm scared."

"Me too."

I hunched my shoulders as the preacher began the welcome prayers, thinking over Maggie and her family moving into the church grounds. That this was my inevitable future nauseated me. I might have won a few days—a couple of weeks at most—but there was no way Dad wasn't eventually going to move us into the camp. I'd do my best to resist, but he'd win in the end. I don't know why it mattered to me so deeply; when the comet hit, I'd be equally dead at home as I would be in a tent.

But it did.

And I hadn't been joking the other night at dinner. What if Emmett came back?

Emmett. Always Emmett. As often happened in church, thoughts of my missing brother filled my head. Where was he? What had happened to him in the last six years, and what was happening right now? The newspapers were full of news of rioting, random violence, looting, all across the country. Food supplies were becoming sporadic as gas supplies dwindled and shell-shocked truckers walked off the job. Gas was running low, and the military had taken most of what remained.

Was Emmett safe?

I closed my eyes during the prayers, mostly to fit in, but if the word of God touched me at all in that moment of stillness, it was only to strengthen my need to find my brother. This couldn't be right. With the end coming so quickly, there had to be something we could do to find him.

I waited until the offering, when people were passing plates and greeting their neighbors, making enough noise to cover me, then I scooted in close to Maggie again.

"Can I stop by later and use your internet? I need to look some things up."

She blinked at me, but then smiled. She was used to this. My parents were so anti-technology that we still had a dial-up modem they kept so locked down we didn't really use it for anything. They had forced Emmett and me to rely on school internet and the kindness of friends for years. "Of course. Come over this afternoon."

Step one in Operation Find Emmett, sorted.

Chapter Three

Interlude: Bazooka

The girl can't know why I'm really here. She'd never accept it.

I didn't mean to set the Earth on the path to destruction. It just happened. It's not really my fault, because those asshole demons could've corrected it in a nanosecond. They left it to teach me a lesson.

I was just trying to win a game.

Here's what happened. Every couple of hundred years, we hold an event called the Interstellar Games. Like human Olympics. The strongest demons against the brightest imps, with the prize being a big trophy and the right to lord it over the other side for a couple of centuries. Often, it's quite close. Demons are bigger and more powerful, but they're not known for their intelligence, so there's often plenty of room for faster, smarter imps to run circles around them and eke out a win.

This time, the imps chose me to compete. And I really, really wanted to win.

The thing with demons is that just because they're strong, they think it means they're the pinnacle of ethereal power on Earth. But the truth is, they're not as great as they think they are.

Like leading humans into evil is even hard. Humans turn evil in a strong breeze. You want hard? Lead a sheep into evil. Or a tree. Or prank someone into insanity like an imp can. All that takes so much more skill and creativity than any demon possesses.

So anyway, the games. We play in multiple events, some of which are much too ancient and convoluted for human brains to understand, but some of the newer categories are based on Earth games. The game the Aztecs used to play with the stone ring and the ball and the chopping off the heads of the losing team? We love that one.

Which brings us to croquet; it's the final, deciding event of the whole tournament. The imps discovered it and, honestly, what's not to love? Croquet masquerades as a lovely activity while seething with passive aggression. Its players titter politely and sip lemonade while viciously knocking their opponents' balls off the playing field. I've seen whole families come to blows over a game gone awry. I've seen siblings stop speaking for years, grudges held for decades, croquet mallets turned into murder weapons.

It's a fine, fine game. So of course, we appropriated it.

Sure, we switched it up a bit. Mainly to allow for space play with small asteroids.

The rules are strict. The course stretches between Mars and Saturn, and the "balls" can't be bigger than a Volkswagen. To score, you must knock your rock through Saturn's rings without hitting anything. You can send your opponent's ball out of bounds, but only on your valid turn. And, most importantly, you hit nothing toward Earth.

I'm not much of one to follow the rules, even on the best of days. So, of course, I spent the entire game looking for a way to cheat.

I soon found myself losing to this big, burly lady-demon named Charazon. No way was I going to let that stand. Then the perfect opportunity hit me. There was this passing comet, too big for play, but if I accidentally hit her ball into it, it would vaporize on contact, knocking her out of the game! Ahh, it was perfection. All I had to do was make it look like an accident.

The best part was: it worked. I waited until she was distracted, lined up my shot, and BOOM. Her ball flew off the field in the wrong direction, smashed into the comet, and disappeared in a cloud of dust and ice.

Which is a win, in anyone's version of the game.

Except Charazon called foul, saying I cheated. We went into instant replay and a whole mini-war broke out right there on the field.

By the time it was over, the survivors had decided I'd acted with intent, and they named Charazon and the demons the winners of the whole damn tournament.

But it wasn't until then that we noticed the critical info. The comet I'd targeted was enormous. And my little jape had changed its trajectory, heading right for Earth.

Although they could've fixed it without raising a sweat, the demons had other plans. What better way to ensure total victory over the imps than to blow our home to smithereens? Even if we followed them to a new planet, it wouldn't be the same. We wouldn't be tied to it the way we're tied to Earth, where we were born from the rocks and trees and water.

And what better way to stick it to me than to leave me here to watch?

Which is how I ended up inside this stupid bird.

When the rock hits and the goose dies, I'll be free,

of course. Able to follow my siblings to wherever they ended up, or stay here, or whatever I want. But until then, I have to sit here and watch the Earth and everything I've ever enjoyed suffer and burn.

Like I said, demons are bastards.

But there's one thing they didn't think through all the way, and that's the fact that I'm insanely creative and still have a bit of power at my disposal. There might be something I could do to lessen the comet's impact. Maybe save a few people or pick one pleasant spot to protect from the blast. But the real question is, do I want to? Are the humans, or anything they've built, worth saving?

Maybe I can use my time in this feathered idiot to figure that out.

Chapter Four

August 26, 2018
Dear Em,
I was hiding in the barn when you left. Same old scaredy-cat I've always been, even though I'm eleven now and should be braver.

The shouting started as I fed the goats, and I came up to the back porch to listen. It sounded bad. Really bad. So I ran back to the barn and waited. I should have tried to help you, but I couldn't. I was so scared. Not only for the awful things that everyone was saying, but because I knew you'd be mad at me all over again when it was done.

So I hid, and buried my face in Mitch the donkey, and then your car started up and gravel went flying. Then... nothing.

No one was around when I came back in. Someone had knocked a lamp over in the living room and there was a big hole in the wall by the fireplace shaped like a fist. I checked your room and some of your stuff was gone. Mom and Dad were in their room, and I didn't want to go in there.

I stood at your door, staring, wondering what it all meant, until Mom found me and told me to go to bed. She looked bad, like she'd been crying.

When I went to bed that night, your pictures were still on the mantel. The one of you in your baseball uniform, and with your arm around Laurie at the prom. The next morning, they were gone.

I asked Mom where you were and she didn't even turn around from the stove, just said you were gone. I kept asking questions, but I finally gave up.

It's been three days now. Are you coming back? Where did you go?

I don't have anywhere to send this, but I'm going to ask around and see if anyone knows where you are. I'll find you.

Love, Lou

****

Maggie lived in a cozy, one-story house in the middle of Davenport. Her room looked out over the back patio, and she'd stuffed it to the brim with the detritus of a more successful teen—posters of celebrities, sports trophies, framed pictures of her doing interesting things. To be honest, I couldn't quite fathom how I'd ended up with such a beautiful, normal best friend. Maggie wasn't in the top tier of high school popularity, but she was so much closer than me.

I'd been popular once for a brief shining moment, somewhere around third or fourth grade. At that age, being the kid who lives on an actual, honest-to-God petting zoo is the golden ticket. Every kid in my class wanted to be my friend and land a playdate at my house, and my birthday parties were one of the most sought-after invites of the year. When you're nine years old, there is nothing cooler than a girl who gets to go home and hang out with a squawking, clucking, bleating menagerie. No one cared if I smelled like I'd been in the barn before school, or if there was a piece of wheat stuck to my coat. I was, for that moment, the coolest thing around.

And then in fifth and sixth grade, everyone else changed, and I… I didn't. Everyone started flirting and play-dating, holding hands on the playground, sending each other notes. For a while, I assumed that most of my peers found it as stupid as I did. Then came makeup and makeovers and sleepovers that had more to do with talking about boys than talking about animals and books and toys. It was like I'd woken up one day and found myself surrounded by strangers who'd learned a new language overnight.

Maggie moved to town during third grade, and I was lucky enough to have her assigned to the empty seat next to me on that first day. She gave me a gap-toothed grin and later passed me a piece of candy under the table, and from that moment on we were inseparable. She changed too, but somehow, she kept more of her old self than some of the other girls did. She still liked books and running in the back fields, watching stars on a blanket in the middle of the night out behind the barn. And most important, she thought all the kids pairing off in elementary and middle school were kind of ridiculous too.

"Hey, you," Maggie said, opening the screen door. "Mom and Dad are out trying to find a Costco that isn't empty. Heavy into the hoarding right now."

She wasn't kidding. As we crossed through the kitchen toward her room, I could see bags and bags of food lying around—mostly rice and dried beans from the look of it, and big jugs full of water.

"Getting ready for the camp?"

"Yep." She led me into her room and waved at her desk, where her laptop stood poised and ready. "What are we researching?"

I slid into the desk chair. "Looking for Emmett. Again."

We'd done this more times than I could count, digging through everything we could find—social media sites, emails of his old friends, genealogy records, random business pages, student lists at various colleges. We never found him. I knew today wasn't likely to be different, but I had to try again.

Emmett Compton, Iowa, I typed in, hit search.

"Only four million results," Maggie said, reading over my shoulder. "Not a lot better than before, right?"

I nodded, scanning my way through the first few screens.

"Let's keep looking. What else could we try?" She bit her lip, thinking. This was why Maggie was a good person. Despite her more sincere adherence to our church's teachings, she still didn't understand why believing in God meant my parents should've kicked my brother to the curb like he was trash. I loved her for it.

We spent the afternoon trying everything we could think of, her on her phone and me on the laptop. Nothing came up that we hadn't seen before. Finally, I sat back, too tired to continue, and rubbed the ache out of my eyes. "It seems wrong to let everything end without trying to reach him."

Maggie looked sad from her perch on the end of the bed. "Yeah. I suppose we all have things we'd like to do before then, huh?"

I got up and stretched and then flopped down next to her, dragging her down on the bed beside me in a comfy pile of limbs. "What's yours?"

Her eyes skittered to the side, then back to me.

"Promise you won't laugh?"

"Promise. You can tell me anything."

"You're going to think it's dumb. It's nothing you care about."

I sighed and pushed up on one elbow so I could see her face better. "Maggie, spit it out! Maybe I can help."

She took a deep breath. "I just… it would be nice to know what kissing someone felt like before I left the planet."

I stared at Maggie, suddenly aware of a strange feeling. Our arms and legs tangled like they always did. We'd always been affectionate, but I'd never really noticed before how pretty the freckles were under her gray eyes. A sudden desire to trace a finger across them overwhelmed me.

"Kissing someone?" I swallowed. "Anyone in particular?"

She grinned. "Oh maybe. I don't know. You know me. Curious about everything."

The moment stretched out, neither of us sure of what to say next, until the front door banged open and closed, breaking the spell. The sound of footsteps made it clear her parents were home. I untangled myself from Maggie.

A moment later, her mom poked her head around the door. "Oh hi, Lou!" she said with a smile. "Are you going to be joining us for dinner?"

I smiled back, but underneath, my head was still buzzing with static. Something in my chest rumbled like thunder. Good God, what had that moment that just passed been? "I don't think so. My parents are expecting me home."

"We just ran into them," she said, running a hand through her hair. "They were filling up gas tanks at the station in town. Your mom said we're going to be neighbors soon—won't that be fun, girls?"

"What do you mean?"

Her eyes went wide for a minute, then she laughed. "Oh no, was I not supposed to tell you yet? I swear, I can't keep a secret. But it sounds like you're going to be joining us in the camp soon. Oh, I'm sorry, dear, I didn't mean to spill the beans."

I looked from Maggie to her mom and back again. Maggie shook her head in a clear sign she hadn't known anything about this. "I—I wasn't aware it was coming up this soon, is all," I stammered, trying to let her mom off the hook. I gathered up my things and made for the door. "Thanks Maggie. I have to go."

****

Mom was nowhere to be found when I got home. I found Dad from the noise of him digging through old equipment in the shed.

"So, something you want to tell me?"

He startled and a string of bungee cords fell to the ground behind him. "Lou! You scared me."

I nodded, eyeing the array of ominous-looking equipment lying about. He'd pulled out an old camp stove, a pile of tent poles, and various other odds and ends of outdoor life. We hadn't used them even once since Emmett left. Me and Emmet had been the ones who liked to camp. "What's all this about?"

A wave of anger bubbled in my chest like heartburn. His eyes didn't quite meet mine as he turned back to his task. Was he going to be honest, or would he pass it off with a lie?

"Getting prepared. I know you aren't in favor of the idea, but we'll need to get over to the church eventually.

It's already filling up." He straightened up and wiped his hands on his pants, looking apologetic. He sighed. "It makes sense, Lou. Things are going to get increasingly crazy around here. There's already been rioting up in Iowa City, you know that, right? Why sit here and be an easy target as a single family on a huge piece of property when we could band together with others and share our resources?"

I snorted. "You think it's going to be easier to defend ourselves living in a *tent?*"

He shifted his weight and frowned but kept his voice infuriatingly calm and level. "I think it will be easier to defend ourselves with a few dozen other like-minded families. We'll have organized watches and patrols. We'll have arms. And we'll have the church."

"Well then, I'm staying here."

He huffed. "No, Lou. We're not leaving our seventeen-year-old daughter here, alone, in a situation that is unsafe for us as a family. When we go, you're coming too." He grimaced, clearly aware he was upsetting me. "You can still come over here and feed the animals. Check the mail, every day if you need to. Not that there's going to be mail all that much longer."

It burned that this was as close as he was going to come to acknowledging my actual concern. The animals. Emmett.

"Dad, come on!" I yelled. "We are literally going to die. Why do we have to do it in a tent? God doesn't care where we pray from."

"I know you don't want this, Lou. None of us do." His voice was gruff with emotion, and I looked at him with surprise. "Do you think this whole situation isn't breaking my heart? If there was any way I could save you from dying, I would."

He reached out to pull me into an unwilling hug. I let him, but I didn't hug back. After a moment, he stiffened and let go, and I felt a flare of satisfaction that my stillness had stung him, followed by my face burning in shame.

He turned away. "Go off and pack up some things. Clothes and essentials first, and then you can figure out what else you want to bring along. We're going at the start of next week." He paused, turning back to me. "Oh, and hey, your friend Maggie's family is coming too! That'll help, won't it?"

"No, it doesn't help," I shouted, my eyes burning with his betrayal. "You don't care at all about what I think or want. You can go if you want. I'm staying here."

He sighed and went back to his work. I stared at him, fists clenched, trying to light a fire in the back of his shirt with the heat of my gaze, then I gave up.

I viciously kicked several clumps of grass on my way back to the house, then I stomped my way up the stairs and slammed the door behind me, before falling on the bed, every limb stiff with fury. My life was screwed up; my parents ensured it at every turn. They threw out my brother, and now they were taking away everything I loved and my last hope of Emmett's return. I hated them and the entire world.

****

Still angry, I headed out to the barn an hour later to take care of my chores. The horde of chickens didn't care if I was upset; they still needed their eggs retrieved and their cages cleaned out. Bazooka was nowhere to be found as I went through my tasks like a robot. When I finished, I headed out onto the property to look for him.

I found him standing at one of the watering troughs in the public portion of the petting zoo, staring quietly at his reflection in the still water.

"What are you doing?"

He jumped, then smoothed down his feathers. "Looking at this body I'm stuck in. It's ridiculous. Do you know geese don't sleep in? Like, ever? This idiot wakes me up at the crack of dawn and wants to find a nest as soon as the sky turns orange in the evening. It takes all my strength to keep in enough control of the nervous system to do all the stuff I want to do."

I blinked. "Like what? What are you spending your time on?"

"Reconnaissance," he said. "I'm trying to find out about the world here. What is this place called again? Iowa? I'm from the Mediterranean. I've never been here before."

Interesting. I reached in my bucket for a bit of corn and scattered some in front of him, and Bazooka took a grateful bite or two while also looking like he resented the prospect with every fiber of his being.

"What have you found out so far?"

"Not much. People are panicking, there's delicious chaos breaking out all over, but everyone here is dull as dirt. I've been listening to the news from your porch in the evenings, and I snuck along to a couple of your church services." He made a sour face. "Not impressed, by the way. They're pretty pallid affairs if you used to hang out with the Greeks and Etruscans. There are no daggers, no one gets drunk or has sex in the woods. There's literally nothing of interest going on here. How do you stand it?"

I laughed, my earlier anger evaporating. "That must

38

really be a letdown. I'm not super fond of the church services either."

He looked at me, consideringly. "What would you say about running away? You and me?"

I almost laughed. This possible hallucinatory, potential nature spirit who I didn't know and didn't trust wanted me to run away with him? It was ludicrous. "Yeah, sure," I said, chuckling. "No problem."

He stepped toward me, eyes glittering. "I mean it, let's get out of here! Nothing is happening here at all. The world is ending, Lou!"

I considered him silently. "I can't leave here. Where would we go?"

He puffed out his chest. "You name it. Isn't there something you want to see? We could watch the end from the top of the Great Pyramid. From the Pantheon in Rome. How about the Eiffel Tower? I could help you get there."

Despite my skepticism, my heart leaped at the visceral pull of these images. I'd barely left Iowa in my whole life. And this creature was offering me adventure? I had to bite my tongue against the sudden urge to say yes.

"I can't, Bazooka," I said instead, the anger rolling back over me, but with an uncomfortable tinge of shame added for good measure. "My family is here. And I have to feed the animals. And anyway, my brother might come back before the end. I need to be here in case he does."

Bazooka flopped, looking discouraged. "Well, aren't you virtuous?"

I left him and headed back to the house.

"Think it over, at least!" he called after me.

****

"Oh, there you are, Lou," my mom said the next morning when I finally made my appearance downstairs.

I ignored her, heading straight for the pantry to find something frivolous to eat. I finally located a bag of chips and ripped it open, eating a handful right there in the pantry, then wiped my greasy fingers on my shirt while I contemplated my mother and her betrayals.

"Did you hear me, Lou? I need your help."

I emerged, glaring at her and still stuffing chips into my mouth. She watched the crumbs fall to the floor and sighed.

"Dad brought me up to date on the big plan. Is it really what you want?"

"What I want," she said, "is for none of this to be happening at all. It isn't just happening to *you*, Lou."

I gaped, trying to land on a feeling. "I know that! But we can't just *leave*. This is home!"

Not for much longer, I thought, a stab of grief hitting me right in the middle of my chest. We looked at each other, mute, and I had the feeling we were both sharing the same thought.

I sighed, and held out the potato chip bag, a weak olive branch, and after a moment's hesitation, she took a handful.

"So, what did you need?"

"The old grain mill," she said, laying her chips down on a clean dish towel. "I think it's in the basement. Could you see if you can find it while I go help your dad?"

We didn't have one of those nice, finished basements with a rec room and a pool table and shag carpeting. What our old farmhouse had was more of what Emmett and I used to call a canning dungeon. It was old

40

and musty, with green stone walls that dripped with moisture in some places, poured concrete floors, and low ceilings.

A series of four squat rooms sprawled around the central staircase, each lit by a dangling, pull-string lightbulb that cast fearful-looking shadows. Shelves lined the walls, filled with boxes or bits of discarded and useless old equipment. An enormous and ancient furnace hulked in the corner of the smallest of the rooms, emitting grunts and wheezes like it might be alive. When I was a kid, I was terrified of that furnace. I had usually refused to come down here at all unless forced to for a tornado warning.

Which was why it was especially odd, when I was eight, when Emmett told me he had a surprise for me in the basement. I balked at first, but he won out in the end, taking me by the hand and dragging my reluctant self down the stairs and into the gloom. When I got to the bottom, I gasped—he'd set up Christmas lights across the biggest and emptiest room, dragged down a tape deck, and pulled our roller skates out of the back shed.

"Come on! It'll be fun!" he'd said.

Looking at the lights and the smile on his face, I wasn't scared. We strapped on our skates and spent the afternoon whirling around the room, the wheels clanging against the stone floor, running into each other and laughing as we tried to outdo each other with spins and dance moves.

It was one of the most fun days of my entire childhood.

I stood there, today, in the middle of the same room and turned in a circle, remembering. An ache bloomed in the center of my chest so hard that it almost made me want to double over.

The sound of my mother's footsteps as she went out the backdoor roused me. I tried to figure out where to hunt for the big hunk of iron that was our ancient grain mill.

A set of shelves close to the doorway was as good a place to start as any. Heavy pots and pans, much too big for regular use, cluttered the top shelves. A quick glance told me it wasn't up there. With a sigh, I sat on the concrete floor and started digging through the boxes from the lower shelves, releasing clouds of dust and grime.

After several explosive sneezes, I hit pay-dirt of a different kind in the second box—not the grain mill I'd been sent for, but a relic from childhood that put an immediate smile on my face. The old cookie jar, its body shaped like a mushroom with the lid as the cute little cap, red with white dots. For years it had lived on the kitchen counter, always full of something Emmett or I couldn't wait to get our hands on. We'd both mastered sneaking into the kitchen and opening it without a sound and making off with a huge handful of cookies to share. When had it disappeared? I hadn't noticed.

I pulled it out and wiped a layer of dust off it with the sleeve of my sweatshirt, and then gave it an experimental shake, hoping for the rattle of one last forgotten ancient chocolate chip cookie.

Instead, the jar made a soft shushing sound, like something papery was inside. Intrigued, I pulled off the lid and tipped it toward the light and found a thick stack of envelopes, held together by a crusty rubber band.

I pulled them out gently, turning them over in the light, and found… my name. My name and address were on the top one, and on the one behind it, and on the one behind that. I snapped the rubber band and paged through, finding each of them the same. Each was a letter, addressed to me, the stamp canceled, the handwriting tidy. There must be twenty of them all together.

I knew that writing. It was Emmett's.

Chapter Five

Six years earlier

It was one of those gorgeous, early fall days you only get in the Midwest, with the air still almost as warm as summer and the grass turned brittle and brown after the annual drought. Mom and I were in the backyard, taking the freshly dried sheets off the line, one of my favorite tasks to help with. Whenever Mom wasn't looking, I liked to bury my nose in them and sniff what I could only describe as the smell of sunshine.

"I'm never getting married," I said out of nowhere, with all the confidence of a kid who thinks she knows everything. "Boys are gross."

My mother removed a couple of clothespins and slipped them into the pocket of her jean skirt, then motioned for me to do the same on my end. The sheet billowed off the line like it had wings. I took the two corners closest to me and we performed the dance we'd done a hundred times, stretching the sheet out between us, snapping it flat, and then bringing the ends to meet in the middle.

"That's because you're eleven," Mom said, a fond smile on her face. "You'll feel different when you're older."

I wasn't about to let that go unanswered. "Nuh uh! Not everyone gets married. Maybe I'll be a doctor or the president or something."

We switched hand positions and brought our ends together again, folding the sheet into quarters, then over twice more into a small bundle she put into the wicker basket.

"Maybe so," Mom said, starting on the clothespins from the next sheet. "Grab the far corner for me, would you?"

I squeezed the weathered wooden clip and freed the sheet, this one bright yellow and destined for my bed, and let the smooth fabric slide over my face as I got the two ends in my hands.

"Besides," Mom continued, "your brother will show you the way. Why, I think any day now he might decide that this Laurie girl is who he wants to marry. It'll be good for you to be a bridesmaid in his wedding."

I pondered that one. Since May, when I saw something I shouldn't have, I'd known a secret: that Emmett was actually dating his friend, Luke. I wasn't supposed to know, but Emmett didn't have much of a choice—he explained things to me and made me swear not to tell our parents.

It made me feel kind of grown up to know something so important, but it was also confusing. I sometimes thought that I was the only person in this family who didn't have big hangups. I loved my parents. I loved my brother.

I didn't think Mom and Dad were going to be as mad as Emmett thought about him dating Luke. Mom and Dad liked Luke, but more importantly, they loved Emmett and wanted the best for him. Yeah, it would surprise them, but they'd come around. Family was everything. They would support him, I was sure of it. Maybe I could even help? He'd be so happy if he didn't have to keep this all inside anymore.

"Don't you want to be a bridesmaid?" Mom asked, as we folded the yellow sheet between us. "You'll get to wear a gorgeous dress and carry flowers and walk down the aisle at church—"

"I don't think Emmett is going to marry Laurie," I blurted out, heart pounding. "What if he didn't? Would you be mad?"

She gave me a strange look. "What makes you say that? Did Emmett tell you he's going to break up with Laurie?"

My face flushed hot. I'd stepped in it now. "No," I mumbled, busying my hands in the sheet, smoothing the wrinkles out. Mom followed along by rote, but she kept her all-too-keen eyes on my face.

"Lou, what are you not telling me?"

"Nothing!" I shoved the remaining corners into her hands so she could start folding the narrow rectangle into a tidy bundle, and then escaped back to one of the other lines where I started frantically unclipping socks, one by one.

"Louise Compton," my mother said quietly, "lying is a sin."

It was the quietness that did it. If she'd yelled, I would've dug in my heels and probably taken the secret to my grave. But the quiet voice and the sadness when she said the word "sin"—it tugged at something deep in my belly, something that thrummed with love and shame and the desire to please. This was my mother, who loved me. Who loved us both. Who was I to keep secrets from her?

I turned back around and glanced at her face. "You can't tell anyone."

She put the last sheet into the basket and turned her full attention to me, her eyes squinted against the bright fall light. "Tell anyone what?"

And so I told her everything. About how I'd found out Emmett had a special friend, a boy. How he'd explained to me that some people don't end up marrying girls, and how sometimes people love someone they aren't supposed to, but that was okay, right? Because God was love. And he commanded us to love one another. So what if sometimes that looked different from what we expected?

I rambled on with growing confidence that, of course, my mother, the number one support of my life, would understand perfectly. I only stuttered to a stop when I realized it had gotten strangely quiet. I looked up at her and froze.

She was pale, her eyes wide, hands clutched to her chest.

A wave of something like nausea broke over me, and I immediately understood that I had just made an enormous mistake.

"Emmett told you all this?" she asked, her voice strangled.

I nodded, and some instinct told me to backpedal. "Or something like that. I might have the details wrong. He might not have been talking about himself, you know. He was just telling me about how sometimes people live in different ways from us."

She nodded, but her gaze wasn't really on me. It was more like she was looking inside herself. Her hands smoothed down her skirt, and she nodded again, as if she'd made some kind of decision. Then she picked up the basket at her feet and held it out for me to toss the socks into. I did, and she gave me a small, empty smile and turned back toward the house.

"Mom?" I called. "You okay?"

"Just fine, honey," she said over her shoulder. "You go play now."

I stared after her, strangely uncomfortable, and then shrugged and set off toward the barn. One of the barn cats was heavily pregnant, and I needed to check in on her and see if the babies had arrived.

****

When Emmett's car crunched into the gravel driveway, I put down my homework and looked at Mom. She stood at the stove with her back to me, stirring a pot of soup. She didn't seem any different from normal when Emmett clattered in the back door in his usual explosion of books and shoes and jacket, dumped everything on the mud porch, and then planted a kiss on her cheek. My fears receded even more when Dad rolled in dirty from baling hay and grunted at all of us in his usual manner before heading off to the shower.

I bit down on my anxiety as I laid plates on the table. Maybe everything was fine. Maybe Mom hadn't said anything to Dad. Maybe nothing would come of it after all.

I held onto that hope until we all linked hands for grace.

"Bless this family," my father intoned, squeezing my hand, "and keep us free of the sinfulness of the world..."

Okay, normal so far.

"And particularly bless our son, Emmett, who is struggling to walk the path of the righteous."

I looked up as Emmett did and our eyes met across

the table, his baffled, mine miserable. I curled in on myself instinctively, trying to make myself small, unnoticeable, like I was of no consequence. Maybe I could disappear if I tried hard enough.

"Dad, what the heck?" Emmett cut in. My father ignored him, finished blessing the meal, and said amen. "Dad?"

My father placed his napkin on his lap and didn't look at Emmett at all. "We'll talk about it after the meal. For now, everyone eat up."

Emmett frowned, looking me in the eye. I shrugged, feeling sick.

The family meeting that followed would go down in history as one of the most unpleasant instances of an already horrible institution. Did anyone, anywhere, ever enjoy a family meeting? At their best, they seemed misguided; no kid wanted to sit around and be forced to talk about their feelings. At their worst, they were nothing more than a way for parents to lord their unlimited authority over their children. This meeting was the second kind.

Dad laid it all bare, everything I'd told my mother, in clear and brutal terms, while I tried to sink into the cushions of the green couch. I stared at my knees to avoid meeting Emmett's eyes.

"None of that is true," Emmett protested. "Lou's a kid. She misunderstood me. You know I'm dating Laurie."

All three pairs of eyes focused on me. I picked at the loose threads on the couch cushion beside me, refusing to look at any of them.

"Are you?" My mother's voice trembled. "Laurie's such a nice girl. I told Lou there couldn't be anything between you and Luke, right? I mean, we've raised you in such a good, Christian home—"

"Being Christian has nothing to do with it. Luke is my friend."

My father sighed heavily. "I didn't want to do this, Emmett, but I think we have to. Let's go have a look around your room, shall we?"

Emmett froze.

"Can I be excused?" I mumbled. No one heard me. I raised my head and spoke louder. "Can I go? I don't see why I have to be a part of—"

"Yes," my mother said, distracted. "You can go. Please go do your homework in your room."

Emmett's room was right across the hall from mine, so even huddled up on my bed with the door shut, I got a front-row seat as Mom and Dad ransacked his room. From the noise, I gathered they were flipping through notebooks, going through drawers, and even looking through his ancient computer.

Whatever they found, it didn't sound good. One of those sources must've proven that Emmett and Luke were more than just friends, and that Laurie was a cover. I wrapped my arms around my knees, pulling them close to my chest. I didn't even pretend to pay attention to the math book open in front of me.

Me and my big, fat mouth. This was all on me. Emmett had trusted me, and I had trusted Mom, and now everything was in an uproar.

"I can't believe you would do this to us!" Dad bellowed from the hallway, before his heavy steps thundered down the stairs and out the back door. Mom and Emmett's voices continued for a while, tense but less loud, and then I heard her leave as well, and the silence that followed was scarier than the shouting had been.

****

I'd never been afraid to enter my brother's room before, but that night, I stood in front of his closed door with my heart in my throat, afraid to knock. The silence in the house hit me like a physical entity, forbidding and fierce. Finally, though, I knocked, soft and quick, making sure he'd know it was me.

He didn't answer, so after another long moment of agony, I peeked in. Emmett was curled up in a ball on the bed, his back toward me, but I could tell he wasn't sleeping. The room was a mess; clothes were hanging out of the closet door, and papers lay scattered everywhere.

"Come to pile on, did you?" he said, his voice hard.

A tight fist of misery gathered in my stomach. "Emmett, I'm so sorry."

He sat up and his green eyes were puffy. "Lou, what did you think you were doing? Why did you do this?"

I stared at him, mute with horror. "I—I don't know. Mom got it out of me. You know how she is."

"Still! You didn't have to tell her *everything*."

"I didn't tell her everything," I insisted, while trying to think of some detail of his secret life that I hadn't babbled away. I was sure there was something. "But you guys will work it out, right? I mean, they love you."

He scowled at me. "Yeah right. You're such a kid, Lou."

I took a step toward the bed, wanting to sit down with him and not sure I was welcome. "I'll talk to them. I can explain that I got it all wrong. Maybe it will—"

"It's too late for that. They looked at my diary and found things. I'm off to talk to the pastor tomorrow. Apparently, I'm a monster. It's not like I didn't know that already."

"They'll come around," I said lamely, not even convincing myself.

He scoffed. "Could you go, please? I want to be alone."

"But…"

He stood, took me by the shoulders, and walked me toward the door, depositing me in the hallway. And then Emmett, my brother who was always kind to me and who had hardly ever said a harsh word to me in his life unless I really, really deserved it, closed the door in my face.

****

We spent the next two weeks collectively shouting, crying, and praying, like we were training for the Olympic gold medal of family drama. If the family was a relay team, I'd started things off by passing the misery baton to Mom, who passed it to Dad, who passed it to Emmett, who was now stuck carrying it for all of us. He wavered between furious and remorseful, alternately crying through whatever insults were being tossed his way or shouting back in complete defiance. This did nothing to help lower the tension at the dinner table.

Luckily, all three of them largely ignored me— Mom and Dad had bigger fish to fry, and Emmett had stopped speaking to me entirely. They sent me to talk to Pastor Freeland, too, but he didn't seem to find anything wrong with me. After that, they left me to watch from the sidelines as our family imploded.

By the end of the second week, my father was more distant than ever. My mother was crying every night as she made dinner, and Emmett was gone. My life would never be the same.

Chapter Six

I stood like an obelisk in the basement, blood pounding in my ears, the envelopes in my hand. Letters to me? From Emmett? What did this mean? Suddenly wary for reasons I couldn't put into words, I slid the letters inside my sweatshirt and tucked the cookie jar back into place, taking care to make it look undisturbed.

While my head swam and my pulse throbbed with enough force to almost break through my skin, my body went through the next two boxes. I found the stupid grain mill and pulled it out, then marched out to the yard and delivered it to Mom. Then we made our excuses, me and my body, headed up to my room, and locked the door.

My hands shook so hard that I dropped the envelopes, scattering them across the rug. Shit, shit, shit. I took a deep, shaky breath as I gathered them up and then sorted them by postmark, old to new. They started a few weeks after Emmett left, arriving about once a month for the next several years. They stopped all together about nine months ago.

A searing shot of pure fear drilled through me as I picked up the first one and contemplated opening it. Inside this envelope was something I'd been dreading for the last six years—confirmation that Emmett blamed me for what had happened to him. As he should. I knew beyond a doubt that it was all my fault. The knowledge had haunted me for years. But to open the envelope and face his anger? His recriminations?

I deserved it. But I wasn't sure I could survive seeing it in black and white.

I squeezed my eyes shut and leaned back against my closed door, and then thumped my head against it, then thumped it a few more times for good measure. There was no point in putting it off. My comeuppance was here. Putting it off wouldn't make it any less painful, and after all, I wasn't going to be alive a lot longer to deal with the aftereffects.

Forty-six days until impact. I might as well get it over with.

I gritted my teeth, opened my eyes, and slid my finger under the flap of the first unopened envelope.

It was time to face the music.

****

September 10, 2018

Dear Lou,

I shouldn't have yelled at you. I know you didn't mean for this to happen, and it was bound to come out eventually. You're just a kid. It was a lot to put on your shoulders, keeping a secret like that, so don't feel bad.

I didn't get to say goodbye—where were you? I feel terrible about that. But I wanted to let you know I'm in Des Moines. Luke's family moved here over the summer, so I headed here first, to stay with him for a couple weeks while I figure out what to do next. Get a job, I guess, earn some money, take classes if I can. Maybe head west. I always wanted to see the Pacific and I guess there's nothing stopping me now.

Much as I'd like to think this will blow over and they'll let me come home, I think we both know Mom and Dad too well for that. I'll give them a while and then try calling. Who knows, maybe they'll calm down. But listen, don't you try to fix this. It's not your fault and you don't have to take that on. Just don't let them make you think I'm wrong inside, somehow, because of who I am and who I want to be.

I won't lie to you. I'm kind of freaked out. I mean, I'm eighteen and that's a perfectly reasonable time to leave home and be out on your own. Lots of people do it. But I wasn't really prepared. And most people who head out into the world can still come home for Sunday dinner or call up their parents for help if things aren't going well. It's a lot to take in. But I'll be fine. You know me. I can adjust to anything.

I'll write to you from wherever I am, so you always know where to find me, and I'll send you my number when I get a phone. You can call me from Maggie's house. Take care of yourself, Lou, and don't worry too much about me.

—Emmett

****

I clutched the paper of Emmett's first letter hard enough to wrinkle it as I read and reread it at least a dozen times. Then I sat back, my vision swimming, and tried to let it all sink in.

Emmett wasn't angry at me. Not even at the start.

Emmett had written to me a few days after he'd left, to let me know he didn't hate me for telling our parents about him.

The tears running down my face were mostly happy, at least at first. I wiped them away, basking. Suddenly energized, I grabbed the next letter in the pile and opened it, then the next, then the next.

Much too soon, I'd reached the end. I emerged from

the last letter, my back cramping from being hunched over the letters. I stretched and looked around at the papers laid out around me in careful piles, and realized I'd gained a good sense of where Emmett had been over the last few years. I grabbed a notebook and listed dates and places.

Most of 2018—Des Moines
2019 through mid-2021—Friend, Nebraska
Late 2021 through June 2022—Jackson, Wyoming
June 2022 through maybe now—Bend

The letters had stopped after he got to Bend, and they were circumspect about what he was doing or who he was with; probably because he suspected my parents would open them. It made sense, but left me burning with questions. What was he doing out on the West Coast? Did he have friends? Was he living with someone? Why had he stopped writing?

The sound of footsteps coming in from the back door below spurred me into a burst of action. No one could know I had these, not yet. My heart pounded as I dug a big yellow mailing envelope out of my desk and shoved all the letters into it, then threw it in the ventilation shaft with fumbling hands.

I realized, suddenly, that his letters were sitting on top of mine. Without knowing it, we'd both been carrying out a one-sided conversation with the other across all the years he'd been gone. If you took his letters and mine and laid them out sequentially, would it sound like we were actually conversing instead of talking past each other?

Once I'd hidden the evidence, I wiped the tears off my face and flopped down on my bed, staring at the ceiling as cold, hard reality broke over me.

My parents had lied to me. They'd lied about so many things—first and foremost that they had no idea where Emmett was. Turns out they'd always had a pretty good idea, at least from the return addresses on the envelopes. And what's more, they'd hidden these letters from me for years. Why? Did they think homosexuality was catching? That I might pick it up from the remnants of Emmett's DNA on the envelope and start ogling girls in gym class? Did they think speaking to Emmett might undermine everything they had ever taught me?

Well, they were right on that front, I suppose. But kicking him out had undermined it even more.

The hypocrites. Suddenly burning, I flipped face down on the bed and stuffed a pillow into my mouth to cover the wordless shouts that broke out of me. I screamed. I pummeled the pillows beneath me. I kicked.

And then I flopped, wrung out and exhausted from my full-on tantrum, and focused on the one thought left to me.

I knew where Emmett was. He was in Bend, Oregon.

And I was going to go find him.

Chapter Seven

September 12, 2018
Dear Emmett,
I figured out what to do.
I'm going to tell Mom and Dad that I lied about all of it. Even if you admitted things, I'll convince them you were protecting me, because you didn't want to get me in trouble. They'll believe that.

And then you can come home! Except I don't know where you are, so I can't send this to let you know. But as soon as you get in touch, we can go back to how everything was before. Whatever Mom and Dad said, I'm sure they didn't mean it. Mom seems upset, like she misses you a lot, and Dad's in one of those moods he gets in where it's better not to even talk to him.

Which is why my plan is perfect. They don't want to believe what they found out about you, so I'll give them a good reason that they don't have to. In fact, I'm going to go do that right now.

——

They didn't believe me.
Dad sighed and left the room before I'd even gotten halfway through the speech I'd planned, and Mom cried and told me I was a good girl and that I should pray for you because you're in danger. And then Dad called for her from the other room and she left. I listened for a while. Words like "delusional" and "hero worship" and

something about how I needed to get counseling at the church as soon as possible.

Are you in danger? I don't really understand why you would be. Is it Luke? Did he do something to scare you? Emmett, if you're in trouble, you need to come home where we can help.

This is all my fault. I'll make them believe me that none of it was true. I'll keep telling them and telling them over and over and eventually I'll wear them down.

I'm sorry.

Please come home.

Love, Lou

****

"So, your parents hid a bunch of letters from your brother," Bazooka squawked as he followed me around on my chores the next morning.

"There was even a phone number in one of them!" I said. "I snuck into the kitchen in the middle of the night and tried it, but it didn't ring." My stomach clenched at the memory of listening to that hollow, endless beeping on the line.

"And they're moving you to live at the church."

I shrugged. "Well yeah, but I'm not going."

Bazooka stopped pecking at the bits of grain on the floor of the barn and came to attention. "What does that mean?"

"It means I have a pretty good idea where to look for Emmett now, and I'm going to go do that."

"But I thought you said you couldn't possibly run away."

"Changed my mind."

There was a long silence, and when he spoke, his voice was taut with urgency. "Take me with you. It was my idea in the first place!"

"I don't even know you! Plus, you're a goose. What, I'm supposed to, I don't know, carry you?"

He looked offended. "I can fly, you know. And do you even have a plan? I'm good at planning. I've run away more times than you."

I didn't have a plan. What little I knew made my prospects look grim. In the two weeks since the initial announcement came out, the evening news had shown things going pretty sideways. Now, with only six weeks left, the government was gathering up important people—scientists, politicians, generic rich people—and stashing them away somewhere. As a result, huge riots had broken out, asking why more ordinary folks weren't being saved. The riots led to many things that were going to make travel difficult—curfews in major cities, road blocks on important routes, and even rumors about martial law. I wasn't sure what that meant, but it didn't sound good. Whenever I thought about it too much, I wanted to curl up in a ball and rock.

"You could steal their car," the goose said.

"I realize you're a demon—oh, no, excuse me, an imp—" I yelled, cutting off his protest before it really got started. He looked at me with disdain but let me continue "—but you don't know everything and you're wrong about this one. The roads are getting tough, the trains are for official use only, and I couldn't afford to get a flight even if there was one available. We're stuck."

Bazooka turned his gaze to the far corner of the barn. "There's that."

Emmett's old Vespa scooter sat in the corner, dusty and deserted. No one had ridden it in at least two years. It was old and slow, but it was functional, and most important, I knew how to ride it.

"Does it even still work?" I mused, walking over to look at it.

"Only one way to find out."

I looked up and grinned.

****

I wheeled the scooter out into the sunshine, checked the tires, and pilfered some gas from the containers my parents had filled up last week. Bazooka and the goats followed along and watched me with interest.

I stood over the seat, flipped the ignition, and then hit the clutch and pressed start, like Emmett showed me years ago. To my surprise, the engine revved into life.

I eased out onto the dirt road that ran into the fields, trying to remember how everything worked. Throttle on the right. Brakes in front of both handgrips. Lean into turns. I stalled it several times, but after a few false starts, I got the hang of it. The smell of exhaust filled my noise and the putt-putt of the engine sounded deafening as the scooter jolted over bumpy dirt roads. My hands ached after just a few minutes from gripping the handles much too hard. I took a deep breath and tried to loosen up.

After a few minutes, I wheeled back around to where Bazooka was waiting. He gave a high-pitched call as I pulled up. It sounded approving.

"Okay, now," he said. "Give me a ride so we can see if I fit."

I turned the scooter off and looked at him. "Fit where, exactly?"

Bazooka shoved his way past my legs and climbed onto the flat, open part of the frame between where my feet rested. "Plenty of room right here, I'd say. C'mon, try it. What do you have to lose?"

My life. My sanity. Maybe my immortal soul?
"I only have one question," Bazooka continued.
"What's that?"
"How fast can this thing go?"

I settled back into the seat, one leg on either side of Bazooka's warm, solid body. It was easier this time to get the scooter going, and to his credit, Bazooka stayed put for the entire ride out to the end of the wheat fields and back.

"I don't know if this is a good idea," I said as we wheeled the scooter back into the barn and hid it away. "How do I know I can trust you? I don't know what imps want. Why do you even want to go?"

Bazooka looked steadily at me. "I'm an ethereal creature who's seen the entire history of the planet. Believe me when I tell you I don't want to die stuck in a petting zoo in Iowa."

I could relate. I didn't want to die in a petting zoo either. Still, I couldn't believe I was considering this.

"How would I feed you on the trip?"

Bazooka folded out his wings and stood large. "Number one, this body eats grass and bugs, and I can feed it myself. Number two, have you ever seen this idiot goose fight?"

"Not really, no."

"Geese are deadly. If I'd been here earlier, I'd have told you to set up a betting parlor for goose fights. Would've made you a ton of money, way more than this stupid petting zoo."

I frowned at him. "Even so."

"Want me to show you? I'd be happy to kick Mitch's ass."

I stepped between Bazooka and the donkey. "Don't

you dare!"

He cackled.

The gravel outside crunched as my parent's car pulled into the driveway. "Gotta go. I'll think about it."

****

Over the next few days, I outwardly played the role of the obedient daughter, packing up my things for the move, while inside I spent every second planning my escape. The thread of family loyalty had snapped clean through upon discovering the letters. They'd lied about everything that mattered. I didn't owe them the truth.

I told myself that over and over as I sat across the dinner table, part of me dying to confront them and ask how they could do such a thing. But I also knew their reasons already; they thought they were protecting me from forces that would lead me astray. After Emmett had left, they'd gone through several strange fixations. They'd cut off the internet to the house and doubled down on the "no phones" rule—I guess so I couldn't read about gay people on the Internet. They got strange about the books I was reading. They dragged me to counseling at the church.

Finally, though, they gave up. I was only eleven. Buried beneath my pain and anger about Emmett's sudden disappearance from my world was a small, rock-hard mountain of terror. I'd had no idea parents could kick out a kid. It made my place in the world feel absurdly fragile, like the ground might shift and I'd find myself next. If there was one thing I knew, it was that my eleven-year-old self would not survive on my own. To prevent it from happening to me, too, I spent those first years bending myself into the perfect child. I did whatever they wanted me to. I never complained. On the surface, I acted like I believed what they'd done was right.

It was the only way to be safe.

Seventeen-year-old me no longer had those illusions. There was no longer safety on offer, either from my family or from the world at large. Although part of me hated my parents, I loved them too—but I loved my brother just as much. I had learned, painfully, over the last six years that they could be wrong. And although a part of me hated to leave them, I was still going the first chance I got. Some things were too important.

One good thing—packing up for the move provided an excellent cover story for my preparations. I could ask where my favorite sleeping bag was or search for a lantern and some batteries without raising suspicions. If they asked, I told them it was for the camp. No one noticed that I'd started hiding bags of stuff under the tarp out in the barn.

Mom didn't even balk when I went through the pantry, pulling out a big jar of peanut butter, some crackers, a loaf of frozen bread, a dozen cans of soup no one would miss, and as much jerky and granola bars as I could fit into my pack.

As I did this, I pondered whether to bring Bazooka with me. On the one hand, having an ancient, sentient being along on the road trip couldn't hurt. He seemed clever, and it would be reassuring to have someone to talk to. On the other hand, I had no idea if he was telling me the truth about his motives. And also, this sentient, supposedly good-at-planning creature of mischief got himself *trapped in the body of a goose.*

****

"Okay, you can come," I said to Bazooka the next

morning. "But we're leaving tonight. What do I need to bring for you to eat?"

Bazooka flapped his wings. "A bag of corn wouldn't be unappreciated. Or grubs, if you wanna go crazy. Live ones, please."

I gave him a look. "Corn yes, grubs no. I'm not going cross-country on a motor scooter with a bag of live worms in my jacket pocket."

The scooter had a decent amount of storage. A large compartment beneath the seat fit my backpack. I rolled up my sleeping bag and blanket and tied them to the rack behind the seat, and put a bag of food in the glove box. That left the saddlebags on either side of the seats—my notebooks, pens, and water jugs filled one, and left the other for whatever else we needed.

Bazooka poked around at the empty saddle bag, made of smooth, worn leather and actually the perfect size for him. "I could maybe sit in this? I might need a helmet or something."

"I'll see what I can come up with," I told him.

****

After several false starts digging through multiple boxes of old stuffed animals, I found the perfect solution—an old stuffed bear that had come with a small, plastic football helmet. One quick beheading and a bit of added padding, and I had a functional helmet. I took it out to the barn for a trial run.

"This isn't what I meant!" Bazooka sank to the floor and flung his neck out straight in a posture of absolute defeat. The plastic helmet flew off and bounced off the ground. "I meant like a pilot's helmet. Maybe leather. With goggles."

"I don't know," I said. "I think you looked pretty

great. And it's either wear this, or I'll have to get a baby harness for you, and you can ride held against my stomach. You won't be safe on the highway just standing on the floorboards."

Bazooka shuddered. "No thank you, I'm not interested in any more touchy-feely stuff than this stupid goose body already makes me do." He took a deep breath and honked. "I'll wear it, if that's what it takes."

****

As much as I doubted Bazooka's essential trustworthiness, he countered my impulsiveness. I would've hightailed it off into the wind that very second, but he pushed me to think things through. Together, we tore pages from an old road atlas, made a list of routes and stops in my notebook, and most important, lashed one of the gas cans to the back grill. Gas stations had become unreliable, tankers were coming through only irregularly, and frightened people everywhere were stockpiling gas in plastic jugs.

Together, we calculated the distance and the time it would take. Forty days to go 1800 miles and find my brother. It was frighteningly brief, but it had to be enough time. If we drove straight through at a good, steady clip, it would take twenty-six hours. Of course, we weren't driving straight through; I wanted to stop at several of the places Emmett had lived, to see if we could find people who knew him and get his current phone number. And we were heading out on an ancient pile of bolts that probably topped out at forty-five miles an hour and might be prone to overheating if we drove for too many hours straight. So maybe three or four days. A week, tops.

I should have been more worried. I really should.

But somehow, it felt predestined. Like fate meant for me to steal this scooter and go. Emmett's existence was calling to me, with a pull as strong as the momentum of the comet, dragging me toward whatever cataclysmic impact lay in my future.

"Maybe get some rest," Bazooka said, nuzzling my leg by goosy instinct before he caught himself and recoiled. "We'll be on the road most of the night."

It sounded like a good idea. I plead exhaustion to Mom and Dad, skipped dinner, and went to take a nap.

Chapter Eight

September 8, 2019
Dear Emmett,
Sometimes I think I hate them. I don't understand how anything is worth throwing away one of your children. Maybe if your child murdered someone. But honestly, even if you'd murdered a lot of people—which I know you wouldn't—I'd still visit you in jail and try to be a good sister. Or write you letters if you were in scary jail, with one of those metal masks over your face to keep you from biting people. Or held in those clear cells with magnetic locks that only a supervillain could open.

I've been watching too many movies at Maggie's.

But still. I don't understand. What does the fact that you like Luke have to do with whether we should love you and live together as a family? You could tell me you were going to marry a carrot, and I'd still love you.

I'd maybe stop eating carrots. You know, out of respect.

I'm tired. More soon.
Love, Lou

****

When my alarm rang just before midnight, I woke thinking about Maggie and how much I wanted to see her before I left. My chest ached at the thought of leaving her. I wasn't sure who I was without Maggie as my touchpoint. Maybe I could convince her to join us.

Maggie could drive. Maybe we could take her parent's car and... no. She'd never do it. Still, the urge to stuff her into a duffel bag and bring her along was insanely strong.

"I'm going to feed everyone before we go," I said to Bazooka when I got to the barn.

"Why? Aren't you letting them go? I thought that was the plan."

I'd completely forgotten. "Should I? Mom and Dad are still here. They might let them out before they go."

"Who knows if your parents will let them out or decide to put everyone down or just abandon them when it comes right down to it?"

Right again.

I started with the chickens, feeling torn between the thrill of leaving and guilt for abandoning my animal friends. I took my time, giving them each a pat on the head as I opened their pen and scattered big handfuls of corn to ease their fears and encourage them outside. The sheep and goats were easier—they were more adventurous. My favorite of the goats, my star performer, nuzzled me and chewed on the corner of my jacket, wanting treats, and I bent over and gave him a big scratch.

I freed the horses and alpacas and shooed them out into the open field. Finally, I turned to Mitch the donkey, my favorite. I gave him a long hug around the neck, nearly undone by the idea of leaving him.

"Goodbye, Mitch," I whispered. "I love you too."

And then they were all out, baying and clucking in the dark, wondering why they weren't asleep and what had happened to the sun.

"One last step," I said to Bazooka. I pulled out his

little helmet and shook it at him.

He hissed, but he let me fasten it on. Then I helped him settle into the empty saddle bag beside me, which I'd lined with a soft blanket. It was a good fit—his body was snug in the bag, and his head and neck were free to look around. It wasn't perfect, but it was as good as it was going to get.

I strapped my helmet on and wheeled the scooter down the road out of hearing range before starting it.

"Ready?"

Bazooka tilted his neck back and let out a loud honk.

I pulled on the throttle and we set off.

Bazooka gave me a questioning look as I pulled into town and wound our way to the front of Maggie's house. "I'll be right back," I said. "I need to say goodbye to Maggie."

Their backyard looked larger in the dark, and the glass in her bedroom window reflected the moon almost perfectly. I stepped up on tiptoe and knocked as lightly as I could, hoping I didn't scare her to death. What time was it? Thank God they didn't have a dog.

I knocked again, and Maggie's face appeared between the curtains, pale and frightened. She slid the sash up.

"Lou, what the heck?" she whispered. "You scared me to death!"

"Need to talk to you. Can you come out?"

She looked back into the darkened room. "If my dad catches me, he'll kill me."

I made enormous eyes she couldn't say no to. "It's really important."

"Hang on."

Soon, Maggie eased open the sliding door and

joined me on the deck. She'd wrapped a thick, fuzzy bathrobe around herself and put on sneakers. She made it look great, like something you'd see in a magazine. I marveled at her perfection one more time while she sat down next to me on the edge of the deck. I swung my feet and tried to decide what to say.

"So…" she said after an awkward silence. "Didja bring me out here to look at stars or what?"

I swallowed. "Maggie, I'm leaving."

"Leaving what?"

"Town. Leaving town." I brushed my hair out of my eyes. "I found letters from Emmett, and I think I know where he is."

"Oh my God. Wow—he wrote to you?"

I nodded. "He's been writing to me for years. Mom hid them. I found them all when we were packing."

Maggie winced. "Ouch. That sucks."

"Yeah. But now I know he's somewhere in Oregon, and I'm going out there to find him."

"Oregon? How? Right now?"

"Right now. I'm taking the scooter. Unless you want to come, of course, and then we have to steal a car." I faked a laugh, but my heart swelled with the impossible hope that she'd leap at the chance.

"Ha ha," she said. "Hilarious."

Maggie wrapped her arms around herself to fight the chill and I could imagine all the objections running through her head. It was crazy. It was dangerous. What would my parents say? I waited for her to say them all, because someone had to. But in the end, she surprised me. Instead of pointing out all the flaws in my idea, she reached over and took my hand.

"Do you think you're coming back?"

Hit the nail right on the head with that one. My throat tightened and my nose prickled. "I—I don't know. I hope so. But who knows?" I gestured at the sky. "Depends how long it takes. We only have forty days before it hits. Forty days to find him, and maybe get back."

She leaned over and laid her head on my shoulder, and neither of us said anything for a while.

I looked down at her, so pale that I could almost see through her, her hair and eyelashes bleached out by the moonlight to a pale silver. I could see the dark blue of the veins in her temple, and the delicate curl of the top of her ear. An absurd rush of something moved through me, and I leaned my head down on top of hers.

"Maggie."

"Yeah."

"About that last wish you mentioned before?"

She pulled her head off my shoulder and leaned back enough to see my face. Our hands were still linked. The night got quieter, and an odd sort of dizziness started buzzing in the back of my head.

"Yeah?"

My tongue grew heavy. "Could I… would it be bad if… I mean, could it be me?"

Something too wise for her years rippled across her face, and then she leaned forward and placed her lips against mine. A whisper of a touch, and I closed my eyes and hung there, suspended.

She pulled back and smiled, and her eyes were wet. "There. Now we've both had a kiss."

I smiled at her, unable to speak.

"So this is goodbye," she said.

"Goodbye for now."

She nodded. "I'll miss you, Lou. I hope I get to see you again."

"Me too."

She gave my hand one last squeeze, then stood, wrapped her robe around herself more tightly, and walked in the back door without looking back.

****

It took me a minute to remember how to move, but when I staggered back to the street, Bazooka had hopped out of the saddlebag and now sat on the driver's seat, poking around at the steering column with his bill.

"Trying to take off without me?" I asked.

"Checking things over. I think I can make the gas last considerably longer." He looked me over. "Did you get what you needed?"

I pulled my braid back over my shoulder and donned the helmet, still half awash in the mystery of whatever had just happened. "I did. I think so."

Trying to clear the haze, I shook my head. There would be plenty of time to mull over this evening on the road. I had nothing but time ahead of me.

We kicked the scooter into gear and headed out. Next stop, Des Moines.

****

August 28, 2024
Dear Mom and Dad,
I found the letters in the basement, and I'm going to find Emmett. Please don't come after me. I'll try to come back before the end.

I love you.
Lou
PS: I'm taking the scooter.

Part Two: The Road

Chapter Nine

September 28, 2019
Dear Lou,

Just wanted to let you know I moved on from Des Moines. Luke and I had a falling out that was probably a long time coming. And to be honest, I've been living over their garage long enough—I'm driving his parents crazy. I can't believe a year has gone by. Time to get on with trying to make a life for myself out here in the world.

Honestly, I've spent a good part of the last year feeling really lost, which couldn't have been easy for Luke. It was hard to process that I couldn't come home, even though I was only two hours away. I sent Mom a letter and asked her to meet me in Des Moines, but she never responded. And I think that because Luke is the one I lost my family for, I decided the relationship with him had to work, you know? But that's not how things work, and Luke isn't the one, and Mom and Dad aren't answering the phone still. So reality has finally settled in.

I drove west, and ended up stopping in a place called Friend, Nebraska, which is nice. Really tiny, like a thousand people, but I got a job here working at the library, and the head librarian is great. Her name's Mari, and she's helped me get settled. Rent is cheap and I'm saving up money to take some business classes at a nearby community college. Not sure what I'll do with that, but I feel like they'll come in handy. One small step at getting my life together.

So that's the current plan. I'm going to call around Christmas. Try to be near the phone, okay? Maybe you can get there first before Mom or Dad pick up, and we can talk. I hope so.

Love you, Lou.
Em

****

The roar of the accelerating motor filled my ears, and I let out a whoop as we pulled onto the highway from Davenport. The cool night air fluttered my shirt and I couldn't tell if my hands were vibrating from the hum of the engine or from the jolts of excitement racing through me. Just being outdoors, alone, at night had its own kind of effervescent joy. Add in finding myself fully independent for the first time, with no one to answer to? It was intoxicating. The days ahead stretched in front of me like the midnight highway—mostly empty, slightly ominous, but also terribly exciting.

At the same time, as the miles raced by, tension clawed its way up my spine. Our purpose was scary and grim: leaving behind nearly all the people I loved to find my missing brother. Relying on no one but my seventeen-year-old self and an imp I didn't fully know or trust yet, on a trip with a firm expiration date. My fizzy excitement bubbled down a bit, poisoned by a faint but palpable trace of worry, deep in my gut.

Our first task was simple—get from Davenport to Des Moines, maybe four hours away at our slow rate, to see if Luke or his family were still there and find out what they knew about Emmett's whereabouts.

Here's what I knew for stage one of our journey:

where Luke had been living when Emmett stayed with him. His family could still be there. People didn't up and move around all that often, right?

What I didn't know: if Emmett had told Luke everything I'd done, and if so, what my reception might be like. Luke might hate me in that way best friends carry grudges for each other. In addition, I didn't know exactly what had gone wrong between him and Luke, only that they'd fought and Emmett left. Luke might not want to talk about Emmett.

Considering what I'd heard about the roads, the first leg of the journey wasn't bad. Aside from a few strange-looking military convoys that blasted past us, there weren't a lot of cars.

I pulled over at a rest stop a couple of hours in, cut the engine, and pulled off my helmet.

"Need a break?" I asked Bazooka.

"Fuck, yeah." He craned his neck from side to side in an un-gooselike way as I pulled him out of the saddlebag. He took a few wobbly steps to get his bearings once I released him.

"That is most unpleasant," he said. "It's bad enough being stuffed inside this ridiculous goose but now?" He bobbed, picking up steam as he went. "Now I'm an ethereal, immortal being stuffed inside the body of a waterfowl stuffed inside a leather bag on the side of a glorified bicycle. Not exactly how I usually travel."

"Well, I'm sorry you hate your saddlebag so much," I said, narrowing my eyes at this complaining idiot. "Why didn't you just take off without me, if you were so miserable?"

"Because," he spat. "Because this stupid goose body loves you so damned much, and I can't control it one hundred percent of the time. If I left without you, it would flap its way back home to you every time I shut my eyes or let my guard down. It's so unbelievably stubborn."

A surge of warmth filled me for my friend, the goose. We'd been constant companions since I was thirteen. It was nice to hear he loved me, too.

Time for a subject change. Get his mind off our travels.

"So, what did you do to end up in this situation, anyway?"

He stepped over to a patch of grass and started poking around, looking for weeds.

"Bazooka? I know you can hear me."

He raised his head. "Let's just say I cheated at a game."

"What kind of game?"

He waved a wing. "You wouldn't understand it. I suppose the closest human comparison would be something like a cross between croquet and Hunger Games."

"So, like, shoot an object through a hoop and then try to kill each other with arrows?"

He honked in amusement. "Something like that."

I checked out the gas gauge by the orange-sodium glow of a streetlamp while Bazooka rustled his way through the grass, eating whatever he could find. To my surprise, the gas level hadn't changed much at all. The scooter had a tiny tank and we should be nearly out by now, but it was only down a notch from where we'd started. I double checked, even taking off the tank cover and peering in, like that was going to tell me anything, but I could tell from the sloshing that it was still full.

Bringing Bazooka along might have some unintended benefits. The question was, what else could he do?

After ten minutes, we strapped back into our helmets and got going again.

****

One thing about riding a scooter—it was interesting for an hour or two, seeing the world breeze by in such an immediate way, air against my skin, no car body separating me from the world. But it had its drawbacks. For one, the scooter had a tiny headlamp, and riding it in the dark was terrifying. Luckily, the weather was decent, so I didn't have to watch out for wet patches, but I concentrated fiercely, on the lookout for cars or animals or anything leaping out in front of us. Not that anything did.

The second drawback is that we couldn't sit and talk, like you do in a car. Too loud, for one. Plus, we had helmets on, and not the fancy kind with speakers in them to let you talk back and forth. Bazooka's was a plastic Pittsburgh Steelers helmet, for God's sake. We couldn't even listen to a radio.

It got dull, and fast.

When we started seeing signs for Des Moines, I pulled over and spread out the map, trying to pinpoint our destination in the pale pink light of sunrise. Luke's family lived in a small suburb on the west side of town, and I hoped we could find the street easily enough once we got there.

At last, around eight in the morning, we pulled into what I hoped was still Luke's driveway. It was a bright blue house, the kind with most of the living space on the main floor and a small, upper dormer level that probably contained uncomfortably slant-walled bedrooms. It sat back from the road with a long sloping lawn, a stand of maple trees, and the remnants of what looked like summer lilies, but were now khaki-colored straw. The gravel driveway wound down the side and continued toward a detached garage, painted the same blue as the house, with an old, worn basketball net on it. A faint hint of music came from that direction.

Bazooka nudged me from the saddlebag. "Think they still live here?"

"One way to find out." I straightened out my braid from the mess the helmet made of it, then climbed the steps to the porch.

My mouth was dry and my stomach an empty pit as I raised my hand to knock, then dropped it, then raised it again. Finally, a loud honk from Bazooka startled me into knocking for real. The sound echoed into the house through the narrow wooden door.

Tired footsteps shuffled toward the door and someone peeked through the glass pane. I tried to assume my least threatening stance. A rail-thin woman opened the door, her face familiar despite the many years since I'd seen her.

"Can I help you?" the woman asked.

"Mrs. Montegro. It's Louise Compton. From Davenport."

We'd known each other a little. Everyone in Davenport knew each other, especially the farming people. Which is why it surprised me when she stared at me with no recognition. "And?"

"I—I'm looking for Luke. Is he around?"

Her eyes traveled over me, and I fidgeted under her scrutiny but took the chance to study her back. The Mrs.

Montegro I'd known always looked put together, but today she wore a worn pink robe and well-scuffed slippers. Her white-streaked blond hair hung in a low ponytail, and her face was lined and worn. Behind her, I could see piles and piles of newspaper, shipping boxes, and mail stacked up on every surface. There didn't seem to be anyone else in the house.

"He's in the garage. Help yourself," she said finally, before turning and closing the door in my face.

I gaped at the door. I don't know what I'd expected, but I thought there'd be some sort of welcome, not this distant, almost suspicious response.

Confused, and with an unusually quiet goose at my side, I headed for the garage.

The door to Luke's apartment hung open to show a staircase heading up, but my childhood training in good manners compelled me to knock before entering. I don't think anyone could hear me over the thumping music blaring from inside, so I pounded harder. After a second, the volume of the music lowered and heavy footsteps pounded down the stairs.

Luke. In the flesh. Staring at us politely and with no sign of recognition.

He looked almost as I remembered, except older. His hair, still an Iowa-wheat shade of pale blond, hung longer and shaggier, and his eyes were still that clear blue, but his chin was stubbled and he clutched a beer can in one hand, even though it was barely eight a.m.

"Hey. What's up?"

"Luke? Luke Montegro?"

He looked more closely. "Nah, it can't be—is that Louise?"

"Lou. And yeah, it is. Could we come in?"

His gaze tracked down to the creature beside me. "You mean both of you? The goose too?"

I smiled and patted Bazooka on the head, hoping he wouldn't kill me for this later. "I do. He's terrified of neighborhood dogs, so I'd hate to leave him out here alone."

He turned, and we followed him up the stairs.

"You'll pay for that one," Bazooka muttered under his breath.

****

Luke and I sat on opposite ends of a ratty brown couch with a faint aroma of beer. He picked up an acoustic guitar that had been laying on the floor in front of him and strummed its out-of-tune strings idly.

Bazooka settled down near an electric space heater, where he busied himself cleaning out various bits of road debris from his feathers.

"What're you doing out here, little Lou? Man, it's been ages. You look great!"

"We're on our way out west. Looking for Emmett."

His face clouded over. "Ohhhhh, man, Lou, Emmett's not here. Hasn't been here for years. If that's why you came, you've wasted a trip."

"No, I know. This is our first stop." I explained the essentials. How Emmett had written to me, how I hadn't received them until now, and what we were doing.

"That's so epic, man. A fiery ball of death bearing down on us and you, Emmett's little sister, are going on a road trip. I should write a song about that." He looked up and winked. "Could be my last song. You never know."

Luke strummed a few misshapen chords on his guitar, and I took that as a signal to get down to business.

"I wanted to ask you a few things about Emmett. He came and stayed with you, right? When Mom and Dad kicked him out?"

Luke gestured around him. "Yeah, he lived right here in this very apartment."

He treated us to more power chords. I tried to look appreciative as Bazooka gave up all pretense of politeness and burrowed his head under a nearby pillow.

"I don't think your goose likes music much," he observed.

"He has simple tastes. He only likes grubs and lady geese."

Luke laughed, and something between us relaxed.

"You and Emmett were... were in a relationship, right? It was you that Mom and Dad found out about that summer." I could see him wince and jumped to correct my misimpression. "Not that it's your fault. It was one hundred percent my fault that people found out. If there's any blame, it's all on me."

Luke put down the guitar and stared at me. "What do you mean?"

I told him how I let my mother goad me into revealing Emmett's secrets, how I'd foolishly thought they'd accept it if I was just convincing enough, and how our entire world had blown up after.

"Ah," he said, voice quiet. "So, I had you to thank for that."

That stopped me cold. Somehow, it had never occurred to me that in unintentionally outing Emmett, I had also outed Luke as well. A hot swell of shame bloomed inside me. Here was another life that I had maybe ruined.

"Oh God, Luke, I'm so sorry. It never occurred to

me before now that you took the heat from this, too. Did your parents hear about it? I—I don't even know what to say."

In his corner, Bazooka pulled his head out from under the pillow and looked at me with sudden interest.

Luke struggled for a minute, then he gave up and offered me a sad smile instead. "Yeah, they heard about it. It made for a tough couple of weeks, but in the end, I convinced them that none of it was true. Everything calmed down after that, at least until Emmett showed up."

"And then what happened?"

"Well, Emmett was a mess when he got here. And he wanted comfort, and to continue our relationship, if you could call it that. Emmett and I were never really together—we weren't open enough or out enough. It wasn't a big, passionate affair.

"But that fall, when he was here, he was so… hurt. And lonely. And he pushed for all these emotional things he needed, but that I didn't necessarily feel."

My stomach ached like someone had stabbed it through with a sword, and my eyes leaked. Poor Emmett. Good God, how we'd hurt him.

"And it was too much for you."

He nodded. "Yeah, man. My position here was shaky. I pushed back. Pushed him away. I wasn't very good to him." He met my eyes. "Don't hate me, Lou."

I wiped my eyes with the back of one hand. Part of me wanted to rail at him for hurting my brother when he was lost, for not giving him everything he'd needed, but most of me understood. How could you give someone that much when you didn't know who you were yet?

"How could I hate you? You were a teenager. It

must've been a lot."

"It was. It was definitely a lot." Luke looked around for his beer and took a long sip. "Anyway, after a while, Emmett told me he was going west, and he wanted me to come with him. I said I wasn't going to do that, and… well, that was that."

I hugged a throw pillow to my chest for comfort. "Do you know where he went after that? Do you have any contact information for him, even if it was old?"

Luke shook his head. "He said something about Seattle or Portland. But he was between phones at that point, and when I tried his old email, it bounced." He paused. "Weird though—I've been thinking about him now, since the comet."

I nodded. Knowing we had less than two months to live seemed to have a clarifying effect on most people's thinking.

Luke gave us a few supplies—mostly canned chili and toilet paper—and then pointed out the best direction to get back on the highway from his front yard.

"If you find him," Luke said as we hugged goodbye, "tell him… tell him hi. And tell him I'm sorry."

****

"I don't understand," Bazooka said as I strapped on our helmets. "Why wasn't he angry at you? Why weren't you angry at him? You should've been screaming at each other and yet you…" He broke off and squawked, unable to put what he had observed into words.

"Forgave each other?"

He made what can only be called a rude noise. "Humans. You have such an instinct for causing suffering, and yet you're capable of so much mercy. I don't understand you at all."

I stopped to think about it. Why hadn't we been harder on each other? For sure, the comet bearing down on us made it blindingly clear how pointless it was to entertain old hurts. But it was also more than that. It was a kind of mutual recognition that we'd caused suffering and suffered in turn, in ways that we never intended, and that our mistakes held devastating consequences. What is there to do with the recognition that we are, all of us, capable of great selfishness in the face of love, except to face each other with some kind of compassion?

I leaned over and helped fasten Bazooka in, and we set off in the late morning sun, heading for the state border.

****

We hit Nebraska in the late afternoon, after endless slowdowns. The sight of the big green sign saying "*You are leaving Iowa*" should have brought a cheer to my lips, but a sharp pang caused me to hit the brakes.

"Hang on," I said, pulling onto the shoulder. I turned off the engine, my breath catching in my throat. Bazooka made inquiring noises behind me, but I ignored him and climbed off the scooter to look behind us. "Just hang on."

I wrapped my arms around my stomach. It hadn't hit me before, but now I couldn't avoid the realization. This wasn't some grand adventure. I was leaving my home, possibly forever. Who knew how long it might take me to find Emmett? If it worked out and I found him, there was no way to tell if he'd want to come back to Iowa with me. Could I even ask him to? No way would it be a good thing to drag him back to the people who rejected him just in time to get wiped out by a giant rock from the sky.

I knew one thing—if I found him, there was no way

I would leave him again. If he stayed put, I would stay put with him. I'd lost six years of time with my brother; I wasn't going to lose him again if I was lucky enough to get him back.

As my nose prickled with impending tears, the facts became crystal clear. Chances were, I would never see my parents or Maggie or the house I grew up in again. Ever. We were going to die on opposite sides of the continent, smashed to smithereens by Comet Lucinda.

Something soft nuzzled my leg. I looked down to find Bazooka there.

"You're leaking again," he said acerbically. The way his goose body was rubbing reassuringly against my side took the edge off his tone. "I'm beginning to think you aren't emotionally stable."

I half-laughed. "Yeah, no," I gasped, still preventing my insides from detonating by holding everything in with both hands. "No, I guess I'm not. Just realizing that all my choices here suck. Like totally suck, you know?"

He nuzzled again, looking so simultaneously concerned and disgusted with himself that I couldn't help but crack a small grin.

"You're gonna kill me with all this emotional bullshit, you know that?" he muttered, but his voice was soft. "Now come on, let's get back on the road before someone runs us over. You promised me sunflower seeds for dinner and I'm not letting you off the hook."

"Okay, fine," I said, sniffling. "You're a hard taskmaster, Falthaom the Repulsive."

He chortled in a way that sounded almost like he was choking on a bug. "That's why I'm here."

Chapter Ten

March 28, 2020
Dear Emmett,

It's my birthday. Thirteen doesn't seem like such a big deal, really, but I woke up excited because I'd been thinking all week: maybe this was it. The day you come back.

On Sunday, Mom said she had a surprise for me after church, so of course I decided it was you. That's what I would do in your place. Take some time away, let everyone calm down, and then make a surprise reappearance for my birthday.

I wore my best dress to church, the new one, because I apparently grew two inches overnight, and because you've never seen it. I wanted to look nice when we came home and found you here.

Which we didn't. Not only were you not sitting there waiting when we got home, but it turned out that the surprise was... a new goose.

I mean, he's a great little guy, and normally I'd be super excited to get a new animal for my birthday. If only I hadn't worked myself up into such a fit, expecting you. Even when they dragged me out to the barn, showed me the newcomer, I was still looking around, waiting for you to pop out from behind a hay bale. It took me a lot longer than it should have to figure out that the goose was the surprise. He's a special breed that they only have in

Europe. Gray and white with an orange bill. A greylag, they called him.

I tried to act enthusiastic, but really I wanted to cry. I kneeled and hugged him—he really is adorable, even if he tried to bite me—and tried to hide my face from them, because I could tell they were disappointed.

And then today came, my actual birthday, and despite my best intentions, I started thinking you were going to show up again. Which you didn't. We had cake, and I pretended it was great, and then I went to my room as soon as I could, and now, here I am, writing to you.

Did you even try? Did you try to call? Send a card? Are you really that mad at me?

I hope you're okay. I miss you.

Love, Lou

PS: I named the goose Bazooka.

****

Men and women in robes clustered on the side of the road just outside of Omaha, holding protest signs and standing in groups of three or four. They appeared to have rifled through the local churches for choir robes, resulting in a mishmash of satiny gowns in shades of purple, gold, and white. The result was more Easter-Sunday-celebration than sackcloth and ashes, but I guess you had to take what you could get.

I read a few of the closest signs:

"Repent. The End is Near."

"The Coment is a Judgment From God."

"Baptisms, Free of Charge."

A few hundred yards later, we came around a bend and squealed to a halt behind a handful of angry, honking cars. In front of them, a dozen or more of the protestors had linked hands and blocked all the lanes. I pulled over to the side before we reached them, taking a second to get my bearings.

"Who are they?" Bazooka muttered as the engine cut off.

"Fundamentalists. Leave it to me. I speak their language."

By any rights, I could easily have been one of them, hoping to help a few more souls repent before the comet reduced us all to ashes.

One of the robed women noticed us and came over with a bright smile. Did they operate on some kind of personal quota system? Like at the end of the day, they'd turn in their punch card to Jesus himself and see what prizes they'd won? I made myself smile and steeled myself for some hypocrisy.

"Can I talk to you about our Lord and Savior?" she chirruped. She was holding what looked like a water pistol. Bright green. It clashed with her yellow robe. When she saw me looking at it, she shook it once, letting the water inside it slosh around. "We're baptizing as many people as we can out here today."

"With squirt guns?"

She shrugged. "Desperate times mean desperate measures. We've got a tub over there too, if you're more into full immersion."

I looked past her and saw a small kiddie pool behind the cluster of her friends, who were all watching with what looked like jealousy. A few of them broke off and started wandering among the idling cars, knocking on windows and then spraying people when they rolled them down.

"I'm already baptized," I said. "Been a churchgoer my whole life."

She looked momentarily disappointed, then brightened again. "Well, it can't hurt to repeat it, can it? Add a second coat, just in case?"

There didn't seem to be any way I was getting out of this without getting squirted. I eyed the gun with suspicion. "You sure that's just water in there?"

"Water, and the love of God!"

"And we can go through after?" She nodded. "Okay, go ahead."

She lit up like a candle, and I shut my eyes as she laid a hand on my forehead in prayer, beseeching God to take me in when the comet came, and then, before I could move or regret it, water hit me on the forehead in a frigid stream.

"Well, that was… good…" I said, opening my eyes and letting the water roll down my face. Was it bad manners to wipe away baptismal water? I wasn't sure.

"That was ridiculous!" Bazooka burst out beside me.

The woman gasped, staring at him.

"What?" he snarked. "Never seen a goose before?"

She burst into motion, backing up several feet. "Rosalie! Bert! We've got a demon over here!" she shrieked. "Everyone! I need prayer warriors here right now!"

Bazooka stepped forward and spread both of his wings out to full. "Oh, just try it," he trumpeted. "I dare you!"

"Bazooka!" I hissed. "This isn't helping!"

Within seconds, a ring of rainbow-colored robes had encircled us, their wearer's faces lit with fervor as they murmured prayers. Bazooka circled in the center, hissing at each of them in turn. I just stood there, chewing my lip to pieces. How was I supposed to defuse this?

One man stepped forward and distracted Bazooka from the front, and before I realized what was happening, someone else grabbed him from behind and tucked him under one arm.

"Don't hurt him!" I shouted. "He's valuable!"

"Oh, don't you worry, honey," the woman who'd started it all said. "We'll just knock that demon out of him, and you can have your goose back in a second. We're professionals."

The group headed to the baptismal pool, and I followed, twisting my hands and trying to come up with a plan. There were too many of them for me to fight off. Bazooka clearly didn't have the power to deal with it, or he would have already.

"Be gentle with him!" I called as they manhandled him to the edge of the pool. Bazooka turned his head and hissed at me, too. I gave him a look. *You started this,* it said. *Play along so we can get back on the road.*

"The love of Jesus Christ compels you to leave this poor creature," the man intoned, raising a hand to Bazooka's tiny forehead. Bazooka bit him and the man winced but continued. "Torment him no more. Be free from this living creature and return to the depths from where you came."

"I'm not a demon!" Bazooka crowed. "I will not be exorcised by a group of idiots wearing rainbow-tinted polyester—"

They cut his tirade off by dunking him into the pool.

"—and you're not even Catholic!" he continued without fail when he came up. "You have to be Catholic to do an exorcism, you fu—"

They dunked him again, holding him under for a

second. "The power of Satan is strong in this humble beast," the man continued, while the people circled around him murmured and prayed, hands raised. "Please cleanse his soul and return him to peace."

Bazooka came up sputtering this time. "Still here, you fucking morons," he hissed.

I could see it happening in slow motion. The man was getting irritated. His eyebrows furrowed and his face flushed. He tightened his grip on Bazooka's neck.

He was going to drown him.

"Wait!" I shouted. "Wait please! Can I help?"

"She's a friend of the beast," one woman muttered.

"He's my goose. I've had him since I was thirteen. Just let me pray over him, too?"

The man motioned for me to come forward and I did, kneeling at the side of the tub. I laid a hand on Bazooka's chest.

"Please don't let any harm come to my friend Bazooka," I said, looking him right in the eye and willing him to get my message. "Don't let him be killed by the spirit inside him. Please, for the love of God. Help him be just a goose again."

For the love of God, I thought, trying to beam my thoughts into his brain, *shut up, you stupid imp, before they kill you. Or is that what you want? Do you want them to snap your neck so you can be free of that body, and of me?*

Bazooka sagged, and the protestors murmured. The man took hold of Bazooka, who didn't fight him this time, dunked him under one more time, holding him for a frighteningly long beat, then released him in the center of the pool.

The crowd watched expectantly.

Bazooka looked around in feigned confusion, then tentatively paddled his way around the water, acting like he was looking for bugs to eat. I almost believed it, except he threw me a quick wink as he went by.

Cheers broke out. Half of the circle fell to their knees in prayer, rejoicing in their good works.

"Here you go, miss," the leader said, brushing the water off Bazooka and returning him to my arms. "Good as new."

Bazooka did his best to appear dim-witted and confused. I hugged him desperately. "Thank you. Thank you so much."

Let them mistake my relief for gratitude. Instead of liberating me from a demon, they'd nearly killed my only ally, tentative and fraught as that alliance might be.

I ran back to the scooter and strapped him into his sack, then headed for the road. In the hubbub, the protestors had abandoned their lane and the traffic backup was now gone. They waved us off, obviously pleased as punch with themselves for having met and vanquished a demon.

****

We scootered along until we were out of sight, and then I pulled over and stomped the ignition off.

Bazooka turned his head to me. "What? Why are we stopping?"

I flipped up the visor of my helmet and glared at him, gritting my teeth as I spat the words out. "Were you trying to get yourself killed back there?"

He gasped theatrically. "No, of course not!"

"You were trying to get them to kill you so you could leave me!" My voice shook as the betrayal sank in. "How could you do that to me? I thought we were a team!"

He wriggled in his bag. "I wasn't, Lou," he said, his tone almost sincere. "Really. I just lost my temper. Bunch of idiots in their shiny gowns trying to exorcise me? If I'd had my full powers, I could've turned all of them into rocks."

I narrowed my eyes. "I don't know if I believe you."

"I just lost my head. Didn't think they'd really try to drown me."

"I thought we were becoming friends!"

He scoffed, but quietly. "Imps don't have friends. I've told you that before."

I gritted my teeth hard enough to shatter them. Fine. So we weren't friends. I guess I could deal with that. What was I thinking, imagining Falthaom might actually care about me? He'd just wanted to get away from the farm. Part of me already knew that.

He was watching me. "But you're not bad. For a human, I mean. I mean, I find your company tolerable."

I huffed out a breath. "Gee, thanks."

He clacked his bill at me. "And what about you, making me play along with their little exorcism game? How fucking demeaning was that?"

"I don't care! You deserved it. You've got to be careful who you reveal yourself around, Bazooka! If they'd snapped your neck instead of dunking you, I wouldn't have been able to stop them, and my goose would be dead! And I'd be all alone out here!" My breathing grew ragged as that sank in. "You can't leave me, Bazooka. Falthaom. Whoever. I need your help."

He ducked his head down in a gesture that looked like acceptance, then fixed me with one glittering eye. "I won't," he mumbled. "I'm here."

We stared at each other for a few breaths, and then I flipped down my visor without another word and started the engine.

I had no choice but to believe him, but good God, I hoped he meant it. I wasn't ready to be out here alone.

****

I continued to fume about Bazooka's antics as we puttered through eastern Nebraska, but as the second hour passed, the scenery sliding by pushed it from the forefront of my mind. When Bazooka nudged me and suggested we stop to let the scooter cool, I was feeling friendly enough to see his point. The scooter got persnickety after a couple of hours of steady driving, and letting it rest from time to time was smart. I had no idea what we'd do if the engine overheated or something broke. Better safe than sorry.

"Besides," he said. "We could use a break, and it's time for dinner. Want to stop for the night and start fresh tomorrow?"

Did he have a point? Friend, Nebraska wasn't too far, but as excited as I was to get there, I had to admit I felt a growing exhaustion. I wasn't used to riding a scooter for long periods. Everything from my wrists to my lower back ached from sitting static in position for hours. I hoped I'd get used to it.

"Okay," I said, looking around. "Where should we go?"

Bazooka wriggled in his bag. "Let me out and I'll take a quick scan from the sky. See if there's a barn or something nearby."

I helped him out of the saddlebag and helmet. Bazooka stretched his long neck and wings. Soon enough, he'd limbered up to his satisfaction and flapped his way into the sky. He circled around me overhead, once, then again, and then he was off across the field beside me.

My hands went clammy and my head spun. Was this a trick? He was a trickster, after all. Imps, as he described them, were the kings of mischief. What if Falthaom found it utterly hilarious to leave me on the side of the road and never come back?

My breath came faster. He wouldn't do that, would he? We had a connection. Still, as I pushed the scooter into a more hidden spot and sank down to wait, I was all too aware of how absolutely naive I was. Stupid, stupid, stupid. I was a literal child, and I was out here, putting my faith in an imp, stuck in a goose?

I pulled my knees toward my chest, clutching my arms around them. And I waited.

****

I'd almost given up hope when a faint honking hit me on the wind. It had to be him, right? I jumped to my feet and scanned the sky, waving my arms even though I didn't know who I was waving to.

Sure enough, he landed at my side a few moments later.

"Miss me?" Bazooka said. It wasn't possible for a goose to smirk, but somehow he conveyed the expression, and I could tell from the glittering intensity in his eye that he had read my discomfort.

"Nah. It was good to have some alone time."

"Liar." He stopped to take a bite of a wheat stalk next to me, then spat it out. "Anyhow, there's a barn that looks deserted about a half mile back. Hop on and I'll show you."

I blinked. "You're not going to ride along?"

He shook his neck vigorously. "No, not getting back into that thing until I have to. I'll go slow. And it's a scooter. It's made for going over fields and stuff."

It wasn't. Dirt bikes might be made for this sort of thing, but motor scooters weren't. The wheels had a hard time gripping on the loose soil, and several times I nearly laid the scooter flat—especially with all our heavy baggage—before Bazooka redirected us to a narrow country road that wound through the surrounding farmland. There, it was easier to follow him and we ended up pulling into a single lane dirt track and winding our way to our proposed campsite.

The barn's formerly white walls were nearly gray, half its roof had blown away or fallen in, and the hayloft at one end had collapsed. Every board in the building seemed to creak randomly, and the scatterings of old grain and the musky smell of long-gone animals showed it had once been well-used. The nearest house was visible in the distance, but I didn't see any telltale lights shining in its windows. There was nothing to show anyone had been here in the barn for a long time.

Bazooka wobbled off into the fields to find insects while I laid out our tarp and bedrolls, then set to work making a small fire just outside the entrance to the barn. Emmett had taught me how to make a fire with two sticks and string when I was younger, but tonight I didn't have the patience for the slow way of doing things. Instead, I pulled out the candle lighter I'd brought along and lit a crumpled newspaper I'd picked up earlier. In no time, I had a smoldering pile of sticks.

"Nice work," Bazooka said as he emerged from the surrounding fields.

"Did you find food?"

He bobbed his head. "Would still welcome a little corn, though."

I pulled out our supply bag and laid out a generous scattering of seed corn for him, then dug out the peanut butter and crackers for me.

"Are you going to be okay eating just peanut butter?" Bazooka eyed me. "Don't American teenagers need burgers to stay alive?"

I snorted. "What kind of television have you been watching?"

He shrugged. "No sweat off my back. If you keel over, I can just, you know, keep flying to wherever." I was just about to make a smart remark when he appeared to lift one wing and hit himself in the head with it. He staggered.

"What the heck was that? Did you just slap yourself?"

Bazooka wheeled in a circle, craning his neck and looking for an interloper who didn't exist. "I did not!" he snarled. "The goose did it. The stupid goose just smacked me in the head with its wing."

I laughed. "Are you telling me that Bazooka's brain overrode your control and out-and-out smacked you because you said you didn't mind if I died?"

Bazooka turned and glared at me. "And why is that amusing?"

I shouldn't have kept laughing, but I just couldn't help it. It was too funny. "Better be careful what you say," I said, between gasps. "Bazooka might just beat the living crap out of you. You know no one in their right mind messes with a goose."

Bazooka gave me his most withering look. "Ah, mockery. Nice. I'm pleased to see a side of you that isn't so goody goody."

I snorted. "I literally stole a scooter and ran away with you a few days after we met. How could you say I'm a goody-two-shoes?"

"That's just surface dressing, and done out of your ridiculous levels of guilt. Underneath, you're as sweet and good as a newborn gosling."

The way he said it clarified that this was not a compliment.

I bristled. "I'm not doing this out of guilt! I'm doing it because I love Emmett. And I don't want to die without seeing him again!"

He settled down, tucking his feet under him, just close enough to the fire for its glow to turn him orange. He turned his head toward me, his eyes reflecting the flames. I sucked in a breath; it was the first time I saw him as the otherworldly creature he was.

"Oh yeah," he said, clearly unbothered. "That too. But it's not the only reason you're here. You just don't want to—" he made a sound like something getting vaporized "—vamoose with all this on your conscience."

I gritted my teeth. "You're kind of a jerk. Has anyone ever told you that?"

He clacked his bill at me, much too pleased. "Only just about every day of my life."

I turned my back on him and crammed peanut butter crackers into my mouth.

****

I couldn't sleep, of course. As much camping as I'd done as a kid, I was no longer a kid with my infallible big brother at my side, stoking the fire and keeping the night terrors away. I was seventeen—old enough to drive, work, and plan out the rest of my life—but old enough to face the coming comet on my own? Laying on the hard ground watching the stars above me made my heart sink. Was one of those dots the rock that was coming to kill us all?

As I lay there, feeling tiny, I remembered the last time I'd gone camping with Emmett and how I'd had no idea that we'd never do that again. Life is like that, I think—people focus on firsts more than lasts. The first baby step, the first day of school, the first kiss. It had never occurred to me before now how little thought we give to the last of something. Everything has an end point. There'd been a moment that was the last time I'd held my mother's hand. Thinking about it now made my chest tighten up, but I'm sure neither of us realized its significance at the time.

I hadn't noticed the last time someone tucked me in at night. The last day of school before this summer turned out to be the last school day ever, although none of us knew it. Would we have acted differently if we had? Marked it? Hugged our friends and lingered over our locker doors when we closed them for the last time?

Now the entire world was nothing but a series of 'lasts.' All over the world, people were marking the end of things. The last month with their family. The last time they'd ever go to the store. The last day they bothered to go to work—because why labor for a paycheck you're never going to see?

Soon, people would have their last dinner. Hug their children for the very last time and put them to bed, or tuck into the couch to stay up all night because bedtimes didn't matter much when a comet was going to hit. There would be last tears, last smiles, last squeezes of hands.

It made everything feel both unreal and

monumental, like every action I took, every step, was historic. There were probably other people like me, making their way on back roads, seeking lost friends or trying to reach family, or even heading to the coast for one last look at the ocean. But not knowing for sure made it possible that I was doing something unprecedented and utterly unique in all human history. The last cross-country drive.

This was the last road trip.

I rolled over and watched the sparks drift upward, finally feeling that heaviness of sleep steal over me. The last thing I saw before my eyes closed was Bazooka's small chest rising and falling, his head tucked under his wing.

Chapter Eleven

September 15, 2020
Dear Emmett,
If you were here, I hope you would've warned me about how middle school is literally the worst thing ever. The least you could've done is come back for me and spared me this hell. I would've gone with you. We could've run off to the woods, camped out for a month, maybe driven to the coast so I could finally see the ocean. I could've gotten a job babysitting or bagging groceries to help. We could've figured it out.

My life sucks. Suddenly no one wants to talk about books anymore, and I have nothing in common with anyone except the school librarian.

Classes are boring. I have to go to gym class and pretend I can dribble a basketball without falling over my own feet, and everyone makes fun of me. They call me Farmer Lou. This one kid started it, some mouth-breather who can't even do simple math, and now everyone's picked it up. I'll never get away from it. I'm stubborn enough not to show them it bothers me, but I hate them all.

Except Maggie. She's still my friend, thank God, even though she wears lip gloss now and is getting boobs and is turning pretty in ways that seem completely unfair. None of that is happening to me. I'm just gawky and flat-chested and my hair is a rat's nest. Nothing changes.

And maybe it's not fair, but I've been feeling guilty for so long, and suddenly, I'm mad. Really mad. How could you walk off and leave me like this, and more importantly, WHY THE HECK DIDN'T YOU COME BACK FOR ME?

What kind of big brother does something like that?

You must know I didn't mean to tell them. You know it was an accident. They taught us all this stuff about forgiveness and family. Do you even remember any of it? Why am I the only one in this family who takes any of the stuff we learned at church seriously? It's infuriating.

I have to go feed the goats. I'm not signing this nicely, because I think maybe you deserve it.

Later.

Lou

*****

March 18th, 2021

Dear Lou,

Happy early birthday!! By the time this arrives, you'll officially be fourteen, or very close to it. I hope you get this. I've enclosed some cash for you to go buy yourself something nice. Nothing practical—get something exciting, like new books or a bicycle or something.

I tried to call you on your birthday last year. Did Mom tell you? I called in the morning, before church, and she picked up. When she realized it was me, she got quiet, and she wouldn't put you on. I guess I'm still a bad influence. But I thought about you all day, and I hope maybe you could feel it, and that you got the card I sent even though it was a couple of days late.

She said I shouldn't call anymore, and the next time I tried, the number didn't work, so that's that. I guess they're serious about not changing their minds.

I'm still living in Friend, Nebraska, working at the library, but I'm thinking about moving on. I like it here well enough, but I don't want to stay in Nebraska forever. I've always wanted to see mountains. I met a guy who works on a ranch out near Jackson, Wyoming. He showed me pictures, and it looks amazing. I might head there in June, when the students get out for the summer so Mari can hire someone to replace me. I don't want to leave her hanging.

I'm doing okay. I've taken about six business courses at the community college and they're as boring as you'd expect, but it turns out I'm sort of good with numbers. Mari helped me find a counselor here who could listen and take some of the weight off from everything that's happened. It hasn't been easy, but I'm making peace with things. With the decisions I've had to make about who I am. It's been a long road.

Don't worry, I'll let you know where I am if I move. I hope you're reading these and thinking about me and just not allowed to write back.

Remember that I love you, and take care of yourself, Lou.

Love, Em

****

Flashback, May 25, 2018

Camping with Emmett and Luke—always one of my favorite things to do.

Emmett set up the tents side by side—a larger one for them and a smaller pup tent for me. I loved having my own. With the two of them right next to me, I never felt unsafe. While the boys finished unloading, I got to work setting up my sleeping area—hanging a lantern from the roof of the pup tent, then stringing up a small set of battery-operated fairy lights. After that, I unrolled my sleeping bag, put out the books and notebooks I'd brought, and laid out my stuffed animals. Perfect.

We spent the first day goofing off. After a big camp breakfast, we hiked, stopping at the nearby lake to play. The boys fished while I jumped in, shorts and all. I paddled around like a dog, enjoying the feeling of mud beneath my toes and the occasional creature that nibbled at my legs and feet to see if I was food.

"You're dirtier than a dog, Lou," Luke complained as I came out.

"I know, isn't it great?" Inspired, I shook myself like a dog too, splashing both him and Emmett with droplets. Luke threw a potato chip at me in protest. I caught it and ate it.

"All right, you two, calm down," Emmett said. I made a smug face at Luke. "No one throws food at my little sister but me."

And with that, he tossed half of a hot dog roll at me, hitting me in the chest. Luke laughed, and I made a face before sitting down on the dock to ball up little pieces of bread and feed them to the fish.

****

That night, Luke and Emmett went to take the food waste to the dumpster, and I stayed behind, feeding pinecones into the fire and watching them combust in a shower of sparks.

CRACK. A branch snapped somewhere behind me, in the stand of trees off to the west of our campsite.

"Emmett?" I called, scanning the trees. "Luke?"

Nobody answered. The hair on my neck prickled. Probably a deer, right? I leaned forward, trying to see eye shine, and then jumped to my feet as another branch cracked somewhere off to the right.

Cougars. Bobcats. Coyotes… Bears!

I made a split-second decision and grabbed one of our hiking sticks for defense, then I flicked on my headlamp and made a beeline for the main loop road in the direction I knew Emmett and Luke had gone.

Campgrounds at night are magical places. The scent of pine and campfires, the way you move from bubbles of firelight and laughter to absolute darkness in the space of a few dozen yards. There are people nearby, but when you're in your campsite, none of the noise reaches you. Normally I loved the silence and the way the stars glimmered through the trees, but tonight I scurried from light to light, anxious to find my brother before whatever was lurking around our campsite shredded our tents and ate our marshmallows.

It didn't take me long to reach the dumpsters. A single orange light on a telephone pole lit the place. It was neat, quiet, and deserted.

"Em? Luke?"

No answer. They must be on their way back, going the other direction. I broke into a light jog and headed around the other side of the loop.

I relaxed when Emmett's voice reached me—although I couldn't see him yet, I'd know his laugh anywhere. A voice that must have been Luke's murmured in return, and on a sudden whim, I flicked off my headlamp so I could surprise them. Why not give them a scare?

I crept closer, ready to pounce, and then I stopped.

As my eyes adjusted to the dark, I could see Luke and Emmett huddled together a bit off the path, near one of the taller trees. Something about their pose, outlined in silhouette by the light of a nearby campground, confused me. They were standing closer than I'd expected, one of them with his back against the tree, and the other leaning in and propping themselves up against the tree with one arm. I couldn't tell who was who.

What were they doing? Were they hugging? Arguing? Whispering to each other?

And then, the outside person leaned in and connected with the person leaning against the tree in a way I recognized more clearly.

Kissing. They were kissing.

I didn't know what I thought about that, but I had the sudden urge to stop it.

"Emmett!" They startled apart. I flicked on my headlamp and they both clocked me immediately. Their faces were bluish in the LED light.

"Lou!" Emmett ran toward me. "What's wrong? Are you okay?"

"There's an animal in the campsite. I was scared."

Luke and Emmett exchanged a glance, then Emmett took my hand. "Okay, let's go back and see what it is."

****

The animal was long gone by the time we got back. Luke disappeared into the tent and Emmett pulled up a camp chair next to me as I sat, pretending to read but mostly mulling over what I'd seen. "Should we talk about this?"

I closed the book. "Talk about what?"

Emmett pulled off his baseball cap and the light from the fire glinted off his coppery hair. "I think you saw me and Luke doing something that surprised you. We can talk about it if you want, Lou."

I swallowed. This was part of why I loved Emmett so much. He never treated me like a kid. If I had questions, he answered them. He never made me feel like I was too young or too silly to hang out with or talk about an idea with.

I struggled for words. "It… it looked like you were kissing?"

Emmett nodded and stared into the fire. "Yeah. We were."

"But I thought Laurie was your girlfriend. Are you dating Luke?"

Emmett blinked at me, surprised, and I felt a little thrill at that. I wasn't some kid. I was a voracious reader and an excellent observer.

"It's complicated, Lou," he said. "To be honest, Laurie and I are just good friends. We go to dances together and do things because we like to hang out. And because I can't go to a dance with someone like Luke."

"Because he's a boy."

"Yeah."

"And that's bad?"

"No, it's not bad. But people here think it is. Everyone expects me to be a certain person, to act a certain way. Mom thinks I'm going to graduate and marry Laurie, like it's all set in stone." He sighed. "To be honest, Lou, I'm not sure who I am. But I'm trying to find out, and part of it, I think, is that I like Luke. I'm just not ready to tell people about it yet."

Silence reigned, punctuated by the distant, spooky call of an owl. I pondered what he'd told me. I knew what our church said about boys who liked other boys. It was a sin. I'd always been taught that. But Emmett and Luke were dear to me, and I knew them too well to swallow the idea that they were evil-doers. So what if they wanted to kiss each other instead of some girl?

"Are you okay with that, Lou?" he asked. When I turned from the fire, his eyes were searching mine.

I shrugged. "Yeah. I'm fine with it. I like Luke."

Emmett grinned, then looked serious. "But you can't say anything to Mom and Dad, okay? This is really important. They wouldn't understand. I think they'd be pretty mad about it."

I nodded. No problem. Emmett's secrets were his own, and I couldn't imagine a circumstance in which I would ever want to share what I'd learned tonight.

****

Back to the present, where the rustling crackle of burned-out coals from the fire woke me first, but I ignored it, wanting to drift back into my dreams about happier days and camping trips and times when our family was still whole. I had almost drifted off when a new sound—a footstep—jolted me awake.

I scrabbled backward, instinctively not wanting to be trapped in my sleeping bag, and scanned the surrounding darkness. My pulse pounded in my ears.

It was still dark, but the sky was brightening in the east in a way that indicated sunrise. And there, kneeling across from me, was the shadowy outline of a person I didn't know. They froze, rabbit-like, and a pair of dark eyes met mine across the embers from our dying fire.

"Who're you?" I jumped to my feet and scanned for something to wield as a weapon. Beside me, Bazooka jolted awake. I stepped between the goose and the stranger, breathing hard.

"Whoa," the person said, "calm down. I was cold, and I saw your camp and thought…"

"And thought what?" I said, still trying to get a good look at them. Their voice sounded female, but it was hard to tell. "Let me see you."

The person moved closer to the faltering flames. It was a young boy, maybe twelve or thirteen, wearing a faded sweatshirt with the hood tied around his head, probably for warmth, and a scrubby pair of jeans that had seen better days. His face was dirty, and he looked more frightened of me than I did of him. The boy held his hands out, showing he wasn't a threat.

"Who are you?" I said, relaxing a little. I could feel Bazooka on high alert behind me, but he stayed quiet. I was grateful for that minor miracle.

"I'm Peter. And I was cold."

Peter looked tired and thin, and I felt like a monster. "Do you want something to eat?" I reached down for my pack and pulled out the mega-sized jar of peanut butter I'd brought along. "I don't have anything interesting, but if you like peanut butter, it's your lucky day."

Peter's eyes lit up in awe. "I love peanut butter! Could I please…"

I dug out a spoon and handed the jar over to him. "Help yourself. I'll never get through that whole jar by myself."

Peter sat back down and shoveled peanut butter into his face with the ferocity of a badger. "Oh my God," he moaned. "So good."

I laughed despite my caution and passed him some water. "How long has it been since you ate anything? What are you doing out here?"

Peter didn't look up. "About thirty hours. And I'm trying to get to my aunt's in Kansas City."

It was the opposite direction from our route. My

conscience twinged.

"On foot? You're a long way from Kansas City."

He pointed behind him, where I could make out the outline of a bicycle on its side in the grass behind him, with a lump I assumed was a backpack beside it. I sagged in relief, knowing that this kid wasn't entirely without resources.

"But why are you alone? Where's your family?"

"Gone," he said. "They're gone. My parents taught at the college in Omaha, in the physics department, and about two weeks ago they disappeared while I was at a friend's house. The neighbors told me some men in a black SUV stormed the house and stuffed them in a car." His voice broke a little as he said this last bit, and my heart did a flip for him.

I frowned. "Government?"

The kid nodded, swallowing hard. "People are disappearing all over the place. There's rumors of some big bunker out in the western edge of the state where important people are being stuffed away. Probably that's where they took them."

"And they just left you?"

The kid faltered. "Well, I wasn't there. The neighbors said my parents fought like hell. Maybe they would've taken me too if I'd been home."

I stared into the fire as he took another big, gloppy spoonful of peanut butter. I'd heard rumors; everyone had. Secret underground facilities where important people were being squirreled away like nuts against the coming winter. The critical point was that "important people" in this context meant very smart or very rich people. There wasn't much room for anyone else, but I'd never expected they'd bust up families. I figured if you lucked out and had a planetary geologist or a nuclear engineer in the family, you'd hit the jackpot; you were safe. It sounded, instead, like people were getting kidnapped and spirited away, with or without their loved ones.

"Why do you have a goose?" the kid asked.

I turned to look at Bazooka, who was still pretending to be a regular barnyard fowl. "Oh, well, he's a pet." Bazooka made a rattling noise that I had no trouble interpreting as outrage. "I couldn't leave him behind when I left."

I told him a little about our mission. After that, we passed the next half hour in silence, sharing the warmth of the fire and the occasional bit of granola bar. The sun peeked over the horizon, and in the dim light of dawn I could more clearly see how hungry the kid looked.

"Are you sure you need to go to Kansas City? You could come with us to Oregon. We'd be happy to have you along." Bazooka stirred at my feet, clearly not sure about this offer.

"I couldn't keep up on my bike," the kid said. "And yeah, I want to go find my aunt and cousins. It should only take a couple days. I can make it."

I frowned, then made a decision I knew was rash. "Bring your pack over here," I said, grabbing my own and unzipping it next to the fire. "What do you have and what do you need? We can spare some things."

Bazooka waddled around us, fussing as the kid and I laid out our inventories at my feet. As I suspected, he hadn't planned very well. He had a box of cereal and some string cheese, two bottles of water, and very little else. I split our supplies as best I could, trying to ensure the kid had more calories to get him through several days

112

of athlete-level hard work. I halved our granola bar supply, split out a whole sleeve of crackers for him, and gave him some of our precious jerky. I even found an empty plastic bag and slopped about a quarter of the peanut butter into it. It wasn't pretty, but he'd be able to get some protein.

"I'm sorry I can't help you more," I said, a whirlpool of guilt churning deep inside my gut. He was only twelve; he should come with us instead of heading off to a family who might not even be there. A better person would take a detour to make sure he got to Kansas City, then return to their own quest. If only it was even somewhat in the right direction! Still, the countdown was ticking away—it was now somewhere between four and five weeks until impact day, and I had no idea how long it would take us to get across the country, and to find Emmett once we did. I only knew that we couldn't afford a week's detour to run off to Missouri.

I pushed a few extra pieces of jerky into his pile to help assuage my conscience. "I'm sorry we can't go with you."

"It's okay," the kid said, stuffing everything into his bag. "Thanks for the food! I really appreciate it." He stood and stretched, looking at the sky. "It's light enough to get going, I guess. Good luck. I hope you find your brother."

"I hope you find your aunt and your cousins. Be careful."

He picked up the bike and wheeled it around the barn, then he stopped and looked back. "Oh, by the way, if you see big black SUVs, get off the road. It's not just kidnappings going on. I've heard all kinds of crazy stuff."

He hopped on the bike and started wheeling it through the grass back toward the road.

****

Bazooka fumed. As soon as the kid was out of hearing range, he rounded on me in all his feathery fury. He spread his wings wide and raised his neck to full height, advancing toward me one orange foot at a time. I squashed the instinct to step back.

"What in the bloody *hell* are you doing, giving that kid so much of your food? You gave him over *half* of our supplies! *Your* supplies, that is! You can't eat bugs and grass like me!"

"He needed our help. He's a kid, completely on his own. I mean, I at least have you."

"Exactly," Bazooka said. "I'm responsible for your dumb ass. And how the hell am I supposed to get you to the other side of the country if you're starving to death?"

I raised my chin and glared down at him. "I've got enough food left for at least a week. And I've got money! We can buy more if we need to." I'd packed a wad of tens and twenties I'd been saving up from babysitting and hay bailing jobs over the last couple years.

"Oh yeah, because capitalism is going so amazingly well right now," he groused. "I'm sure every grocery store between here and Oregon is full of yummy snacks and healthy vegetables, dropped off by the supply chain, right on schedule."

I knew as well as he did that grocery shelves were emptying, but I was sure we could find something if we needed to. "What do you make of his warnings about the black SUVs?"

Bazooka settled down a bit. "It's not all that surprising. You know how humans are. Always looking for a new excuse to do terrible things to each other."

"Is that really what you think of us?"

"Should I not?" Bazooka turned away and rooted in the grass for a few last bites. "Let me have a quick snack and we should get on the road again."

I started rolling up our supplies, pondering our next steps. Today's goal: make our way into Friend and find the woman Emmett had stayed with.

If she was still alive.

Chapter Twelve

August 2, 2021
Dear Em,
Happy birthday. I can't believe you're twenty-one. I hear that's a big deal. You can drink, right? No idea why you'd want to, but still. It sounds so adult. Weird.

Things here are going okay. The new goose, Bazooka, is turning out to be a lot of fun. He's smart and good at tricks. I've taught him some funny ones that visitors really like. When he's in a good mood, he carries around a bucket full of candy in his beak, handing it out and collecting tips. And he can make rough marks on the ground with a stick. We've even tried it with a bit of paper and a marker. The kids love it. When he's in a bad mood, he bites, but that also seems to make people want to leave a tip even faster than usual, so I don't know if it's entirely a bad thing. But I watch him and try to keep the violence to a minimum.

I had to do my confirmation at church this summer. You must've done that, although I don't remember it. Me and the other kids my age took all the classes and tests and recited stuff and then got dunked in this big tub. Boom. Full member of the church.

It was so embarrassing. That stupid white dress dripping everywhere. Everyone staring at us and smiling like we're such special little angels. When all I wanted was a towel and a blow-dryer. I think I have one of those faces that shows everything I feel because Mom scolded me later for not looking pleasant enough through the whole thing.

It's not that I'm against religion. God and I might have some stuff to work out, but I believe in him. I just don't like the actual church. Following the rules. Being the perfect little lamb. Acting like what matters most is that we do and say the right things at all times. Wearing the right clothes. Believing the right things. Saying what we're expected to say.

I've never been so glad to get home and get my overalls back on. Mucking out the stalls in the barn is a much more preferable task. I got extra dirty to make up for it. Mom sighed when she saw me an hour later, but she didn't say anything.

I'm wondering how you spent your birthday, this year, and the last couple of years, and if you have someone to celebrate with. I wish I could send you a card. Instead, I try to beam my thoughts to you through telepathy or something, so you know I'm thinking about you. Maybe you can feel it. I want you to know you're not forgotten.

I miss you Em. Please write to me.
Love, Lou

****

Two things struck me about Friend, Nebraska, as we pulled into town: one, it was tiny, and two, there was no one there.

We puttered our way down the brick-lined main road, sheltered on both sides by old buildings with elaborate little cornices on top, curlicued white window frames, and awnings leaning out over the sidewalks announcing the names of the businesses below. We saw

117

a gift shop, a pharmacy, an old opera house that was now a wine bar, and a few other businesses. A train track ran through at the far end, abutted by a huge concrete grain elevator.

It was adorable in that way of small midwestern towns, and obviously a popular tourist stop. It was also a ghost town. The street was devoid of cars and people, shops boarded up. I dumped the scooter into a parking slot. My scalp tingled, my senses on high alert for the slightest sound as I looked around. Memories of every zombie movie I'd ever seen played in my head.

"Remind me why we're here?" Bazooka muttered.

"Because Emmett lived here for almost two years. He worked in the library. They might have a phone number for him, so I can find out for sure where he is."

I could tell from the way Bazooka's feathers raised on his neck that he was nervous. "Why isn't there anyone here?"

Even with fall approaching fast, the morning sun pounded down on the back of my neck. I stopped to tie my jacket around my waist, and then peered in the window of a former brewing company. It looked like someone had swept and tidied, carefully placing chairs on top of tables.

Bazooka poked me hard in the side of the knee. "Down there," he said, gesturing with a wing.

Sure enough, someone had stepped out onto the sidewalk about a block away and was waving in our direction. He didn't look like a zombie.

"*Tourist Information*", read a bright gold sign swinging from two short pieces of chain, and beneath it we found an older man with a navy baseball cap over his white hair. He waved to us with a huge smile, one hand holding the door of the office behind him open in welcome.

"Hiya, visitors!" he called as we drew closer. "Don't get many of you anymore. Come in, come in! I'm Michael. Welcome to Friend."

I hesitated, but Bazooka pushed past me into the office and so I followed. The man directed us toward comfortable wooden seats, then went back to his desk, which was spread with a variety of pristine-looking pamphlets.

I introduced myself, shook hands, and sat. "What's happened here? It seems like a ghost town."

"Oh, well, you know. Most people stopped going to work, for one, so the shops closed. And all the sporting goods and food stores got cleaned out quick. Most folks left town, going down to the bigger cities or heading out to shelters outside Omaha."

"But you're still manning the visitor's booth?"

He smiled and readjusted his baseball cap. I could see army insignia embroidered on it. "Well, you know. Been doing this a long time now, almost thirty years. It's what I do. Didn't see any reason to stop now."

I smiled back. "Do you have anyone? Here, I mean." I hoped he wasn't alone.

He nodded, a faraway look in her eyes. "My kids are all off on the east coast, but my wife is here. She's passed, of course, but she's buried here in town. I figure at the very end, I'll pack a picnic and go out to the site, spend my last day at her side."

Bazooka clucked beside me and our host, Michael, turned his gaze on him. "And who is this fine fellow?" He leaned in, holding out a hand to Bazooka.

"He bites!" I warned. Bazooka gave me a disdainful

look and nuzzled against the man's hand. I shrugged. "This is Bazooka. He's a greylag goose."

"So what's your story? Just traveling the country with your goose friend?"

"More or less. We're heading to Oregon."

The man nodded. "I hope you weren't looking for supplies. There's not much to be found here. Seemed like every day, for a while there, someone was coming through town and breaking into another storefront to steal whatever they could."

"But everything looks so orderly."

"I've been cleaning up after them as best I can. Civic pride, you know. I want to put our best foot forward, even if our visitors don't always appreciate it." He fanned himself with a brochure. "So what brings you to our neck of the woods?"

I filled him in on our itinerary. How I was following a series of letters Emmett had sent from each of the places he'd lived over the last six years. How I hoped that would help me double check I was heading to the right place. We didn't have time to get this wrong. "He spent a while here in Friend, back in 2021. I think he worked at the library with someone named Mari Kalouh?"

The man's face creased with pleasure. "Oh, everyone knows Mari! She's a wonderful woman. And you're in luck. She's still here." He dug around on the desk and selected one pamphlet. "Would you like a map? I can show you how to get to the library."

We didn't need a map. I took it anyway.

"The library is still open?"

"Not exactly, but that's where you'll find her." He pulled out a pen and uncapped it with obvious pleasure.

He circled two spots on the map and pointed at the first. "You're currently here." He tapped the second. "Here's Gilbert Library. I assume you have some kind of vehicle? You can follow this route here. Park around back."

I made appreciative noises. It seemed to bring such purpose to his life to have a tourist to assist.

He circled a few more spots. "There are some public bathrooms here, and if you follow this route out of town, you might find some produce available at this farm stand on the edge of town. You could freshen up your supplies before you leave."

"Thank you so much, Michael," I said. "I can see why they gave you this job. You're good at it."

"Oh, thank you." He gave Bazooka one more scritch. "Beautiful bird you have here. Best wishes to the both of you!"

Michael walked us to the door, and struck by some sentimental impulse, I gave him a hug before we left.

****

"Why did you hug him?" Bazooka complained as soon as we were out of sight. "Do you make a habit of touching strangers?"

I shrugged. "I liked him. He's doing a sad thing, but it's kind of beautiful, you know?"

"It's beautiful to sit in a tourist office and hand maps to people who don't need them and then go die in a graveyard?"

I didn't know how to explain it to him, but yes, it was. This was a man who loved his job and his town and his role greeting people and his dead wife so much that even the end of all things couldn't inspire him to leave them. I couldn't claim to have a reference point for that in my life, but I had always imagined that when I grew up, life would involve finding a place in the world where I belonged and people who I would love and care for until the end of time. Who wouldn't want that?

I wouldn't get to find out now. And the thought made tears prickle my eyes. I would never find out who I would love that way, where I'd wander to, where I'd settle, what I'd do. But it helped to know that love was out there.

Gilbert Library was a small, neatly kept, two-story building made of dark brick. The roof glowed with terracotta half-pipe tiles, and a small bronze sign announced its name and founding date of 1906. Bronze books bracketed the sign, piled as if on a shelf, with one lying open in the center. I leaned in and ran a finger over the pages of the open volume, worn to a shine by many other fingers over the last century.

Like most of the town, the library looked deserted. Its small-paned windows were unbroken—apparently, no one wanted to loot a library. We walked around back; the door there showed signs of more recent use. I knocked on the wooden frame.

A few minutes later, it opened to reveal a woman of indeterminate age. The only signals that she was a little older were creases around her dark-brown eyes and streaks of gray in her black hair. Spectacles sat atop her head, holding back tight curls that had escaped her messy bun.

She did not open the screen door.

"Can I help you?" she asked, peering at us with clear suspicion.

"Um, Michael sent me? From the Tourist Information booth?"

Her face got friendlier. "Oh Michael. I suppose it

made his day to have a customer again, didn't it?" She looked past me. "Is... is that a goose? What on Earth?"

"I'm Lou and this is Bazooka. He's traveling with me. He won't hurt you," I said, hoping this was true. "I think you knew my brother? Emmett Compton?"

She gasped. "Oh dear. Emmett! You must be... well please, come in!"

She unlocked the screen door, and we followed her into a dusty hallway piled on all sides with books, some on shelves, some on the floor. There was barely enough room for one person to walk between them.

We emerged into a tiny library, just three main rooms: one for children, one for adults, and a reading/periodical room whose shelves were mostly empty. High, rectangular windows bathed each room in light, and cream-colored walls gave a sense of calm, contrasting nicely with the heavy, old oak tables and shelves. Decades of use had worn the table surfaces, but they gleamed with recent polish.

The disorder from the back room continued here. Books were everywhere, in large stacks, this time with hand-printed signs on them. "*Top priority— agriculture/farming*" one read. "*Basic engineering.*" "*Mathematics.*" "*Outdoor skills.*"

She led us to a section where three comfortable reading chairs sat around a small table and invited us to sit down.

"So you're Emmett's little sister! He spoke about you so many times." Her face creased with happiness as she said his name.

I smiled nervously. "I'm on my way out west to find him, and I'm visiting the places where I know he stayed. I found a stash of letters he sent me over the years, including some that mentioned working here, with you…"

"Your parents hid the letters from you, I assume?" She peered at me over her glasses. "Oh, don't look surprised. He told me what happened. Any parents that could do that to their own flesh and blood are capable of all kinds of wretchedness."

I swallowed, my anger rising in a hot, red tide. She was right. Although I'd set the process in motion, it was my parents who made the critical decisions: rejecting Emmett, throwing him out. It wasn't the first time I had wondered if I blamed myself too much; they were the grownups, and they were supposed to be the ones who knew how to handle things. I blinked rapidly as it all roiled together into a dark pit in my stomach. Would I ever be free of the effects of that day? My thoughts buzzed with darkness, and I was barely aware of my surroundings.

Oddly enough, Bazooka chose that moment to reveal himself, even though we had agreed he'd pretend to be an ordinary goose whenever we were in human company.

"You'll have to pardon my companion. She's frequently paralyzed by unnecessary emotion," he said, stepping over me in my frozen state. "Greetings! Don't be alarmed. I'm Falthaom, but you can call me Bazooka."

Time slowed way down. Mari blinked and blinked again, frowning deeply, then her expression transformed to one of sheer curiosity. She reached up, pulled off her glasses, and leaned forward for a closer look.

"Well, doesn't that beat all?" she said, eyebrows drawn up. "And what exactly are you?"

He straightened up, looking pleased. "I can see you're not the average, superstitious human," he said, then repeated the gesture he'd first greeted me with, offering a wing tip instead of a handshake. Mari got the point faster than I had, and reached forward to gently grasp it.

"Nice to meet you," she said, shaking and then releasing his wing tip.

Bazooka settled his wing back at his side. "I'm an imp."

"Oh," she breathed. "I've read about imps! Not the little helper demons, but the mythical, mysterious imp, borne from the trees. Never dreamed you were real, or that I'd meet one!"

Bazooka turned to me, every line of his posture smug. "I like her."

Mari turned back to me. "You're going to have to tell me the full story over dinner, but I can see Emmett was right about you—you're something special. What can I do to help you find him?"

I told her. That Emmett had written from here, that the next letters had come from Jackson, Wyoming. That I had proof that he'd made his way to either Seattle or Portland and then, well, then the trail went cold somewhere around Bend, Oregon nine months ago.

"I guess I was wondering if he stayed in touch with you, or if you have any contact information for him? Or if you know anything else that might help me find him?"

She thought for a minute. "He stayed in touch for quite a while, but I haven't heard from him in a bit. He used to send me a postcard or a letter now and then."

An absurd spear of hope lodged in my chest. "Do you still have them?"

"You know? I think I put a few of the postcards on one of the bulletin boards." She stood. "Come with me, let's go look."

Mari led us to a huge bulletin board in the kids' area that was covered in pictures and postcards and pieces of maps showing different locations around the world. I scanned it, feeling like no one could ever find one individual important piece among all the many items on it, but Mari knew what she was looking for—she went right to the lower left corner where she ran a finger across a dozen items before pulling off a card there, then two more nearby. She handed them to me and then smiled.

"I'll be back in the reading room when you're finished with them."

I sat at one of the kid-sized tables and examined the three cards. They were from tourist locations I'd only vaguely heard of. I held my breath as I touched them; it was as close as I'd ever come to understanding how people might feel when touching a religious relic, like I was drawing a finger across the bones of a saint. Emmett had touched these. Emmett had stood in each of these places, selected the card from a stand, scrawled a message on it, and sent it on its way.

The messages were brief. A few words of greeting, a joke or two, maybe a comment on where he was going next. Love, Em, he signed each of them. My old nickname for him. He'd cared for Mari.

The postcards didn't add a lot to what I knew already; each of them meshed with what I already knew about his cross-country trip. Even so, seeing them made me feel closer to him. I put them back on the board with a last reluctant look, then Bazooka and I made our way back to the front room.

Mari was typing away on a laptop when I came back in. She looked up and smiled at me. "Did they help?"

I nodded, unable to say more, and she stood and gave me a hug. I sniffled into the shoulder of a total stranger and wondered what had become of my life.

When we separated, Bazooka nudged his way into the conversation. "If I may, Mari, why are you still here?"

Mari nodded. "I'm glad you asked." She gestured around the room at the piles and piles of books. "This is my legacy. I'm scanning them."

"You're digitizing a few piles of books?"

"No. Librarians are digitizing their books all over the world. We call it Project Thoth. You know, the Egyptian god of sacred texts?"

"I know Thoth," Bazooka said, and I side-eyed him. He meant 'know *of* Thoth,' right?

"And then what happens to the works after you've digitized them?" I asked. "Are you thinking there will still be people somewhere with computers and the internet?"

"No, probably not. But there's a group in England who developed a way of writing files to crystals that can survive high temperatures and last for thousands of years, and the main scientist at their lab is collecting every book sent to them and storing it as fast as possible on that medium. Before impact, he'll take the crystals and store them somewhere secure, a cave I think, hoping someday people will recover enough to find them and read them." She smiled sadly. "It's a long shot that anyone will ever use them, but if we can preserve some kind of knowledge for future generations of any survivors, why wouldn't we try?"

Bazooka clucked indignantly. "You've chosen to spend your end here in this little library, alone, digitizing books for humans who may not even survive?"

I glared at him.

"Someone will survive," Mari said. "We always do. And think about how much knowledge we lost in the past, every time a civilization fell into darkness. Rome, Alexandria. This time we've got the benefit of foreknowledge, and the technology to do something about it. We can give them everything from Plato to the instructions for how to perform surgery."

I pondered that; how men and women like her all over the planet were sitting in libraries digitizing beautiful works of literature and the most important nonfiction in their collections—books that would help people remember how to plant a field, build a radio, invent penicillin. Books that would remind us of where we started, of how to be human.

"I love books," I said. "I read all the time. I think it's beautiful, what you're doing."

"You could stay and help?" she said, eyes bright with hope. "We could digitize twice as much with two people working on it. I've got an extra laptop and there's a scanner sitting idle in my old house that we could drag in."

I wished I could, but I couldn't choose to save books any more than I could have taken a week-long detour to help Peter. It was maddening how the hard limit of impact day choked off my options; there were so many things I'd like to do, to see, to take part in. I guess I thought I'd already made my hardest choice when I left home, leaving my parents and probably ending my days far away from everything I'd ever known, but the more we traveled the more I realized that this might not be true. There were still painful choices to be made, every step of the way.

"I'm sorry," I said, my throat suddenly tightening. "I wish I could. It's worth doing. But I have to find Emmett. I left my family and my friends for this…"

She didn't look surprised. "I know, but you can't blame me for asking, can you? Anyway, how about I put you two up for the night, and you tell me more about this magical goose of yours?" She turned to Bazooka. "I assume you don't lay golden eggs or anything, do you?"

Bazooka looked confused. "I've got the wrong equipment for that, but even if I could, would that really be helpful at this juncture? Do you ask every waterfowl you meet this question?"

Mari and I both laughed. "Perhaps I need to read you a bedtime story."

Chapter Thirteen

August 24, 2021
Dear Lou,
Guess where I am.

Jackson, Wyoming! You know, that place I've been mentioning for a couple of years now? With all the mountains and the snow. And did I mention the MOUNTAINS?

Oh my god, Lou, I've never seen a place like this. I got here in the summer, which was pretty great on its own, but I'm really looking forward to October when the snow falls. I wish you could see it. I've never smelled air like this—it's like living in a pine candle.

I'm working at one of the hardware stores. It's decent work and I make enough for my rent. Most of the fun here is outdoors and free. Hiking especially. Skiing's expensive, but a buddy of mine hooked me up with some used gear that I'll learn how to use later this year. I suspect I'll spend more time flat on my ass in a snowdrift than whooshing down the slopes.

I think about you a lot, Lou. You started eighth grade this fall, right? Man, I wish I could see what you're up to. I've written to Mom a few times, and I keep writing to you, but I don't know how to reach you by phone anymore. I've sent my number to you, but it doesn't seem like you've gotten the letters. I hope you'll call sometime. I'll try to keep that number.

Things are improving for me. The first couple years were lonely, and I had a lot of feelings to work through, but lately things are making more sense. I've had a lot on my mind the last two years, thinking about how I want to live, who I want to be. I've come to some decisions, although it's too much to write out in a letter. Maybe soon.

I think one of my greatest fears is that, with me gone, Mom and Dad might brainwash you into seeing things their way. Like they were right to kick me out. To call me an abomination. To say my life is a mistake, that I'm full of sin. It would break my heart if you were against me, too.

You aren't, are you, Lou?

Of course you're not. If there's anyone on the planet I know, it's you, Lou. Stay open and keep reading all the books (go read all the ones I left in my room too) and remember your brother, who loves you very much.

Love, Em

****

No matter how much I intended to get an early start, the pleasures of sleeping in an actual bed again were irresistible. I woke up much later than I'd intended, and followed the scent of pancakes down to the kitchen, where Mari had left a plate for me. I could see her through the window over the sink, and picked up my plate and headed to the backyard.

"Mari, do you have a working phone here?" I asked when I'd finished my breakfast. "Emmett sent me a cell number a long time ago, but it didn't work the first time I tried. Could I try again?"

"Sure! My cell is pretty unreliable, but the landline still works great." She led me into the living room, where an old-fashioned, mustard yellow phone hung on the wall. It was very like the one we had in the farmhouse, and a pang of homesickness swept over me.

I dug through my pack until I reached my notebook, flipped for the page where I'd made notes from his letters, and punched his number with trembling fingers. I held it to my ear as the line clicked and whirred, processing. I stopped breathing entirely, the entire focus of my world contracting to the headset of the phone pressed much too hard against the side of my head. Would it ring?

Your call cannot be completed as dialed. Please check the number and dial again.

Damn it. I resisted the urge to slam the phone back onto the base. It was Mari's phone, Mari's home, and I had no right to treat her things with disrespect. Instead, I hung up. Then, struck by another idea, I dialed Maggie's number. This one rang. It rang and rang and rang. I almost imagined I could hear the sound echoing through her empty house. They were undoubtedly in the tent city by now. Who knew if she'd brought her phone, or if it was even still working?

I put the receiver down gently and stayed where I was, facing the wall, my stomach a hollow pit. Everyone I loved was out of reach. I missed Maggie with an intensity that left me dizzy. I don't think we'd ever gone this long without speaking, not since third grade. What was she doing? How she was feeling, stuck in a tent, waiting for the end? The urge to talk to her built up in my throat like a storm, ready to spill over.

I examined the small notepad Mari had placed on a table below the phone, the calendar on the wall with scribbled notes about appointments gone by, old engagements, friends' birthdays. I took a few deep breaths, trying to work the disappointment into a smaller package—something I could hide—before I turned and headed back out into the yard.

"Any luck?" Mari asked.

I shook my head. "Doesn't work. It might have been his number once, but I don't think it is anymore."

"Or maybe it is, but you can't get through. From what I've read, cellular networks are getting pretty iffy." She grimaced. "It's a new world out there. Only going to get worse before the end, too."

I nodded and folded myself into a seat beside her, picking at my pancakes. The grass in her backyard was still green, and some late season vegetables grew in a small plot that backed up to her slightly ramshackle garage. I saw cabbage, kale, and maybe garlic, some of it not yet ready to harvest. Bazooka was wandering between rows, eating the occasional bug and digging here and there. I hoped she didn't mind.

"By the way," she said, pointing at a big fat book on the patio table. "I brought home a book about basic scooter maintenance. Time to learn a thing or two before you get back on the road."

I shuffled myself to the edge of the seat, idly turning the pages, trying to muster up any enthusiasm for this task. But Mari was right. If I was going to drive another 1400 miles, I needed to know things. Where the oil went. What to do if the engine overheated.

Mari and I wheeled the scooter into the yard and spent a couple of hours working together. She went through the basics and then pulled out a few tools and we practiced tightening various things up that might come loose. She gave me the wrenches as a gift, and I tucked them into my pack. Finally, she reviewed our maps and made notes on them about better road options, things she'd heard about the path ahead of us, and where we might find shelter.

"Just as well you're using paper maps and not relying on a phone," she said. "Like I said, my cell almost never works anymore. And you'd lose your signal where you're going, anyway. Lots of wilderness between here and there."

"We're doing this old school," I joked, trying to keep my voice light.

"I hope you find Emmett," Mari said. "But you should know that he was going through a lot of changes when he was here. He had a lot of things to process and work out."

"What do you mean?"

"Just that the Emmett you find might not be the Emmett you remember."

I wasn't sure what she meant, but I nodded. "It doesn't matter. As long as I find him. He's still family."

She smiled, satisfied, and hugged me. "Be careful. And if you can't get through, you're always welcome to come back. I'll be here until the end."

That was sobering, but also a comfort. I hadn't considered a backup plan, but it was nice to know I had one. If the worst came to pass and I couldn't find Emmett, if there wasn't time to get back home, maybe I could get as far as Mari's before the end.

"Thank you," I said. "I'll try to let you know if we find him."

I fumbled with my helmet, every part of me aching with regret. Between missing home and fearing I might never find Emmett, part of me longed to stay here in

Friend with Mari and join her mission. My goal suddenly seemed almost impossible: getting across the country amid a huge crisis? Before heading out with Bazooka, I had never pumped gas on my own, gotten a hotel room, or even been out-of-town overnight by myself. What was I thinking doing this? I wavered, helmet in my hands, and looked at Mari as if she might hold the answers.

Somehow, she read my mind. She stepped forward and put her hand on my shoulder. "You can do this, Lou. Emmett believed in you, and so do I. I have a feeling you're going to do okay. Stay off the main roads if you can."

"Thank you. Really, thank you. For everything. I can see why Emmett liked you so much." I took a deep breath, double checked Bazooka was secure in his seat, and then I headed for the highway.

****

It was a long way to our next planned state: four hundred miles across the rest of Nebraska, eventually turning north and heading into Wyoming. Even in a car, it would be a long trip, but puttering along like we did? We'd undoubtedly have to stop and sleep at least once, maybe twice, with regular breaks along the way to let the scooter cool down. I hoped the scooter was up to the trip, even with my new knowledge about how to take care of it a little better. How many miles could a small scooter like this go?

We spent the next couple hours zooming along the back highway. It was gorgeous and barely traveled. The golden wheat fields flickered by in the bright sunshine. We stopped for an hour at midday to let the scooter recover, then pushed on further.

I'd almost relaxed when we hit our first big issue a

few hours later, on an empty stretch of road between two small farming towns.

"What the fuck?" Bazooka said, examining the mess in front of us. A bridge across a rushing river with steep, rocky banks had somehow come loose of its moorings and the entire structure listed to the side at a frightening angle. It looked like a light breeze might be enough to take it down. Rough wooden sawhorses blocked off all lanes in both directions, and from the look of things, there was no way to sneak across without risking our lives.

Apparently, folks here didn't put up detour signs. I looked around and saw nothing and no one to show what we should do. "Can you, like, magic us across or anything?"

Bazooka hissed. "No, of course I can't."

"Don't hiss! I don't know what you can do!"

"I've told you, I don't have a lot of powers while I'm all... all befeathered." He made that last word sound like a curse. "Is your hearing impaired or just your memory?"

"Fine, I'll figure it out." I flopped down on the side of the road and spread out the paper maps we'd brought. I located the town we'd recently passed, then traced the route back a little and saw a road heading north that would put us back on the interstate. The one Mari had suggested we stay off.

It gave me pause. It did. Even so, any other route would add hours and hours to our trip, and it was already late afternoon. I was hoping we could get much closer to the border before we stopped. Would it really be that dangerous to be on the interstate for a while? We could get off it again—I traced my finger along the route—

once we got to a town called Sidney. Two, three hours tops.

"Highway's not too far north," I said, looking up from the maps. "Do you think we should head back up?"

"It's that or swim for it."

"Hilarious. I know, why don't you just fly and we'll, I don't know, meet you in Oregon?"

Bazooka stiffened his neck. "Don't tempt me, missy. You have no idea how much I don't want to sit in this stinky leather pouch anymore."

A thrill of fear spiked through me. Bazooka wouldn't leave me, would he? I tried to play it cool, rolling my shoulders out and stretching.

"You're welcome to fly ahead." I tried to make my voice casual, like I didn't care at all.

He honked. Loudly. "Nah, someone has to make sure you don't get smashed by a truck, or hauled off by a death cult, or... or..." He stopped, clearly trying to come up with more frightening scenarios.

I narrowed my eyes, unable to resist needling him. "I think you're all talk. You act like you don't want to be here, but I think you actually like me."

He twitched. "Shut up. Don't say things like that."

"I think we're becoming friends. It must be killing you."

He hissed at me. "We should get on the road, unless your new plan is to just stand here and irritate me all day?"

I grinned, but let it go. "Shall we?"

He hopped onto the floorboards between my legs instead of into his pouch. "I'm gonna ride here for now."

At least we were moving again. That was all that mattered.

****

Traffic grew increasingly terrible with every mile on the interstate. More and more trucks went by, usually military. Once, a huge bus zoomed past, its windows darkened so that I could see only the dim silhouette of people inside. Who were they? Where were they being taken?

One of them placed a hand on the window with their fingers splayed out as if asking for help, and for a second, I thought I saw a face pressed against it too, pale, with wide, helpless eyes. Startled, I veered off onto the exit for an upcoming rest stop and pulled into a parking spot.

"Did you see that?" I asked Bazooka as I cut the engine. "That woman on the back of the bus?"

"No. Who? What? Someone look at you funny?"

I shook my head. "No, just weird. Where's a bus with blacked-out windows going at a time like this? It wasn't a greyhound or any kind of commercial bus."

"Maybe what Peter mentioned? People being spirited away to somewhere?" His head turned toward the tree line. "Oh look, clover!"

He flapped off to the weed in question and I hesitated. Was it safe to leave the scooter here? There weren't too many people around—one woman down at the far end sat by a beat-up red car, eating a sandwich, and there was a pickup truck parked with no owner in sight. Caution was probably the best policy, and I wheeled the scooter over to where Bazooka was grazing and tucked it in behind a couple of bushes.

"Guard this, would you? I'm gonna go use the bathroom."

He puffed out his chest. "You got it."

****

There's nothing like rest stops in rural America. This one had a huge map behind glass with a cheerful "You are HERE" dot in the center, a series of pamphlet stands about nearby attractions that I plundered for kindling, and a now-deserted welcome center whose sign said that weary travelers should help themselves to coffee and cookies. I was sad to see it empty.

The bathroom was cold and dirty. I counted myself lucky to find a couple of paper towels, but the toilet paper was long gone. I cleaned up as best I could, then I checked the tampon dispenser on the wall, but it was empty; I hoped the handful I'd packed would be enough when the time came. I hurried through my task, my danger senses tingling for no good reason, and then stepped back out and smacked into an enormous man. He stood at the end of the walkway exiting the bathroom—I was stuck between the cold brick wall of the building and the open cement blocks forming a breezeway on the other side. I skidded to a halt.

"Hey there," he said, sliding one hand into his pocket. "You by yourself?"

I looked him over, pushing down a wave of panic, feeling like a rabbit facing a predator. He was tall and had a body that was probably once strong but was now running to fat around the middle. His hair was brown and longish in the back, and he had a strange, floppy mustache that upped his ick factor by about a hundred. My skin crawled just looking at him, and the hungry expression in his eyes made it worse. I swallowed hard.

"I'm not alone," I said. "I'm here with my friend."

He smiled and stepped forward until he was even more in my way. "I don't see anyone else here but you and me, darling. C'mon, I won't hurt you. What's your name?"

Subterfuge, then. Pretend to cooperate, look for an opening. I gave him a weak smile. "Name's Lou."

"Lou? Like Louella? Louisa?" He grinned. "Pretty. Like you."

He had to be kidding. I was wearing the same shapeless jeans I'd had on for the last three days, a dirty tee shirt, and a sweatshirt. I hadn't washed my hair since we left home, and I was sure my face wasn't in much better shape.

"Falthaom!" I called as loudly as I could, instinctively feeling that calling out 'Bazooka' would be a mistake. The name did not inspire fear. "Falthaom, I need you!"

The man frowned and grabbed me by the wrist and I stiffened, trying to twist away. "What now? Who the heck are you calling?" He started pulling me along, heading for the abandoned pickup truck in the lot. The woman and her sandwich were long gone. A sudden, blinding rage overtook the buzzing panic in my head, and I dug in my feet and shrieked, kicking and punching any part of him I could reach, until he turned around and raised a hand toward me. I flinched from the coming blow and then…the world exploded in a chorus of honks and feathers.

"What the—" the man grunted, before Bazooka was on him, all flapping fury. I stepped back and tried to make sense of what was happening. One of Bazooka's wing joints connected with the man's shoulder with a sickening thud, but then a hand reached out and grabbed feathers and the two of them rolled into a writhing pile.

"Bazooka!" I shouted. I looked around for a tree branch or something I could use as a weapon, my hands shaking with intensity. I had just grabbed a large rock that had a satisfying heft when everything fell silent. I whirled to find Bazooka panting with effort, his head craned up and wings flared out to the sides and the man… well the man was hovering in the air three feet off the ground, his expression a rictus of fear.

"Oh my god, Bazooka! How are you doing that?"

"Shh. Concentrating."

I stopped. Bazooka continued to stare at the man, the sheer tension in his body palpable in the slight shiver of his wingtips. After a second, he slid his gaze my way. "Now might be a good time to get the scooter?"

Oh. Duh. Of course. I grabbed it, wheeling it as close to Bazooka as I could. He closed his eyes and concentrated, then the man flew back a few feet and collided with a maple tree behind him. The resulting thunk left him passed out and stuck in its branches, like some kind of man-sized kite.

Bazooka sagged in exhaustion, and I stuffed him into his saddlebag, then zoomed away at top speed. I couldn't tell if it was the vibration of the bike or if all of the muscles in my body where trying to shake themselves apart. I held onto the handlebar for dear life and tried to steer straight.

We grimly motored on, both of us shaken. I took a random exit off the interstate and headed a few miles into the middle of nowhere until I found a field that looked safe for the night. The house on the property looked deserted; most of its windows were boarded over, and the driveway had more weeds than gravel. Just to be safe, Bazooka pushed his way in through the back screen door and poked around, confirming no one was there.

We made a cooking fire behind a decrepit garage,

since the power was out to the kitchen, and cooked a couple of sausages Mari had sent us off with, and then we rested in the house's living room for a while before deciding whether to continue.

"The sun's going down soon," Bazooka said. "Do you want to sleep outdoors with a fire or indoors?"

I hesitated, indecision knotting my insides. On the one hand, I was desperate to be indoors where it would be warmer; the nights were chilly and sleeping on a bed with blankets sounded great. On the other hand, occupying someone's empty house felt creepy and wrong. What if someone came back to check on it? Either way felt vulnerable.

"Indoors, I think," I said finally. "A fire feels too dangerous after what happened. We don't want to attract any attention. Is that okay?"

"Sounds fine to me. I'll be warm either way. I have down."

Then I realized.

"Wait a second." I said, slowly putting the pieces together. "You said you had almost no powers in this form, and yet you've made a single tank of gas last for days and you levitated that man at the rest stop without even breaking a sweat."

"Geese don't sweat." His voice was curt and even his posture was surly.

I dug my fingernails into my palms, ready to meet his aggression with my own. "That's not the point! I think there's more to you than you're telling me."

Of course, he looked more comfortable now that he had irritated me. Bazooka was always at his best when he'd angered someone. He turned to face me dead on, eyes gleaming. "Well, of course I haven't told you everything about myself. Why would I do that?"

"I don't know, maybe so I can trust you?"

He wriggled in annoyance and the feathers on his neck formed little fluffed up rows. "Is it a bad thing that I'm keeping you out of trouble? Did you want me to let you get kidnapped or murdered or anything else that comes up? Cuz I can sit back and start letting whatever happens happen, but I thought that what mattered to you was getting to your brother."

A horrible idea occurred to me. "Oh my god, do you know where he is? If you've known this whole time and haven't told me—"

Bazooka snapped his bill at me. "I do not have a database in my head with the location of every human on Earth. To be honest, keeping track of one of you has been exhausting."

I calmed down. "Okay. But here's what I don't get—if you have the power to throw a big guy like that into a tree, why can't you do anything about the comet?"

He shook his long neck. "Levitating that idiot is about a thousand levels of intensity lower than levitating a comet."

"But there must be something you can do. Who said you have to levitate it? Can't you vaporize it? Or like send it a thousand miles off course?"

"Nah," Bazooka said, scuffing one webbed foot on the carpet. "I mean, as a group we could've, but it would've taken a bunch of imps, maybe all of us, working together with singular focus and intention."

I sat up straight. "So, let's do it. Let's get all your friends and let's get to work on moving this comet into another dimension."

"It's too late for that," Bazooka said. "Like I told

you, they're all leaving. Mostly gone. I'm probably the only one left, unless anyone stayed behind to laugh at me."

I froze, absorbing that, then put down my cup. "You're the only imp left? Like on the entire planet?"

"As far as I know, yes. The demons all went on permanent walkabout when they heard about the comet. Decided to find new sentient beings to torment. And the imps went too, out of self-preservation."

"But not you?"

Bazooka was up and moving off toward the kitchen in a flurry. "I wasn't invited," he called over his shoulder. "C'mon, let's see if there's anything worth scavenging in here."

I could tell he didn't want to talk about it, but I couldn't help myself. I followed along and bit back the follow up question for at least thirty seconds, a major accomplishment. "Why weren't you invited?"

Bazooka turned, and I expected aggression, but instead his wings sagged and he looked spent. "Because they didn't want me around anymore, okay? I'm stuck here. Now you know all my secrets. Are you happy?"

I opened and closed my mouth, unable to find anything to say. "I'm sorry to hear that," I finally stammered.

He looked me in the eye, expression unreadable, and then he went out the back door, after a grasshopper or a piece of grain or maybe a quick escape. The growing dusk enveloped him, but I could hear his footsteps crunching on the dry ground.

I let him go.

Chapter Fourteen

Interlude: Bazooka

Okay, I know what you're thinking, but what I told her wasn't untrue. I couldn't completely remove the comet, or vaporize it, or levitate it out of the way. Even at full power, the laws of orbital mechanics are serious matters and not subject to the whim of individual imps. And being locked inside this fleshy, feathery prison significantly reduces my powers. All that is true. Mostly.

So what if I have more powers than I was letting on? I know how humans are. Once they know you can do things, they ask for stuff. Small stuff at first, and you think, oh, no problem, one little favor won't hurt anyone, but before you know it, you're at their constant beck and call, expected to solve all their fucking problems. I'm not interested in being anyone's genie, granting wishes left and right. Not even for Lou.

I only wanted to get off that farm, to get out into the world and see what was happening. I never intended to become the sidekick to a teenager on a stupid quest. How did this happen? How did I end up feeling responsible for the wellbeing of an emotionally unstable teen who's dealing with grief and loss and mortality in a way that humans her age aren't built to endure? I'm not without some level of compassion for her issues. Still. She could carry herself with a little dignity, you know? So much weeping. I'm going to have to toughen her up or we're never going to get through this trip alive.

It's not like I haven't had opportunities to escape, either. Did she think I wasn't coming back when I flew off to find our first campsite? To be honest, I wasn't so sure there myself. Finding myself free of that ridiculously tight bag and the endless vibrating monotony of the scooter was better than the finest nectar—as I soared away from her, a thrill of freedom rushed through me that I haven't experienced in much too long. Not since the games.

But the damn goose still partly controls my brain. While it can't make decisions, it has a persistent webbed foot wedged into my emotional centers, and the goose, sap that it is, is shouting at me about love and loyalty and taking care of Lou who is taking care of us and how I can't abandon her and on and on and on until FINALLY, just to shut it up, I agree with it.

Fine. We'll stay with Lou. I'll do what I said: keep her safe, make sure we get through the night. I'll spend my semi-useless powers to make that stupid scooter keep running despite the total lack of gas and maintenance. There is no way, without me, that she's going to make it to the west coast in one piece. The scooter would give up the ghost long before we got there. Does she really think that thing is going to cross the mountains on its own?

My goosier half, mollified, settles down.

As for my big questions—is it worth any potential punishment I might face to interfere in what's about to happen? Are the humans worth saving?

For now, the jury is out.

What I've learned so far is that Lou is a good person, if foolish and ill-equipped for survival without me. She's a terrible liar and hopelessly sentimental.

Look at how she gave that grimy child Peter nearly half of her food supply. Shared her fire without checking him for weapons or even for ticks, and probably would've strapped him onto the back of the scooter if he'd been heading our way. Why would someone do that? Even humans, altruistic as they think they are, they're primed to focus on their own survival first.

But that idiot kid wasn't Lou's offspring, or a member of her clan. Why would she put her own survival at risk that way? It's a damn good thing she has me along, and that this ridiculous waterfowl is so fond of her. Its feelings are clearly leaking into my own, as her survival is beginning to matter to me in a way it didn't before.

But inside, I know the truth.

It isn't that I care so much for Lou. It's the fact that even if I left her, I would still be trapped. It's not like I'd actually be free. Charazon's restrictions would still prevent me from freeing myself of it, and I could easily find myself at the mercy of any idiot with a hunting rifle who caught sight of me.

I might as well stay with Lou, who is at least predisposed to take care of me. She feeds this stupid body, scratches my stupid neck, hands me those revolting nuggets of corn that my feather-self is constantly thinking about.

It isn't loyalty; it's sheer practicality.

That alone.

Nothing more.

Chapter Fifteen

August 19, 2022
Dear Emmett,
Big milestone today: I started high school. It's really not that exciting. I didn't even get to change buildings—I moved from the junior high side of the school to the high school side. My locker is in a new wing. Same gym, same band room, same kids, same teachers.

Oh, that's right, you don't know that I took up the trumpet after you left. Mom said it would be good for me, getting my extra energy out. I'm officially in the marching band, out on the practice field sweating my way through August, wearing a stupid hat and the world's itchiest uniform and performing at halftime at football games. I guess she was right because it tires me out, which leaves me with less time to brood, but it still hasn't helped me make friends. I talk to people at practice, but it doesn't seem to help. I don't know how people do it, talk to kids their own age. I'm so much better at talking to teachers than to teens.

I'm taking all the normal classes—algebra and English and biology and history. My electives are art and band. Art's my one sunny spot during an otherwise boring day. I've already read everything we're going to read in English, and I can write circles around most of the kids in that class. But art is fun. I like watercolor especially. My teacher says I've got talent.

If I only lived somewhere where I could change to a different, bigger high school, with new kids added into the mix, my life would be so much better. But nothing ever changes here outside of Davenport, and you can't start over when everyone already knows you and has seen every iteration of you since kindergarten.

Some days, I don't even want to get out of bed. Everyone said high school is supposed to be the best days of your life, so what does it mean when it's looking like it might be the worst?

I miss you, Emmett. How come high school looked so easy and fun when you did it? It's just not fair.

Love, Lou

****

September 2, 2022

Dear Lou,

I moved again. Are you surprised? Jackson was great, but I still had this idea in my head about wanting to see the Pacific Ocean, the western edge of the continent. It seemed wrong to go all that way and not take that last step. So, this past August, after saving up for a while, I bought a secondhand truck and took off for the coast. I drove straight through to Astoria, Oregon, and then straight down the coast from there.

Lou, let me tell you—I've never been so blown away as I was by the Oregon coast. The beaches here are nothing like the ones you see in movies with actors soaking up the sun. Most of the beaches are rocky, with these enormous stones standing in the water shaped like haystacks. And there are tide pools, where you can climb around and see starfish and anemones of all different colors and pick up shiny rocks the tide left behind. It's amazing. I spent almost a week on different beaches,

Megan Zalkan

collecting jaspers and agates and shells. Totally amazing.

After that, I kept going straight down to the redwood forests in California, camping as I went, and spent a couple of weeks marveling at the biggest trees I've ever seen. You wouldn't believe it, Lou. There are trees here that are thousands of years old. I saw one that would take twenty of us to link hands around it.

And then? After a few months of being a tourist, I was running out of money, so I headed back up to Oregon, taking on odd jobs along the way, and ended up making my way to this town called Bend. It's a really cool place, in the middle of central Oregon, full of artists and outdoorsy people and dogs. A little bigger than Davenport, so there are lots of jobs and places to live. A huge river runs right through town and when it's warm, everyone is out floating on it in inner tubes. You'd like it here, I think.

Right now, I'm bagging groceries and doing odd jobs, but I'm meeting people and making friends and hope I can find something more interesting. Maybe farming, since that's what I know. There are some cool organic farms around here that grow weird things. I heard of some lady who farms only mushrooms, and another guy who runs a fish hatchery, and a couple who farm only bullfrogs. Can you imagine? Don't worry, I'm not going to go work on the bullfrog farm. That's some nightmare stuff, right there.

Anyway, I'm settling in, and I think I might have found the place I'm going to stay for a while. I need to find some adopted family out here, some people who accept me exactly as I am, and start figuring out how to make a place into a home. You know what I mean?

150

I miss you, Lou. I'll write to you again.
Love, Em

****

Without a fire, the chill night air clawed at me and I tossed and turned, wishing I was still back in Mari's cozy house. At around three a.m., I even missed home. My room. My comforter. My parents.

Maggie.

I forced myself to burrow deeper in the sleeping bag, reminding myself that, even if I hadn't set off on this road trip, my comfy bed at home would no longer be available to me. By now, we'd be sleeping on cots at the church. The reminder worked. I suddenly didn't mind my present circumstances so much.

Then thoughts of Maggie invaded my brain, and that hollowed out feeling crept back into my solar plexus.

When I finally slept, my dreams plagued me with troubling images. The creepy man in the trucker hat kept popping into them, his hand around my wrist, but this time, Bazooka was nowhere to be found. I startled awake, more than once, trapped by the sleeping bag around me, trying to free myself. I sat for a while, staring into the dark nothingness, holding my knees hard against my chest until my heart stopped pounding. My eyes got heavy, and I slumped back to the hard ground.

Then I started dreaming about Maggie, about that kiss we'd shared before I left town, about the way her lips felt when they'd brushed mine. This jerked me awake too, but more out of urgency than fear. I was so glad to see her in my dream that I think I woke up hoping she was really there. Of course she wasn't. I stared into the sky for a while, remembering how that felt, wondering if I'd ever get to see her again.

Finally, after the last jolt awake, I got up to drink some water and then wandered out the back door to look around. The horizon was lightening in the east, so dawn couldn't be too far away. Perhaps it was safe to risk a small fire. I lit the sticks with a brochure from the rest stop and stared into the small flames, lost in my thoughts of saying goodbye to Maggie.

It was ridiculous. The world was about to end, and I was sitting in the middle of Nebraska thinking about a kiss and what it meant. Was I attracted to her? Or was it just the monumental events around us, the pain of parting and the overwhelming love and friendship I held for her that made me feel strange? It didn't feel exactly like friendship; it felt swoopier, mushier, warmer.

I didn't know what it was. But I didn't regret it.

How would my parents react if they knew I'd kissed Maggie? With crying and shrieking and the tearing of clothing, I supposed. They would've assumed I'd been afflicted by the same demon as Emmett, maybe sent me off to conversion therapy. To people like my parents, you were good, or you were sinful. There was no in between. It was confusing how they could be decent people in so many ways, and be so close-minded and judgmental in others.

But life wasn't as simple as they made it out to be. And how ironic, that I might discover the capacity for this immense new feeling, all these cliché first crush things, at the last possible second when it couldn't do me or anyone else any good.

The sad reality was there was no time left to find out whether this was real or some kind of cometary madness. Whatever I may have felt for Maggie, whatever we might've explored if I'd still been in town, there was no time, either for us as individuals or for us as a species. The end was coming and my feelings would never have time to blossom any further than this.

It surprised me how deeply it could cut, this regret for something that hadn't even happened yet. It was like being slammed in the chest by a softball. It ached all the way through, like a bruise blossomed beneath the surface of my ribs.

In the end, all I could determine was that I was glad to have known Maggie, to have been her friend for the last decade. To have gotten the chance to kiss her even once, whatever it had meant.

Bazooka roused himself as the tiny fire I'd lit popped loudly. "Decided to risk it, huh?"

"Needed something warm," I said, as I used my one cup to heat water over the fire and then mixed in a bag of the instant oatmeal Mari had given us. I stirred and took a deep and satisfying breath of the scent of apples and cinnamon wafting out of it in curls of steam. "Oh my God, that smells good. I've never appreciated oatmeal more in my life." I looked at him. "Do you want some?"

"No, of course not. I don't eat—" Bazooka staggered. "Oh fuck. Apparently yes I do. The feathered idiot is very interested."

I grinned and spooned a little out onto a patch of grass for him. Bazooka waddled over and pecked at it, looking suspicious, then dove in to inhale the whole thing. I scooped out more for him and dug out another bag to make for myself. Might as well fill up; we had a long ride ahead.

"The plan today is to cross the border into Wyoming," I said, poring over one of Mari's maps in the light from the fire. I measured the map scale against one of my fingers and tried to estimate how far that was going to be. "Looks like two hundred-ish miles? So, maybe five hours of driving? With one break in the middle to let the scooter cool off?"

"Shouldn't be too hard," Bazooka said. He wandered over and poked around at the empty oatmeal wrappers, gathering a few extra bits of dry oats from inside them. "What's our next stop?"

"Jackson, Wyoming. Emmett sent a letter from there. He worked on a ranch for a while. We'll get there the next day, hopefully."

As we rolled things up and secured them on the scooter, the sunrise kindled a feeling of hope blooming in my chest. With luck, we'd check another state off our journey by the end of the day. We were getting closer and closer to where I wanted to be.

****

The fantasy of a quick exit from Nebraska died almost instantly. We scooted along at a decent clip for the first hour through scant traffic, the occasional vehicle passing us. I clung to the far right lane, hugging the shoulder as much as I could to avoid aggravating other drivers, only moving fully out into the lane when abandoned cars on the shoulder blocked my way.

Those were becoming more frequent, too. Some had white fabric tied around their antennas. Others hand-lettered signs saying "*Out of gas*" or leaving a contact number. At least the main traffic lanes were still mostly clear.

I clearly jinxed us with that; we rounded a bend and my heart sank. Ahead of us, a forest of red brake lights gleamed as an infinity of cars stretched out in front of us.

"This is the backup from hell," I muttered,

unstrapping my helmet.

"Not literally." Bazooka squawked wildly at his own joke.

I snorted and looked around. Although we were high up, it was flat as a pancake here. Open fields, grass burned into sepia tones, stretching around us with distant tree lines and rock formations here and there, the view punctuated by small, rolling hills. The road curved to the right, not far ahead, cutting off our view. Cars toward the back of this mess were committing questionable three point turns in open fields to go back the way they came, but the folks in the middle were stuck. Most of them had their engines off and were standing around in clumps, bitching, drinking coffee, or smoking. The exhaust and nicotine assaulted my nostrils, along with the smell of dirt and sweat. The growing frustration of everyone waiting was so profound I felt like it almost had a shape, a color.

"Well," I said, strapping the helmet back on, "this is what a scooter is for, right? Might as well head toward the front and see what's up."

Bazooka made a noncommittal noise that I took for approval.

We puttered our way up the shoulder, continuing through a line of traffic that stretched for at least a mile, until the source of it came into sight.

Concrete barriers were blocking all lanes of traffic, with big "Road Closed" signs and two camo-covered convoy trucks pulled together behind them, and even a hastily erected guard tower to one side where the silhouette of two men and their guns was clearly visible. Several more soldier-types stood in front of the barriers, heavily armed. The exit to Sidney was out of reach, beyond the blockade.

"I changed my mind. Let's go back and wait with everyone else."

"Too late," Bazooka answered. He nodded. One of the soldier types had spotted us coming and stepped forward to speak with me. Apparently, I had to go ahead with this.

"Can I go through?" I asked, my voice coming out in a high-pitched squeak. "We're not going very far, just trying to cross the state border up ahead."

"Road's closed to all but military traffic from here through our base at Kimball." The man shifted his sunglasses and peered more closely at us. I got uncomfortably sweaty under his scrutiny.

I felt every inch my seventeen-year-old self, a child facing off with GI Joe, but I tried to keep my voice steady. "How long will it be closed?"

"Indefinitely," he barked, then he looked at me closer. "Wait, are you a kid? What are you doing out here?"

"Heading to my brother's." It was getting easier to lie. "In Wyoming."

Bazooka chose that moment to shift uncomfortably in his saddlebag, and the man's gaze tracked directly to him. "Is that a goose?"

I cursed inwardly. It was too attention-getting, traveling with a goose.

"Yeah," I said, unable to think of anything else to say. He continued to stare at me, and the words spilled out of me in my desperation to fill that quiet. "He's my brother's. I'm returning him. He's a special breed, very valuable."

Bazooka hissed at me in a clear 'shut up' warning.

"How old are you?"

"Seventeen."

He removed his finger from the trigger, which was a relief, but he stepped forward and placed one hand on the steering column of the scooter. "Please come with me, Miss."

I held up my hands. "No, no, that's okay. I don't need to have questions answered. We'll head back the way we came."

The man tightened his grip on the scooter. "I'm asking you to come with me. You can bring your livestock with you."

I sighed and got off the scooter, then grabbed Bazooka out of his saddlebag. The soldier helped me wheel the scooter through a gap in the concrete barriers and over to the nearest truck. He sat us down on a rock at the side of the road, where we cooled our heels for at least an hour before anything more happened.

A sick feeling grew in my stomach as the soldier had conversations with various people, including two men who didn't seem to be enlisted; they wore the obligatory khakis and button downs, heavy boots, but had radios, earpieces clipped onto their ears. They looked from the soldier to us several times, then one of them started talking into his radio and the other one stepped out of sight.

One car in the back was a black SUV.

Spots swam in my vision. We might have a serious problem here. I clamped down hard on the desire to flee. It was too risky. Instead, I focused on keeping my breathing calm and even, even as I ground my teeth.

Finally, Mr. Buzzcut came back with another man who was almost his identical twin, except his buzz cut was darker and he was taller. By the decorations on his shoulder, he was maybe in command.

"Sergeant?" the first man said, gesturing at us. "We have an unaccompanied minor out here."

The sergeant towered over me, checking us out. Satisfied, he held out a hand.

"Sergeant First Class Wilson," he said, offering us a smile. "And you are?"

"Lou Compton." I shook his hand.

"May I see the goose?"

I gaped. "He bites sometimes."

"You wouldn't believe the things terrorists will stick a bomb into," the man said. "You don't look like much of a terrorist to me, but I'd be remiss not to check. Oh, and please keep your hands where I can see them."

Oh God. This would not end well. I looked down at Bazooka and tried to let my eyes implore him. *Don't get us shot. Don't do anything stupid. And for god's sake, don't bite the man.*

I handed Bazooka over with as much confidence as I could muster, and placed both hands out in front of me, palms up. "Please don't hurt him. I raised him."

Sergeant Wilson tucked Bazooka's head and neck under one arm and probed his body with one big, beefy hand. What the hell was he looking for? The hard edges of an explosive device in his belly? Pockets of lethal gas? Given the state of Bazooka's digestive system since the oatmeal, the search might be successful. Bazooka, to his credit, waited at least ten seconds before the first bite. The man's backside was closest to his bill, which I assume from the resulting jump is where he aimed. The man dropped the goose.

"What?" Bazooka said, flapping his wings as he ran

over to me. "He was fingering me!"

Everything stopped. I sucked in a breath and waited for the repercussions.

"Your goose can speak?" the sergeant said.

My brain kicked into overdrive and I snagged the first lie I could think of.

"Oh no, that was me," I said, and forced a laugh. "I'm... I'm a ventriloquist. That's why he's so valuable. I've been training him since birth to do tricks. We live in a petting zoo, and he's the main attraction."

I was more than aware of how made up this sounded, even though every statement except one was the truth.

The man narrowed his eyes. "Do it again."

I picked up Bazooka, fear sweat beginning to pool on my lower back, and held him to me. "Let's introduce you, okay?" I whispered to him. Then I turned Bazooka to face the sergeant and laid a hand on his feathered back. "Ready? Okay, here we go."

The nice thing about pretending to be a ventriloquist is that you're not supposed to move your mouth at all, so my part was easy. I gave Bazooka a quick squeeze when he was supposed to talk, and bless him, he played along.

"Hello," he squawked out. "My name is Bazooka."

I squeezed again, and he cleverly stopped talking.

The man peered back and forth between the two of us, and then, to my endless relief, he laughed. "Oh my God. I couldn't see your lips moving at all! And how do you get him to move like he's really speaking?"

"Years of training," I said. "He can also carry a pail, draw a circle with a marker, and do a couple of other things."

The man laughed. "Wait right here. I need to go get James. He needs to see this."

As soon as he was out of sight, I leaned my head down close to Bazooka's ear. "Now what? How do we get out of here?"

"We need a distraction. I'm pretty good at distractions. You want me to—"

"No!" I cut in, panicked. "No, I don't want you to do something that will undoubtedly be ridiculous and life-threatening! Just let me think."

Bazooka bristled. "I don't *only* do things that are ridiculous and life-threatening. I just enjoy it when things go that direction. I can be subtle."

"Bazooka, please, please don't. These men have guns and we are at their—"

"Shhhhhh."

He somehow flung a wing tip toward my face, covering my mouth completely.

I stilled, dropped my hands to my sides, unable to do anything. This was it. This was where it was going to end. Whatever Bazooka was about to do, we were going to be shot, or arrested, or blown up, or… or… I couldn't think of anything worse.

But Bazooka, oddly enough, was still and silent as a statue. Was he concentrating?

After a minute, he shook himself and removed his wing from my mouth. I resisted the urge to check for feathers on my lips. He looked almost smug.

"What did you do?" I whispered.

"Wait and see. Oh, and maybe let's turn the scooter around. Just in case."

I looked around, but no one was paying a ton of attention to us, so I wheeled the scooter over to the edge of the road, pointed back the way we'd come. Then I waited, counting time by the pounding of my heartbeats.

They were so loud I didn't see how everyone around us couldn't hear.

"There they are," Sergeant Wilson said from about fifty feet behind us. I turned and saw him and another man heading our way. "Hey, I found him. You gotta show him the trick."

"Whatever you're doing, Bazooka, it needs to happen now…"

Just then, a loud ruckus emerged from a group of vehicles about five car-lengths down from the barricade. One man shouted something at another man, and then a second joined in. Someone pushed someone else, and the yelling got louder, and before long, people were streaming out of their parked cars to join in. It was a complete bar brawl, minus the bar, and it was getting bigger by the second.

"Oh shit," the sergeant said, reaching our side, waving a hand toward us. "You guys stay back. We gotta go take care of this before it gets out of hand."

The two soldiers ran off toward the fray, most of their companions heading the same direction to plunge into the crowd and, I assumed, stop this from turning into a riot. In the distance, someone hurled a rock through a car windshield, and the yelling became something more like screaming.

"Shall we?" Bazooka said. If a goose could look smug, he certainly was.

I glanced up at the soldiers still in the makeshift watch tower. They weren't looking our way, and even if they were, we weren't harming anyone, or under arrest, or anything. I waved at one of them, who nodded back, and started easing the scooter around the barricades and onto the open road.

With one last glance at what now was a brawl involving dozens of people armed with rocks and window scrapers, and strangely, a pile of flaming luggage, I started the engine and we puttered back the way we came.

Chapter Sixteen

September 18, 2022
Dear Emmett,
So I'm grounded again. Honestly, I don't even care.
It was worth it.

*Today at church, the pastor mentioned gay people
in his sermon, and not in the "we are all God's children"
kind of way. It was more of a brimstone and damnation
thing. And I could feel it, in all the pews around us,
people stiffening and side-eyeing our family, like the fact
you even exist is something to feel shame about.*

*And then, you know what? He said something about
the strength of character it takes for us to turn against
the evil of the world (meaning you, I guess) and keep our
souls pure, and stupid Mrs. Haynes sitting next to Mom
reached over and squeezed her hand like Mom was some
kind of hero. And Mom smiled at her. She actually
smiled.*

*I kept it to myself until we were back home, but when
Mom asked what was wrong as we finished making
Sunday dinner, I told her. I said it right to her face. "I
don't think you're heroic for throwing Emmett out. I
think you were wrong."*

*She looked at me for the longest time, concentrating
so hard it was like she thought she could back up time by
sheer force of will and make me not have said that. When
that didn't work, she sighed and wiped her hands on her*

apron and reached out for me. I wasn't going to let her touch me.

Then she started with her preachy voice: "I know it's hard for you to understand, Louise." She only ever calls me Louise when I'm in trouble. "This is one of those ages where you think you understand everything, but really, you don't."

I don't think I've ever felt so angry, Em. I had a horrible vision of throwing something heavy at her and storming out. Of course I didn't do that. Instead I said, well, perhaps I was yelling by this point, "I understand my brother is gone and no one but me seems to care! You even get congratulated in church for doing it!"

I felt awful right away. Her face seemed to crumple up, and she sat suddenly on one of the kitchen chairs, covering her face with her hands. When she looked at me again, she'd clearly started crying, which made me feel even worse. Then she spoke in this hushed up, wobbly voice: "Do you think this was easy for me? Do you think I don't miss him with every fiber of my being? Because I miss him every single day."

Then Dad came along and wanted to know what was going on and Mom told him what I'd said to her, and he got mad at me and sent me to my room. But that's fine because where do I go anyway, other than to Maggie's house?

But Emmett—this is good news, don't you see? Mom misses you. She cried! Maybe if I talk to her about it again, I can get her to change her mind. Take it back. Maybe we can find you, and bring you home, and we can all be together again.

If I could just hear from you, sometime. It would make such a difference. Do you think about me, or are you so far gone that you've started to pretend I don't even exist?

Love, Lou

****

By unspoken agreement, we spent the rest of the day trying to get the hell out of Nebraska, pushing the scooter to maximum speed for as long as we could. Whatever was going on with the protestors and dark vans and mysterious buses, my instincts for self-preservation had kicked in hard. Nebraska suddenly felt like one long disaster after another.

I pulled over and flung my arms out to the sides in glee when the "*Welcome to Wyoming: Forever West*" sign appeared in front of us, with its bucking bronco and cowboy silhouetted across a gorgeous, ice-blue mountain range.

We stopped for a break and I considered hopping off the scooter and kissing the ground. Another state crossed off the list! 700 miles off the overall trip! Only 1100 to go? Not even halfway and we'd been attacked at a rest stop, targeted by protesters, detained by the military... ugh. I shut down that line of thought and focused on the issues at hand.

"Mind if I look for some bugs?" Bazooka asked. "Anyway, the scooter is getting warm again. Best to let it rest."

I nodded, and while he foraged, I tore through another couple pieces of jerky and a big swipe of peanut butter. That made me thirsty, and I realized our water supply was getting low. We hadn't refilled since Mari's place, and we would need to find another refill site soon. I took a few sips of what remained.

"It's very brown here," Bazooka observed, reappearing beside me.

I looked around. Most of the surrounding landscape was dry, scrubby grass, with the occasional rocky butte popping out near the horizon. It had its charm. And seeing the landscape change from flat, grassy fields to something more western felt like progress.

"What do we do next?" he continued, not noticing that I hadn't responded.

"Let's put as much distance between us and whatever the hell was going on between the roadblock and the border as possible."

Bazooka honked thoughtfully. "Bunker, probably. You know those buses we saw go by with the dark windows and people crammed inside? And the rumors about something happening in the western half of the state?"

"You think so? Right there in 'Nowhere,' Nebraska?"

"One hundred percent," Bazooka said. "You saw the news about how people were rioting about being left out. There's probably some missile site around there where they're stashing the locals who have value. Scientists, power brokers, the rich."

More power to those who wanted to hole up underground, but I wasn't convinced I'd want to be part of the crew who had to pry open a bunker door after a year or two and come back out onto the surface of a wasted planet. Maybe I was morbid, but I'd never seen a disaster movie in which I wasn't imagining that I'd be glad to die early. Fighting off vampires, eking out a living on a radioactive planet, running from zombies—I knew myself, and such heroics were not for me.

I said as much, and Bazooka wriggled indignantly.

"You should be more interested in survival. You're young! It's probably why that soldier got so interested when he found out you were a minor." He snapped up a grasshopper and choked it down with his bill in the air, then returned his attention to me. "He was probably gonna add you to the next bus out as a potential child bride."

The thought honestly hadn't occurred to me before, but it made a certain sense. That's what always happened in disaster movies. People who survived had to have lots and lots of babies, so young women were very much in high demand.

I shuddered. "Oh my GOD, don't say that. It's so disgusting!"

We continued on for another two hours before finding a place to camp for the night again, this time at a mostly deserted campground near Caspar.

For once, a night out in the open passed peacefully, with no surprise visitors or threats of violence. The campground was almost entirely empty, just an attendant who took our entry fee and let us know which bathrooms still had working plumbing. We filled our water jugs, had the rest of Mari's sausages and part of a loaf of bread she'd given us, and got a decent night's sleep.

****

A cranky-looking goose poked me awake the next morning. "Are you aware that you snore?"

"I do not!" I sat up and rubbed the gunk from my eyes. "What time is it? Have you eaten?"

He had, but he sat gamely by while I heated water and made oatmeal. "So the plan today is to get to Jackson?"

"Yep."

"It's a long way," he said doubtfully. "Almost three hundred miles. You sure the scooter can make it that far in one go?"

"We'll take a lot of breaks." I patted the steering column of the scooter affectionately. "She's been doing great, right? And we have literally all day to do about seven hours of driving. She can make it."

He shrugged. "If you say so."

****

The scooter stood pinging and steaming in the pullout for a small scenic overlook. The parking lot was empty except for us. I was working my way loudly through every swear word I knew, combining them in new and creative ways.

Bazooka was in no mood to give me space. "I told you so! You humans never listen!"

"I thought you were protecting the scooter!" I shouted back. "Shouldn't you be able to keep this from happening?"

"I've been keeping the gas tank full. That's all." He snapped his bill at me. "This is all on you."

I went back to my swearing and added in kicking rocks. Behind me, smoke rose from the scooter's engines, smelling of burned rubber. I'd started looking for a spot to pull over once it started making a sound like a handful of pebbles had gotten stuck inside it, but things had worsened fast. And now, here we were.

We were hours outside of Jackson, stranded with a scooter that wouldn't start, and only thirty-six days left until the world ended. Bazooka was right: I *was* a fucking idiot. I sat down on the curb, deflated, and stared at the ground.

"Maybe it will start after we let it cool down for a

while?" Bazooka said.

"I hope so, because we're in the middle of nowhere and there's no one to help us."

"We could hitchhike."

I sighed. "Bazooka, hitchhiking is dangerous."

He cackled, and after reflection, I laughed too. We could suspend the regular rules of life at this point. Being kidnapped while hitchhiking was a danger, sure, but so was absolutely everything else happening to us right now.

Leaving home at my age to make an impossible trip? Dangerous.

Driving across the country on an old scooter, while taking advice from an imp? Dangerous.

Sneaking away from military arrest? Dangerous.

A giant rock streaking down to end civilization in roughly five weeks? So dangerous, the word hardly applied.

It put hitchhiking into perspective.

"All right, maybe we can hitchhike," I said, wiping my eyes as my laughter died down. "But not now, in the dark. Let's get off the road and find some shelter for the night. We passed that little town not very far back... what was it called? Should we walk back?"

Bazooka shook his head. "No. It's rough terrain, and I don't think we should risk it. Might be animals around."

I sucked in a breath. "Oh shit. Are there bears here? What are we gonna do?"

Bazooka stretched his wings wide in obvious pride. "If I can lift a man, I can lift a mountain lion. I'll protect you."

"If you have so many powers, can't you magic the scooter fixed?"

"I'm not a mechanic."

I muttered to myself about how a mechanic might be more useful, but I dropped it. Bazooka's powers, or lack thereof, made no sense to me, and I could tell there were things he wasn't telling me. But honestly, that he was still here with me meant something. Technically, only I was stuck here. He still had wings. He could fly away any time he wanted. I hadn't messed up his wish to see the country at all, just my own. And yet, he was sitting here beside me, sharing in my misfortune.

Like a friend.

I knew better than to say it out loud, but the concept made me feel a little less lost.

We wheeled the scooter over to a small picnic area amongst some overgrown trees where we could find minimal shelter and were out of sight of the parking lot and road. Bazooka wandered off to forage, no doubt thinking about what an idiot I was to have burned out the engine. He wasn't wrong.

The chill wind at this higher elevation soon had me scrambling through my pack for a long-sleeve shirt. As hot as it had been during the day, I could practically see my breath tonight. I hesitated about making a fire, but in the end, we used one of the rickety barbecue pits that stood beside an ancient picnic table to warm up.

I fell into a fitful sleep, tormented by thoughts of the scooter and what we were going to do next.

****

The next morning, I prayed for the first time in ages. *Pleasepleaseplease. God, if you're there, I've gone to church my whole life. Will you fix this, please?*

My heart was in my throat as I pressed the ignition switch in the morning light. Nothing. Not a click. No purr, no hum, no trying to start. Just nothing.

God—if he existed—was clearly not on my side, no matter how much of my childhood I'd spent in a pew. I wasn't all that surprised.

"Dammit," I muttered, as I poked around as Mari had shown me, trying to see if I could spot any problems. Not that I would know what to do about them if I did. All I could do was to open the seat and confirm that yes, there was an engine down there, and yes, it had oil. I held the wrench she'd sent with us, trying to find anything to use it on, but her careful instructions had fled my mind.

Great. Great work, me. Really making a name for myself as a mechanic.

After that, I slumped on the picnic bench beside the scooter and twirled the wrench in my fingers, trying to regroup, while Bazooka stood a short distance away, not speaking to me. Until, that is, the rumble of distant engines announced company. I leaped to my feet, too numb to land on a feeling. Should I be nervous? Hopeful? Should we hide? Stay where we were?

I had no idea. Instead, I quickly hid the scooter behind a bush and we edged back toward the parking lot, taking shelter behind a group of trees. Four vehicles pulled in at the other end of the parking lot and rolled to a stop. Three pickup trucks, the kind with enormous wheels designed to go off-road, and an open-top jeep. One truck was full of cargo, boxes and crates covered with a bright blue tarp. The other two trucks held a combination of more crates and people. I counted as they climbed out and noted that there were about a dozen of them, young to middle-aged, men and women, all dressed in camo or worn-out denim.

Most of them headed into the rest stop buildings to

use the facilities, but two of them, a man and a young woman, stayed with the vehicles, talking. Should I reveal myself? We were screwed without help. I shuffled out of the bushes and stood nervously on the edge of the concrete parking lot.

They looked my way, and I looked down, nervous. Should I retreat into the grass behind me? Pretend I hadn't seen them?

The young woman said something to her companion, then headed toward me. I waited, muscles tensed.

I needed help, after all. Maybe it was worth the risk.

She was a couple of years older than me, dressed in overalls and a blue thermal shirt, and her hair was insane—frizzy chestnut-brown curls sticking out in every direction. She stopped a few paces away and smiled at me. It was one of those smiles that transformed a face from average to gorgeous. I smiled back without even meaning to.

"You okay?" she asked. "I'm Ivy. Are you all alone? You and the goose?" She smiled down at Bazooka.

"I'm Lou. And yeah. My scooter died. No idea what's wrong or how to fix it."

She pointed behind her at the man who was still standing beside one of their trucks. "That's my brother Dan over there. He's pretty good with engines. Want him to look?"

"Where're you guys from?" I asked, playing for time.

She ran a hand through her curls, and I caught sight of a lot of freckles that dotted her olive skin as she looked up toward the sky. "Missouri. Ran into some trouble out there with looters and riots, so we're making our way to a kind of family home base on a ranch out in Idaho. You?"

"I'm from Iowa. Trying to get to Oregon where my brother is before... you know."

She nodded seriously. "Just you? That's so dangerous! There are a lot of crazy people out here right now."

"We've had some help on the way, but yeah, me and him." I motioned to the goose. "He's a pet. I couldn't leave him behind."

Ivy kneeled and clucked at Bazooka, holding her hand out to him, and he gave me a dubious look but eventually waddled over to her. "Oh, isn't he the handsomest?" she cooed. "What kind of goose is he?"

"Greylag. Oh, and he can do tricks."

She looked up, interested. "You'll have to tell me more about that sometime. So what do you say? Want to meet Dan?"

What else could I do? The scooter wasn't going to fix itself. Ivy seemed nice, and it wasn't like sulking was going to get us moving again. "Sure," I said, and we wheeled the scooter over to where her brother stood.

She made quick introductions and explained my situation.

"Nice to meet you, Lou," Dan said. Like her, he had olive skin and dark hair, cut short but showing a bit of curl. He was tall and dressed for efficiency—sturdy boots, camo pants with a gazillion bulging pockets, a warm shirt, and a bandanna around his neck. He smiled at me with the same bright smile Ivy had. "Mind if I look?"

I stepped aside as he examined the scooter. He seemed to know what he was doing. He pulled out the seat cover to access the engine and then systematically poked and prodded at things, testing the start button. After a few minutes, he straightened up.

"Looks like it's a spark plug problem. You've worn out the one you have. Do you know when you last had any service done?"

"It's, um, been a few years," I said. "The scooter's been in storage for the last couple years. No one's been riding it."

"Well, that's your problem. Easy fix if we can get the right part, but unfortunately I don't have anything like that on me." Dan made a sympathetic face. "Tough break, kid. I'm sorry."

Ivy pulled her brother aside. They spoke for a few minutes, and when they came back, she had a hopeful look on her face. "Lou, I know you don't know us, but you said you're heading to Oregon, right?"

"Yeah, although I'd planned to make a stop in Jackson to look for someone who knew my brother. But after that, I'm heading straight to Bend."

"We're going to Jackson!" she said. "And from there we're going all the way to southwest Idaho. It'll get you a heck of a lot closer to where you're going. Do you want to come with us?"

"I know you don't know us," Dan added, "but I promise you'll be safe with us. We're good at protecting our own. And we can off-road if needed once we get through the passes."

"But what about my scooter?"

"Well, we could throw it in the truck and bring it along, try to fix it up when we reach the compound," Dan said. "Would that work?"

It seemed like a dream come true. Help from

friendly strangers, a ride for over half the remaining distance we had to go? And maybe, in this Ivy girl, a friend? The relief I felt in my chest had me wanting to both laugh and cry, both of which might have convinced them I was too unstable to bring along. I stuffed the reaction down and simply smiled instead. If my smile was a little wobbly at the edges, no one commented.

"I'd love a ride. Honestly, I can't thank you enough."

Dan grinned back. "Just get your things off the scooter and I'll start working on fitting it in somewhere."

Ivy gave my arm a squeeze that nearly had me bawling on the spot. She seemed to sense my emotions close to the surface and made light conversation while we emptied the contents of the saddlebags, repacked my backpack, and tied my bedroll to the bottom.

Before I knew it, they'd bundled me and Bazooka into the back bed of one truck, Ivy beside me and two other women and a man seated across from us.

We pulled back out onto the highway. I could hardly stop smiling. We'd been saved.

Chapter Seventeen

Interlude: Bazooka

One thing I've noticed about humans over the millennia I've been observing them: they're much too suggestible. They see and believe what they most want to see and believe, latching on to whatever attunes with their own values and blocking the rest. Sure, this Ivy person seems nice and her brother is a decent sort, but then again, what exactly are they doing out here? What kind of compound are they heading toward in Idaho? Why are they so eager to help? Does Lou think to ask any of these questions?

No, of course not.

While Lou all but hands over the keys to Dan within seconds of meeting him, I wander around unobtrusively and examine the people and their belongings. There are thirteen of them, seven men, six women, most under the age of forty. Nearly two-thirds of them carry guns. While that seems like a pretty wise idea in the current political climate, it also raises a red flag. If their intentions turn out to be less than pure, Lou is going to be at a severe disadvantage.

From what I can see of their vehicles, they're traveling hard. I see food supplies, water tanks, some crates that probably hold ammunition, a couple of ladders, bundles of rope, and various other odds and ends. There are even a handful of chickens in a crate in one of the truck beds, squawking away like idiots. I don't bother introducing myself. Try having a conversation with a chicken sometime. You'll rip your fucking ears off before you're five minutes in.

By the time I make it back to Lou's side, she's thrown in with the new humans whole-heartedly.

I can't really fault her; people need other people, and it isn't like I can magically resurrect a dead spark plug. And we have over seven hundred miles left to reach Bend. Getting a ride for nearly four hundred of those miles makes sense, no matter the consequences.

Plus, we have a secret in our back pocket. As long as I let the feathered portion of my biology take over, none of them will know that Lou has a powerful imp on her side.

I'm here to watch her back. And to kick ass if necessary.

Fine, then. Let's go.

Chapter Eighteen

April 3, 2023
Dear Em,
At school today, the guidance counselor called me in and said we had to make plans for my future. Junior year is looming, and I've apparently got a big brain and good grades, and it's time to think about the rest of my life.

I suppose that's fair, but the rest of my life is something I have a really hard time picturing. Is it that way for everyone, or is it just me?

Do you ever think about time, and how we can get stuck in it? Like something bad happens and a part of us freezes there, even though time keeps ticking forward. Like we just stay there, living in that moment?

I guess what I'm trying to say is that I feel like part of me is still eleven, sitting in that barn. My life divided neatly into two parts. Before that, when I felt safe and loved, and trusted everyone and hadn't done anything really bad. And after that, when I suddenly knew more than I wanted to about the ways people can fail each other.

Is that why I never grew into the self-assured teenager that everyone else seems to be? The kind who actually has a life and career interests and big dreams? Other kids have plans they're looking forward to, but I don't, not really. I've been okay with that for a long time, but now? Now I'm feeling like something isn't quite right.

I think it's partly that I don't trust myself. I've made so many poor decisions over the years. I either trust the wrong people and share way too much of myself, or I trust no one, shutting out people who are probably very nice and might be good to have around. The only person I really trust or talk to is Maggie.

It's like there's an invisible wall inside me, and people can get right up to it, but no closer. I think I'm going to have to do something about this, eventually, if I don't want to be lonely my whole life.

I think maybe I need counseling. Or drugs. Or both. Probably both. But that's a problem for future me.

So much for deep thoughts. I know I don't want to spend the rest of my life at the petting zoo, though, so I guess I better start at least going through the motions of making plans. Getting ready for the college prep exams, looking into schools, learning about scholarships.

If I at least set something in motion, maybe the rest of me will eventually catch up, right?

This letter is depressing. It's a good thing you aren't going to read it.

Love, Lou

****

Ivy, Bazooka, and I curled up on a pile of blankets in the back of the truck. She played with the goose while I enjoyed the luxury of taking in the sights. It was the first time in ages I'd been able to fully admire the gorgeous landscape around us—sharp, snowy mountain peaks, huge trees, even hawks and eagles circling overhead—without keeping my focus on the road to avoid smearing us into the pavement.

We heard Jackson before we could fully see it. After so many half-empty ghost towns, the signs of life here shocked me. Even before we turned onto the main drag, the shouts and whoops of many voices reached us, accompanied by loud music blasting from somewhere.

It got louder as we pulled into the business district, a strip of old-West style buildings, all with long overhanging roofs. Most of the shops had varnished tree trunks as columns, and the storefronts were natural wood, trim painted in shades of blue, green, and orange.

More astonishing, there were people everywhere—I counted at least two dozen near us—in various stages of dress or undress, small children and dogs running wild between them. People were hanging off balconies, sitting in the street, dancing in a clump further down the road. Nearly all had an alcoholic beverage in hand.

Ivy and her people looked tense, but we soon realized these people weren't rioting, or recruiting, or anything scary. They were having a party, and it looked like an excellent one.

Dan laughed as he pulled into a parking spot. "Okay," he said to me and Ivy. "I'm gonna drop you guys off to do your research while I head to the other side of town to pick up our fuel supply. It might take a couple hours. Try not to get into too much trouble." He leaned over and passed her what looked like a small handgun.

Seeing my alarmed look, Ivy smiled reassuringly. "Don't worry. It's in case anyone tries to hurt us. You've seen what things are like out here."

My brain still prickled with discomfort as she tucked it into the deep pocket of her overalls. I helped Bazooka out of the truck, and Ivy climbed out beside me. Before I had time to even ask what was going on here, two of the party-people approached.

"Welcome to Jackson!" the taller of them shouted, tossing her long brown hair back behind her shoulder and pulling me into an impulsive hug that crushed my face against the sparkly bits bedazzling her jacket. "The last and best party on Earth! No bad vibes allowed!"

I examined the other girl over this one's shoulder. She was tiny, almost elfin, with platinum blond hair cut pixie short, and piercings and tattoos all over her body.

"I'm Christina," she said when her friend released me. She nodded toward the person next to her. "And this is Max. Where're you folks in from?"

"Nice to meet you. I'm Lou and this is Ivy. I'm from Iowa, and she's from Missouri."

"Road trip, huh? Well, take a break here with us. You're in good company!" Max grinned, her smile infectious. "Let me go find you a drink."

"We're just passing through, heading west."

Christina winked. "So is everyone who comes here. Most of 'em end up staying, though, once they realize they can cry away their last few weeks or stay here and have fun."

"So you've what, taken over the town?" Ivy asked.

Someone put a can of something alcoholic in our hands, and Max slung an arm around me and pulled the two of us into the fray. "Not taken over. But did you know that there used to be more billionaires here in Jackson Hole than almost anywhere else in the country? When the comet got announced, they all took off in their private jets or went to live in their undersea bunkers, and they left a lot of good shit behind. Food, drugs, wine cellars, vehicles, you name it."

"And we," Christina cut in, "the regular folks who

aren't getting whisked away to survive the blast, simply decided to... well, help ourselves to whatever they left behind."

They bumped hips and Max took a long drink. Ivy excused herself to find a bathroom, and Bazooka, who had until this point been listening, tilted his head toward the sky and made his gurgling honk-laugh sound.

"Is your goose laughing?" Max asked me. "Oh man, so cool. This party needs a goose!"

Bazooka gave her what could almost pass for a wink, then flapped his way up to the high roof of one of the local businesses, where he could, I assume, get the best view with no one touching him. A few people behind me cheered his passage, and I heard a few shouts of "Goose! Goose! Goose!" followed by the chugging of beverages.

He favored them with his loudest, raunchiest honk. They cheered.

"So you're what, going to have a party from now until the end?" I asked Christina.

"I mean, what else are we supposed to do?" Her face went pensive, but then she grinned, threw her arms wide, and looked around. "We're in the most beautiful place in the whole damn world, and there's nothing we can do about what's coming. Might as well make the best of it."

Lots of people were smoking; I coughed when we walked through a blue cloud of tobacco smoke. Max rejoined us, waved a hand in the air and wrinkled her nose apologetically at me.

"Sorry about that, it's just, with the end coming, why not smoke all the cigarettes? You know?" Max grinned at me and then raised her voice to address the people nearby. "This is OUR town now, baby!" Hoots and cheers followed.

"How old are you, anyway?" Christina asked, peering at me more closely.

"Seventeen," I said, and before I knew it, I was telling them my life story. By the time we were done, we'd gathered a small crowd, who were listening raptly.

"Oh my God," one guy who looked completely spaced out said. "It's so sweet that you're going all this way to find your brother! And your parents are, like, supervillains, man!"

"No, they're really not—"

Everyone was talking to me at once. It was hard to follow. About the hardware stores in town, which store we should check, what years my brother was here.

"There's an Ace Hardware a couple of blocks over," someone offered.

Christina's face lit up. "I know where that is! Let's all go!"

I shot one last glance at Bazooka up on the rooftop and tried to find Ivy in the crowd, but before I could, the wave of be-crystalled, intoxicated humanity swept me along on a seemingly hilarious mission to take me straight to my brother's former workplace.

The hardware store was no longer functioning, but a group of people had taken it upon themselves to set up a barter shop in the parking lot. They were guarding the store against looters while offering trades on items of similar value to anyone who could offer something in return, be it food, blankets, or booze. It impressed me to see something so organized and community spirited. Maybe these party people were onto something.

"Christina!" the guy at the table said, and she swooped around to give him a hug and then punch him in the arm. "What brings you to my fine establishment today?"

"Joel! My new friend Lou here is looking for her brother. Thinks he might've worked here a while back."

The man crunched up his face, thinking. "The office inside is still in one piece, filled with filing cabinets and stuff. I bet you could find employee records in there, if that would help?"

I nodded. "Could you show me?"

Joel conferred with the woman next to him and then stood. "C'mon in," he said. The crowd behind me whooped, and we all headed toward the front door in a bouncing, dancing clump of jingling beads, beer, and smoke.

He threw open the doors, and the party boiled over from the parking lot into the store. Three people hopped up onto the checkout counters and someone else started playing music on some kind of ancient battery-operated tape deck. As Christine and I picked my way around them and followed Joel toward the back corner, it looked like a dance-off was brewing in the yard tools aisle.

Joel pushed open a door and flipped on the buzzy, overhead lights to highlight a grim little office. Framed posters of barns, mountains, and rivers decorated the walls. A small metallic desk stood in front of a long row of shiny black file cabinets, and a green leather couch sat along the opposite wall. A circular Formica table with two plastic chairs made up the only other furniture.

Joel slung an arm around Christina and gave her a peck on the cheek. "Have at it, ladies. I'm gonna go supervise the party. Someone has to make sure no one breaks the light bulbs we have left."

Christina rifled through one drawer after another,

opening them with a swoop and smashing them closed. "Financials… inventory… divorce papers…" She opened the top drawer of the third cabinet and crowed with success. "Here we go. Employee records. Thankfully, Gus, the owner, was terrible at computers. Everything is on paper."

I stepped over and ran a finger over the labels of various files, sorted into groups with dividers by year, then moved to the drawer below when the top drawer was too recent. In that drawer, I found what I was looking for.

Compton, Emmett.

I grabbed it, flipped it open, and froze.

Emmett's face looked up at me, several years older than I remembered. My throat closed; it had been so long since I'd seen his face. The contours of his cheeks were softer than I remembered, like he'd gained weight, and his hair was longer and lighter, maybe from the sun, but his green eyes were the same. It was him. My brother.

"Oh, is that him? What a cutie!" she said, leaning over and looking at the polaroid.

I cleared my throat. "Yeah. That's him."

The picture was clipped to the top of a job application. I unclipped it and scanned through the text. He'd applied in August 2021, listing Mari as a reference, and had a local hotel as his address. Maybe he hadn't found a place to live yet? There weren't many other pages in the file. A photocopy of his driver's license, still from Iowa, and a couple of forms he'd signed. The last page was a hand-scrawled note from his manager showing that Emmett had left his job the following June.

Such tiny bits of information, and yet they felt monumental to me. I ran a finger over his signature.

Emmett had been here, sat at this table, signed these papers, stocked shelves in the store.

Christina laid an inked hand on my arm. "You okay, hon? You look like you've seen a ghost."

I nodded. "It's—It's been a while since I've seen his face. God, I've missed him."

"You wanna keep that file?"

Suddenly, I did.

We shut off the lights and headed back out to where Joel was standing, arms crossed, trying to watch all the various clumps of people messing around in his store at once. "All set?" he said, noting the file folder in my hand. "Find what you needed?"

"Yeah, we did—thank you so much."

Christina hopped up on the main pay counter and stuck both fingers in her mouth to produce the most ear-splitting whistle I'd ever heard. The entire store came to a halt, all faces turned expectantly her way.

"Party people!" she bellowed, arms spread wide. "We have succeeded in our mission!" Massive cheering broke out and someone rattled what sounded a lot like a cowbell. "And now, let's get the hell out of Joel's store! Back to the brewery!"

Like good natured sheep, everyone turned and piled through the front door. I glanced around one more time, then followed.

****

Ivy and Bazooka were waiting at a table near the brewery when I returned. I plopped down happily, showing them what I'd found, except for the picture, which I'd tucked in the back pocket of my jeans. That felt private.

"Didn't really learn that much, did you?" Ivy said,

examining the folder. "I mean, yeah, he was here, but there's no forwarding address."

I patted the messenger bag at my side, the one with Emmett's stacks of letters and my notebooks, as I slid the file into it. "I know where he went from here."

"Then why are you here?" she asked, her face confused. "I mean, if you know where he ended up, why not go right there?"

I leaned forward, feeling my face flush red. "I don't know for sure he's still there. His letters ended about nine months ago. I think he's in Bend, Oregon, but I can't be sure, and I've only got one shot at this. Anyone I can talk to who might still be in touch with him is really, really important. Someone might have his email address or know how to call him."

Ivy looked apologetic. "Okay, I get it. Did you talk to his boss here?"

"Nah, he's long gone. But still. It was worth it." I sat back and noticed a large canvas bag at Ivy's feet. "What's that?"

"Oh, some bedding and stuff from the hotel. Someone let me have a few blankets. We always need more stuff." She didn't meet my eyes. I hoped she hadn't stolen it.

Someone appeared on the balcony of the bar across the street before I could decide what to say. "You guys!" he shouted to the people gathered in the street in front of him. "I got the soft serve ice cream machine working! Sundaes on me!"

Ivy raised an eyebrow. "You want ice cream?"

I shook my head. I didn't feel like being in a tight space with that many people.

"It's okay, I'll go. I'll bring you some back."

After she joined the crowd of people making their way into the building, Bazooka shook himself like he was shaking off a too tight jacket. "Thank God. It's exhausting pretending to be a dumb farmyard animal."

I smirked. "I'm sure it's very tiring."

"This town is amazing, Lou," he said. "I approve of their methods. Are you sure you don't want to stay here? Besides, I'm not so sure about Ivy and her friends."

"What do you mean?"

"I mean, what's with the gun?" He flopped one wing up on the arm of the chair like a little professor holding office hours. "And who are these people? They said they'd drive us through most of Idaho, which is great, but what then? Are you sure this is a good idea?"

Was it? It felt so nice to have other people involved in my quest. These people were headed our way in their big, fast trucks, willing to drag along my busted-up scooter and maybe fix it. With any luck, these guys were going to take days off our trip by driving us to southwestern Idaho.

Bazooka's head shot up. "Oh my. What is that smell? Do you smell it?"

I sniffed. "Chocolate, maybe? And beer."

"No, no, under that…" Bazooka hopped off the table and called back over his shoulder. "I'll be right back. One last snack before we hit the road."

****

"No goose? Oh well, more for us." Ivy returned with three big paper cups filled with ice cream and sprinkles.

I picked up a spoon and dug in. I hadn't had ice cream in such a long time, and despite the cool temperature up this high, it tasted amazing. As we ate, Ivy told me more about life at the compound in Idaho.

She called it a farming utopia. As she talked, I examined her more closely. She didn't seem like she was hiding anything. Her face was open and honest, and her dark eyes were sincere. Then I got distracted by her freckles.

"You still there, Lou?" she asked.

I shook myself. "Yeah, sorry, drifted off. So anyway, what do you think about this place?" I gestured around with my spoon. "Christina said almost everyone who passes through ends up staying."

Ivy glanced around. "I mean, it's pretty. And the people are nice. And they are incredibly lucky they have a ton of resources to work with, with all these stores and big fancy homes and ranches to plunder. They've got a lot of what they need." She took a big spoonful and crammed it in her mouth, then licked the spoon clean. "At least for now."

"What do you mean?"

She lowered her voice. "It depends if what the government is telling us is true. I mean yeah, for sure there's a comet. We should be able to see it soon. But is it as big as they say, and is it possible that every single human on the planet won't make it?"

"You don't think that's true?"

"I think it's bullshit. So let's say you're one of the party people here in Jackson, and you spend the last two months eating and drinking everything in sight, whipping through resources like they're a never-ending pool. And then, suddenly? Say the comet hits on the other side of the planet or something, or it breaks up in the atmosphere and only causes minor issues." She looked up at me and her face was intense. "So yeah, the world is fucked up, but you're still alive, with maybe decades of hard work ahead to re-establish society and all that. What're you going to do if you already partied your way through all the important supplies?"

I sat back in shock. "I never thought about it that way. That's scary. What will happen to them?"

"Chaos. Anarchy." She licked the last bit of ice cream out of the bottom of the cup. "That's where the real struggle begins. And we're gonna be ready."

Just then, Dan's truck pulled back into the end of the street. He got out and waved, and Ivy stood and signaled back. "Time to go. Where's that goose of yours?"

"Let me find him—he went off to forage." For a nerve-wracking second, I couldn't find any sign of him, but eventually I located him in the center of a big circle of people, eating the remnants of a pan of brownies from a ceramic dish while people cheered.

"Bazooka!" I said, pulling him away and tucking him under my arm. "Our ride is here!"

A guy reached out and patted Bazooka on the head, and, much to my surprise, Bazooka permitted it. "Your goose is a trip, man. Hope he enjoys the rest of his night."

What did that mean? I didn't have time to find out. I hugged Christina and Max goodbye, and left Jackson, feeling reluctant.

We drove out of town with Dan and stopped where the rest of the caravan had gathered.

"Dan, what happened to you?" Ivy said worriedly, going over to him and gently reaching out a finger to touch his obvious black eye and a smear of blood on his cheek. I followed closely, still a little shy with most of the crew.

Dan shook her off. "Nothing, Ivy, a little dust-up. We straightened it all out."

I noticed that several of them seemed to have been

in a fight. The backs of the three trucks held more cargo, with various new boxes and barrels covered with tarps. We rearranged, but Ivy made sure that she, Bazooka, and I stayed together as we huddled down in the bed of Dan's truck, and she even grabbed us a pair of blankets for the ride.

"Settle in now, you two," Dan said, leaning over the edge of the truck to check on the three of us. "From here on out, we're likely gonna drive straight through except for bathroom breaks. We'll be in Idaho by morning. See if you can get some sleep."

Ivy, to her credit, conked out like a pro—she was clearly used to sleeping on the go and slept easily and deeply. Me? I couldn't sleep, and apparently neither could Bazooka, who seemed to be in some kind of deep funk. He moved restlessly beside me, changing position, tucking his head under a wing, then pulling it out, turning in circles, sitting back down, and finally leaning up against me with his neck stretched up toward my shoulder and his head near my ear.

"Lou," he whispered, and I started, checking to see if Ivy had noticed, but she continued her soft snoring. "Lou, are you awake? I feel strange."

"I am, but you have to keep it down… what's going on?"

Bazooka craned his neck toward the sky and his pupils seemed… wrong somehow. Too big? Wrong shape? Was he sick? How did one tell if a goose was sick? "Look at all the stars, Lou…" he whispered. "Shoooooo pretty!"

This didn't seem like Bazooka at all. "Are you okay? Why are you stargazing? And why aren't you talking right?"

Bazooka pulled his neck away and seemed to sway, almost drunkenly, before flopping his neck down on my shoulder. "I'm fine," he insisted. "Love the—love the stars." He fell silent and stared up at the sky some more. "You'll be able to see it soon, you know."

"See what?"

"Comet. Myyyyyyyy comet."

"Your comet?"

He thumped his head emphatically up and down against my collarbone, and I flinched.

"Why is it your comet?"

He pulled back and fixed an eye on me. "Cuz I put it there. Should name it after me, acshually. Comet Falthaom. Welcome to Earth." He made a sound that was almost a burp. "What's wrong wifme?"

I thought back to Jackson. "What was in those brownies, Bazooka? Do you know?"

"Oh, I dunno. Tasted like plants? Maybe?" He smacked his beak together. "Damn good stuff. Leafy."

It suddenly hit me. My goose was high. Baked. Stoned. He was tripping. I also suddenly understood that whatever he was on the verge of telling me was something he probably wouldn't normally. I placed a reassuring hand on his back and leaned in.

"So," I said, "tell me more about why we should name this comet after you."

And over the next few miles, Bazooka did just that.

Chapter Nineteen

Interlude: Bazooka

I come to at dawn feeling like I've been run over by a lawn mower in the middle of the night. My feathered head is pounding, my wings ache, and I puke loudly several times over the side of the truck.

Lou makes sure I don't fall out, but aside from that, she refuses to speak to or even look at me. It takes a while, but eventually the memories return as my stomach and head clear.

I got intoxicated on that fine young man's excellent brownies and spilled every single one of the beans about the comet and my responsibility for it.

Damn. I really hadn't intended to do that.

So now Lou hates me. And so what? Let her. Stupid interfering human. Like I owe her my full story or any version of the truth. I don't care. I don't care at all. Let her stew. It isn't like she did anything to stop me from getting half-poisoned in Jackson. Isn't she supposed to be the one who was good at watching over barn animals? This is at least partly her fault.

Besides, it's not like she won't forgive me. She'll have to. We're in this together. And if this means I have to put up with a lot less conversation? That's fine with me.

****

The silence only lasts until our first pit stop after

sunrise. I watch as Lou bounds out of the truck without paying the least bit of attention to me, and I'm so offended by this that I flap along after her as she makes her way into the rest stop bathroom.

"Your goose is in here," Ivy calls as she follows me in. Lou has already locked herself into a stall. "He reeks. You should go let him freshen up in the grass when you get done."

I squawk indignantly at this Ivy character, but sure enough, when Lou comes out, she gives me the stink-eye but motions for me to follow her out to the wide grassy lawn, far enough away from the others that it's safe to speak.

"So, you're pissed off, then?" I say, while she helps me clean bits of last night's vomit off my feathers.

Lou crouches down and glares at me. "You betrayed me," she hisses, sounding rather gooselike herself. "All this time, and you never once told me you're the reason that we're all in this mess? Never thought to mention it?"

I flap my wings and dislodge a piece of grass that shouldn't have been in there. "I didn't think you needed to know. What difference does it make?"

She gapes. "What—what difference? What difference does it make? It makes a lot of difference! You... you're the reason that everyone I love is going to die!"

"Well," I sniff, digging in the ground with one webbed foot and then the other. "If you're going to look at it that way, it's actually Charazon's fault, not mine."

Her face turns so red I am afraid she's going to have some kind of stroke. "Who the hell is Charazon?"

"The demon," I say, slowly. "Try to keep up. The one who decided to not fix my trick shot, and not to let *me fix it either. I told you about the game last night, didn't I?"*

She nods, wordless for once.

"Well, really, it's her fault. I had no intention of sending a rock hurtling toward Earth when I knocked her ball out of play. She's the one who let it complete its route."

She blinks. "So your point is that you're only unintentionally responsible for killing everyone I know."

"Maybe not everyone," I say, trying to be reasonable. One of us had to be. "Anyway, it hasn't happened yet. Maybe we'll think of something."

Her face flickers through a panoply of emotions— anger, outrage, grief—and finally lands on blankness. Her shoulders droop and her eyes don't meet mine as she stands.

"Lou? We all right?"

She turns and starts walking back toward the truck. "C'mon," she calls back to me, her voice unreadable. "Don't get left behind."

I think I like weepy, maudlin Lou better than this new angry Lou.

Chapter Twenty

May 15, 2023
Dear Emmett,
So, guess what? Last month some kids at school wrote up a charter to start the first-ever LGBT alliance club. The principal didn't want to allow it, but we made a big fuss with a protest and a walkout and everything, and eventually he had to give in.

We just did a unit on this in history class—did you know Iowa was the third state to legalize gay marriage? Way back in 2009. It's been legal almost the whole time I've been alive. Not that this means people are especially accepting of it, still. But things are changing a little. Maybe you'd find the atmosphere different if you were here now.

I got in trouble for being part of the walkout, of course, so I'm grounded again. (If you're wondering if I'm always grounded, the answer is yes.) And Mom and Dad made me go talk to the pastor twice, to make sure that I wasn't turning into a bad seed. I heard a lot of murmured late-night conversations at home after all that, and to be honest, it scared the crap out of me.

Because what if what happened to you also happens to me? Not the being gay part—I don't seem to have romantic feelings for anyone yet. I figure I'd have an inkling about it if I liked girls. And anyway, that wouldn't horrify me if it happened.

What I mean is, what if they turn against me, too?

I don't know what I'd do if they kicked me out. I don't know how you did it. Where did you go? How did you survive?

I'm going to have to be a little less rebellious. Because if I learned anything from you being gone, it's that nothing and no one is safe. You can't count on anything, not the love of your parents, not the home you grew up in, not the church that's supposed to love and accept everyone equally.

I'm simultaneously scared and furious. It's confusing as hell. Some nights, I lay in bed and my whole body shakes and I can't tell if it's rage or sadness or what. Sometimes I feel like I just need to hit someone with a frying pan or kick through the wall or something. I can imagine myself doing it. It pops into my head at the worst possible moments.

Every day I feel like less of myself, here. I wish you'd come back.

Love, Lou

****

December 15, 2023
Dear Lou,

It's almost Christmas, and high time I sent you a letter. What's it been, six months since the last time? I'm sorry about that, champ. I'm still in Bend, and I think I will be for the foreseeable future. You'd absolutely love it. There's a great bookstore, and a ton of shops and restaurants, and I swear every single person here has a dog. Usually multiple dogs.

The best part of Bend is that it's just so beautiful. We're in the middle of nowhere, technically the high desert, but you'd never know it with the river here and all the water sports people do. Hiking and rock climbing and wilderness all over the place. We have our very own mountain called Mt. Bachelor, one of like half a dozen snowy peaks you can see from the highway outside of town. Man, you and I could've done some good camping here. I wish we'd gotten the chance. You'd like the American West. What's that guy's name who took all the pictures in black and white of mountains and valleys and landscapes out here? Ansel Adams, I think. It's like stepping into one of his portraits, every day.

I'm doing pretty good. Working a couple of odd jobs, including one out on a farm near here with a friend of mine. Actually, he's more than a friend. I think maybe I've found someone special. We work together, and we're great friends, and he's so damn good looking. And kind. I think his laugh might be my favorite thing in the world.

I guess that's how you know. When someone's smile or laugh fills up an empty space inside you that you didn't even know needed to be filled. File that away for the future, Lou, under the category "good dating advice."

Geez. Are you dating? You're old enough now. How weird is that? Part of me still thinks of you as the age you were when I left, but you're going to graduate in a year or two.

Whoa. Had to put the pen down for a second and reflect on that one.

Anyway, I met him at the farmer's market in town, about a year ago, and we've been together ever since. I know how folks at home would feel about that. But honestly, I don't care anymore. There's nothing wrong with this, or with how I'm living my life.

Isn't it a good thing for people to find someone to love? Someone who's good to them?

I hope someday you get out of there and see the world out here for yourself. There are a lot of things that might surprise you about the life I'm living now, and it's too much to get into in a letter, especially a letter I suspect might be intercepted and read by someone other than you. But I hope someday I can tell you about my new life, and we can get to know each other again.

I don't know if you even get these letters. I'm guessing you don't, which is why I don't write them as often as I used to. I decided you would've answered at some point if you'd read them. Even so, I want you to know where I am. If you get a chance, come find me someday. I'll always let you know if I move.

Take care of yourself, Lou.

Love, Em

****

Bazooka nudged me awake in the early morning. "Wake up, we're here," he whispered.

I didn't answer. I wasn't ready to either speak to or forgive him. Instead, I sat up, wrapping my blanket tighter around me, as the caravan slowed and turned in at a gated drive. A sign overhead announced that we'd reached Harmony Ranch.

Our first view of it was much as Ivy had described it—a long, dusty drive leading back to what had once been a working ranch, tucked in between rolling tawny hills with views to die for in all directions. I had no idea that Idaho was so pretty, but then I'd never pictured Idaho at all. I suppose many people felt that way about Iowa, so I could hardly feel superior.

The ranch house, when it came into view, was a

huge, log-built home, painted brown with pine green trim. Multiple dormers dotted its green shingled roof, and a massive front porch supported a balcony that three rooms appeared to open onto. Next to the house was a two-story building that might be a garage or an office, and I could see a large barn and several other outbuildings in the distance. There were pasture and gardens in all directions, and a decent-sized greenhouse back in one corner. It looked welcoming, homey despite its size. If I'd drawn a ranch from my imagination, it might've looked something like this.

Except for the security features, that is.

A sturdy set of metal gates blocked the driveway. A man materialized out of nowhere to push them open and let us in, and he locked it up behind us with a clang. I looked to the side and saw what looked like a guard tower, made of peeled logs and covered with a slanted roof that would keep the worst of the weather off. I caught sight of two men in there, both holding rifles. A couple of jeeps and an ATV were parked behind it.

Ivy noticed me looking at them and gave my hand a squeeze, her smile as distracting as ever. "Oh, don't worry about them. We keep a watch 24/7 to keep looters or raiders out. You can't be too careful right now."

I supposed she had a point. As the truck pulled further in and took a turn around the side of the ranch house, tons of activity came into view. Men and women fiddled with solar panels, kids ran around playing or carrying buckets from place to place, and lots of other people were working in the fields or caring for animals. Although they couldn't have been here long, it looked like they'd done their best to salvage the ranch and get it functional and self-sufficient fast. We might be in good hands.

A heavy-set older woman with white hair noticed us in the back of the truck and walked over. "Ivy, you're here! It's so good to see you again! What's it been, eighteen months since you were last in town?" She smiled and wiped her hands off on her skirt and held one out to help Ivy down from the truck bed. "And who's your friend?"

She turned to me and offered the same helping hand, and I gratefully took it.

"Ma, this is Lou. We picked her and her goose up in Wyoming. Lou, this is Gina Martin, but we all call her Ma."

"Nice to meet you, Lou." The woman looked me over with glacier blue eyes and must have seen something she liked. She nodded approvingly. "Glad to have another able-bodied young woman joining us here. Oh, and you brought livestock? That's lovely. We don't have any geese here. Can she lay?"

Mad as I was, I wasn't about to let anyone take my goose frenemy away from me. I scooped him up and made a regretful, polite face. "No, sorry, it's he, and he's a pet. I'm only passing through on my way out to Oregon to find my brother. Ivy and her friends were so nice to give us a ride after my scooter broke down."

"Dan said he'd see if he could fix it, Ma," Ivy said.

"Is that so? Well, that's a shame. Anyway, Ivy, you're upstairs in the last of the bunk rooms—why don't you two get your things settled and then meet back down on the porch for a tour?"

Ivy helped me grab my backpack and bedroll from the truck, and we set off into the main ranch house. Bazooka busied himself poking around in the grass, so I left him as we went inside and up a wide staircase.

"Is that your grandmother?" I asked Ivy as we carted our stuff up the stairs.

"Kind of like an honorary grandmother. Believe me, you'll love her."

"Does this ranch belong to someone in your family? Sounds like you've been here before."

"Yeah, we're related to some people here. My great uncle founded the ranch, left it to one of my uncles when he died. We've been out to visit before. We lived on something similar but smaller in Missouri, before things went bad."

Ivy dragged her bag down a very long hallway lined on both sides by doors.

"We're in here," she said, opening the last door in the back corner. Inside were two bunk beds, a couple of dressers, and not much else. But it was clean and smelled good and the beds looked freshly made. "You can take your pick of beds. Oh, and Bazooka will have to stay out in the barn, of course."

I stopped short. "He's... he's all I have left from home. Can't he stay here in the room with us? He's very quiet."

Ivy made a face. "I don't love the idea of sleeping in the same room with a barn animal."

"Well, he and I could, I don't know... is there a smaller room where he and I could hole up together? That way, you wouldn't have to be inconvenienced?"

"I think space is pretty tight here," Ivy said, frowning. "I guess we can ask."

I peered around the room. A door led to a small closet. "What if we make him a bed in here? You won't even notice that he's there." I widened my eyes and tried to look as pathetic as possible. "I know it's silly, but I'd feel so much better if I knew where he was. He's like a pet to me. And we're only staying a couple days."

I could tell how weird she thought I was being. But she liked me. I knew she did, and after a long stare, she sighed and backed down. "Okay, but if he poops in here, he's gone."

"No worries, he's house broken."

She smiled uncertainly and got back to her unpacking.

****

Ma was waiting for us in one of the rocking chairs on the front porch when we came back down. "There you are, girls! Ivy, do you want to come along on Lou's tour?"

"Sure, why not? I'd love to see what you've done to the place since I was last here."

She led us first over to the garage-like structure I'd seen. We entered through a side door and saw a series of ATVs and snowmobiles. "Vehicles for all kinds of weather and terrain," she said. "And of course you've seen we have a sizeable collection of trucks and jeeps outside. The walls are reinforced concrete and we're hoping it'll hold up to the initial blast. But even if it doesn't, we've got a few vehicles tucked away in the bunker site."

"Bunkers?" I mouthed to Ivy.

"Just wait," she whispered back. "It's so cool."

Next, she led us through the barn, which was large and well populated. "Ivy's great uncle Jamie was an odd duck," she said. "Always convinced the end of the world was coming. Turns out he was right, if on the wrong time frame." She stopped and opened a metal hatch in the floor, showing stairs leading down. "He built this underground storage facility for animal feed. We've been sending out trucks to other deserted ranches in the area to bring in as much hay and feed as we can. Should be a few loads coming in today."

We wandered through a smokehouse packed to the gills with meat being preserved, a bustling canning shed, and then out through the pasture to a tall, metal gate with two guards standing on either side.

"And this," she said, as the guards swung the gate open, "is our pride and joy. Welcome to our secret weapon."

In front of us, maybe fifteen small concrete structures dotted an otherwise empty field, each of them little more than a door backed up by bermed earth.

"What is this place?" I asked.

"Old army installation," Ma said. "Ivy's great uncle bought it from them when it was decommissioned and started turning it into a self-sustaining survival complex. He was a man of great foresight, decades ahead of his time."

She led us to the first one and opened the door. I hesitated, not sure I wanted to go down the metal staircase that yawned in front of us, but Ma smiled at me reassuringly. "Nothing to worry about, Lou. I promise it's not a dungeon."

Ivy laughed and flipped a switch.

The stairwell flooded with light. Ma and Ivy headed down, and after a last glance around, I followed.

At the bottom of a long stairwell was a tidy little home, shaped in a long, half-cylinder, its walls curving overhead. Dividing walls split it into a series of workable rooms, all in a row like a train car. We wandered through a small kitchen, a rough living area with basic but serviceable furniture, and then a series of three sleeping areas, each with multiple metal bunks. Beyond that was some kind of storage room.

Each bunker, she explained, could support ten people for a period of up to a year.

"I don't understand," I said. "How did you do all this in the last couple of months? You couldn't have had time to stock all this since Lucinda was first sighted."

Ma laughed. "Oh my dear, you misunderstand. This isn't *new*. We've been prepping for the fall of society here since forever. We've simply sped the process up lately."

I blinked. "You already had all these bunkers down here, stocked and ready for people to flee to, even before the comet?"

"We did." Ma smiled a beatific smile. "Not that we're glad to have been right, but, well, it seems we were."

"Isn't it great, Lou?" Ivy said, her eyes glowing. She sat on the small dining table and swung her feet. "We're safe down here from the blast, from fire, from almost anything."

My brain wasn't catching up. "This is where you're going to live?"

"You can stay with us if you like. Always room for one more." Ivy winked. "We can be roomies."

My face flushed. This gregarious, beautiful girl wanted me to not only stay but to hole up underground with her for a year? I couldn't help but feel flattered. It was nice to be wanted. Still, even without the question of Emmett, the idea of living underground in a glorified tin can freaked me out.

Ma led the way back up to the wind-swept field. I gazed around at the other dozen bunkers and imagined what life would be like here, underground in rural, southwestern Idaho, huddled in like hibernating mice with a hundred other people, waiting for the skies to clear. Would it be hellish? Would it be frightening? Or would there be comfort in being closed in with people who were so well prepared?

I couldn't answer.

I followed Ivy and Ma back to the house with my thoughts churning. Once again, I'd been offered shelter by people who seemed very genuine in wanting to help me. First Mari, now Ivy. The urge to stay was so strong that I almost couldn't fight it.

But I couldn't stay. This wasn't my path. I had just over a month left, and I needed all of it to find Emmett.

****

I found Bazooka out behind the canning shed. He'd obviously eaten his body weight in insects or grain and was lounging in the sun.

"Speaking to me again?" Bazooka asked, turning a glittering eye my way.

I shrugged. "What else am I supposed to do? You're still an asshole, and I'm still mad. But you're my only ally."

He ruffled his wings and then settled back down. "Okay, so spill. What's the story here?"

"They've got a field in the back with old military bunkers they've converted to housing and even a kind of barn where some animals can live," I said, taking care to keep my voice low and my posture casual. "Everyone here is heading underground before the blast to ride it out."

"I suspected something like that. Not a bad idea. Maybe you should join them."

"Wouldn't that be convenient for you?" I snapped. "Relieve some of your guilt about killing everyone if you knew I was going to survive, wouldn't it?"

He rounded on me. "Listen, Lou. I'm sorry about the comet. I truly am. Earth is my home, too. I had no intention of destroying it. If I could fix it, I would." He sagged. "I can't. You know I can't. We're both stuck in this situation."

I sighed. "I know, Bazooka. I do."

We sat in silence for a while. Then he perked up. "Well, maybe you can come back here after you find Emmett and they'll still take you in. It's closer than Mari's place. Wouldn't be that bad, you know. To survive."

I considered it. Would there be time? "Maybe. I have a feeling, though, that this is a one-way trip."

Bazooka wriggled. "Who knows? Maybe when you find Emmett, he'll have some kind of bunker of his own."

****

Clang CLANG. Clang CLANG.

An old-fashioned triangle called the ranch members to supper, held in the large clearing beside the house. A line of women served food cafeteria-style, dishing out courses onto the plates that people held out as they passed down the serving tables. Everyone smiled and greeted me. I sat next to Ivy and tucked into my cornbread.

A man in weathered jeans and a brown and gold flannel shirt stood up near the front of the tables, and everyone quieted down. He wore a cowboy hat pulled back to show his face, which was carved into crags and crevices in the way of someone who has worked outdoors in all types of weather their whole life. Judging by his hair, which I could see was silvering, I put his age at a little older than my parents.

"Who's that?" I whispered to Ivy.

"Jonah. He's one of the leaders here. Listen."

Jonah offered a long and winding welcome speech, stating how grateful they were to be out from under the thumb of the federal government, to have this land, to have each other. He thanked the Missouri contingent— Ivy's crew—who had bravely made their way across the country to bring in fresh blood and much needed supplies. He rallied against the comet and stated that by their hard work and the sweat of their brows, we would all survive.

Bazooka, keeping a low profile beneath the table, nudged against my legs and made a quiet, questioning sound. I reached down and patted his head.

I was confused. Was this a religious group? It didn't really sound like it. More like anarchists? Left wing? Right wing? I didn't know enough about either to answer the question. I'd have to ask Ivy what she knew about the politics of this place. If I'd learned anything on the trip so far, it was not to make assumptions about people before having all the information.

I kept quiet through the rest of dinner, trying to listen in to conversations around me. As I did, I noticed things I hadn't before. Like, most of the men carried guns. There were bits of conversations about some kind of struggle outside of Jackson and I remembered I'd seen some brownish smudges in the back of one of the pickup trucks that looked like oil but could have been blood.

The woman across from us leaned in, her dark brown, shoulder-length bob streaked with gray, and smiled. "We're so glad you're joining us, Lou. We need more young people here. You can keep Ivy company!"

"I'm not staying," I said. "I'm heading to Oregon to find my brother. Ivy and Dan brought me along to get my scooter fixed, and then I'm continuing."

She smiled at me. "Well, you might change your mind. Tough times are coming and we're the best chance you likely have to make it through in one piece."

I looked at Ivy, who continued eating and didn't say anything.

"I have to find my brother."

"Aren't you a dear," the woman said. She picked up a basket and held it out toward me. "Do you want another roll?"

I took it and pocketed it for Bazooka's midnight snack. I wasn't sure he'd be able to come and go from inside the house freely in the night, and I know he usually got up for a bite somewhere in the night. He might be a lying traitor, but he was *my* lying traitor.

****

Dan told Ivy they'd sent someone out to fetch a spark plug for the scooter from a nearby town, and I settled in for a wait that turned out to last a few days. In the meantime, I allowed myself to be folded into ranch life without complaint. It was a comforting life, reminding me a lot of home, but stripped of the need for church and sermons. I found that refreshing. Daily life offered lots of sunshine, fresh air and good, clean work that could lull me into forgetting that everything happening around me was because of the coming apocalypse. It was so enticing to exist here and pretend that the end wasn't coming.

Bazooka wasn't so easy to fool. He cornered me a couple of nights later out in the yard after supper, and I followed him behind the canning shed, where we could talk without attracting notice.

"What are you doing, Lou?" he squawked. "Are we staying here? It's been three days now. Where's your spark plug?"

"I'm sure they're working on it. I'll check in with Dan tomorrow."

"How much time do we have left? The goose isn't so good at math." I shrugged, and he stared me down, unimpressed. "You don't even know, do you? Better find out."

He stalked off and left me standing there.

I huffed the hair out of my eyes, but realized he was right. I didn't know. What day was it, anyway?

I asked a lady cleaning up from supper. September 3rd. Impact day was predicted to be October 8th. One month and five days.

That knowledge was an ice-cold shower. I had to get out of here before I lost my nerve and stayed.

Sleep eluded me that night, so I crept out of bed as silently as I could, not wanting to wake Ivy, and snuck down to the kitchen to get myself a glass of water. I stood at the kitchen window, staring out into the night while I sipped it, then rinsed the cup and put it back in the sink. It was pitch black here and quiet as a crypt, nothing in sight in any direction except for the lights of the outbuildings and the hum of a generator from somewhere. Usually, that felt peaceful to me, but tonight it rang with warning. We were so, so far from everyone and everything.

Bazooka was right. What was I doing here?

The murmur of voices in low conversation hit me as I was making my way back to the stairs. A nearby door stood cracked open, spilling light into the corridor. I ignored it and continued on my way until I heard Ivy's name.

I couldn't help it. I drifted closer to listen.

One of the voice's was Ma's. I didn't know the other; it was a man but I couldn't place it.

"What about the new girl? The one Ivy and Dan brought?" the man said.

"She seems like an excellent addition to the crew," Ma answered. "Young, farm-raised, able to tolerate hard work. I think we should keep her here."

I frowned. They were discussing me like I was a farm animal. I half expected them to evaluate the health of my teeth and gait next, like they would a fresh horse. I took a tiny step closer to see who Ma was talking to, but all I could see was the fireplace and the wrong corner of the room.

"She said she's heading out to Oregon as soon as her scooter is fixed."

Ma scoffed. "We can't in good conscience let her do that. A young girl on the road? With the comet only a few weeks away? It's a miracle she's gotten this far."

The man murmured his assent. "Always good to have another young woman of breeding age around. We're going to need it."

The hallway grew tighter, closer, and my lungs suddenly struggled for air. What the fuck did he just say? I wasn't planning on breeding with anyone, thank you very much.

"You're right about that. With her, we'd have a good

half dozen girls who should be able to bear children after the comet. It's enough to start again when the smoke clears."

"Dan has an eye for them," the man said, and Ma murmured agreement. "With the girls he brought, we're just about set."

"She won't be happy to find out she's staying, but she'll adjust. Once we hit the bunkers, there won't be any other options."

"And anyway, it's not like that scooter of hers is getting fixed. No one has a spark plug sitting around to spare. Maybe we can strip it for parts."

The conversation sounded like it was wrapping up, so I beat a hasty retreat up the back stairs and toward our room. Once I shut the door behind me, I made sure Ivy was asleep, and then I sank to the floor beside my bed. What in the hell had I heard?

Tricked. I'd been tricked again. I felt waves of disgust run up my arms, intermingling with shame. I was so bad at this! Apparently, help that seemed too good to be true was just that. And I hadn't seen it coming. Dan had been on the lookout for new girls for the compound. Had Ivy been in on it, or was she a dupe in the same game? I couldn't tell. I wanted to wake her up and ask her. I wanted to shake her, ask if her smile, if the way she'd befriended me and held my hand, was anywhere near genuine.

Caution won out. I couldn't risk it. She was in on it or she wasn't. Either way, I needed a new plan to get myself and Bazooka out of here. And I needed it fast.

****

Bazooka was curled up on a blanket on the floor of his closet home. His chest rose and fell, and he made tiny, squeaky snoring sounds with every breath. I didn't have time to admire the cuteness.

I shook him.

"Bazooka. Wake up. We're leaving."

He opened an eye. "Who is it? What happened?"

"It's me. Come on. We're leaving right now."

Bazooka came instantly alert. "What's going on? Did something happen?"

"Later. We don't have time."

"Wait, on foot? You want to go on foot? I don't think this is a good plan."

I tried not to lose my temper. "I know it isn't, but we need to get out of here while we still can."

Bazooka looked at me silently for a moment, then nodded and followed.

I grabbed my backpack with its meager food supply, tucked Bazooka under one arm, and crept down the back stairs and out into the parking lot with no difficulty beyond a motion-activated search light coming on behind us. I froze, but when no one emerged to ask us where we were going, I straightened my shoulders and made for the driveway.

"Act confident," Bazooka said from beneath my arm. "Don't look scared. I'll see if I can influence them at all."

By the time we got to the gatehouse, the guards had obviously realized we were coming. They stood shoulder to shoulder in front of the gate, blocking our way.

"Where are you going, Miss?"

"We'd like to leave." I straightened my spine and looked them dead in the eye. "Please open the gates."

"I'm sorry, I can't do that. Not without approval."

"What am I, a prisoner here?" I countered. "I'm not

part of your compound. They gave me a ride here after my scooter broke down, and now I need to get going."

The second man stepped forward. "I can't let you out, Miss. Not without talking to Ma. Put down your bag and your goose and let's head back up to the house to see what's going on."

I stepped back. "I'm not giving you anything."

His partner raised his gun and pointed it at me, and I turned to ice, frozen on the spot. Every hair on my body stood up, each of them screaming danger.

"I think you'd better come with us," the man said. Bazooka bristled under my arm, but I only stared.

I had no idea what to do. They were actual adults, with actual guns that they were clearly well-versed in using. There was a click as one of them adjusted their gun, probably to let them shoot me deader and faster. The world slowed down, and I felt like every cell in my body was vibrating with fear.

"Okay," I gasped out. "Okay. I'm coming. Please put that down."

The man lowered his gun a little, and his partner came and pulled my pack from me and grabbed my upper arm with the other, his fingers digging into me through the thin fabric of my shirt.

Helpless, with no idea what else to do, I followed as he led us back to the house.

"This isn't good, Lou," Bazooka whispered.

"I know, I know!"

I could feel the panic building in me. This was disastrous. I hadn't asked to be taken into their camp. I didn't want their protection. In a show of fake clumsiness, I stumbled. My captor let go for a moment, then watched in disinterest as I leaned down to untie and retie one of my shoes, setting Bazooka down in front of me.

"Should we make a run for it?" I whispered.

"They've got guns. You wouldn't make it halfway to the fence line. Maybe later."

Soon enough, the man grabbed my arm again, and we continued our forced march. The house came into view, and my heart fell when I recognized a familiar figure on the front porch.

Ma. Arms crossed. Waiting for me.

Part Three: Bend

Chapter Twenty-One

September 7, 2024
Dear Emmett,
Thirty-one days until impact.
I'm writing this from a small, locked room in a survival compound in Idaho.

If you're noticing that I haven't written for a while, you're correct. I've been kind of busy stealing vehicles and trying to fight my way across the country to reach you. You'd be proud of me. I got really far. All the way from Davenport to this ranch in Idaho, but I think I've reached the end of the road now.

The people who threw me in here left me with my bag, which had my notebook and a pen in it, so I thought I'd write to you again, if for no other reason than to keep my sanity. Let me tell you how strange my life has gotten in the last four weeks. Let's see.

First, they announced the impending end of the world.

Then my trick goose started speaking to me in real, honest-to-God English, convinced me he had an imp trapped inside him, and started counseling me on what to do with my life.

Then I found your letters, realized I could find you, and I stole your old scooter and left.

Then I got attacked, but the goose saved me (I realize how this sounds), then we got held up by the

216

military (yes, I know), then the scooter broke down, and then these people who seemed really nice offered to help me. But it turns out they had an agenda of their own, and they're, like, a full-blown doomsday cult. Which I'm now a part of, against my will. Any day now, I expect to be tossed into a bunker and hear the door sealed closed behind me. They'll let me out in a year, when it's time for me to bear some children.

It's nice to have my life all planned out, I think. Takes away all the uncertainty. I assume my first child will be named Jebediah or Noah or Mad Max.

And then it turns out that this imp I've put my faith in isn't particularly trustworthy either. He's been lying to me. He put the comet on its path toward Earth. Not on purpose—he said he hadn't meant to destroy the planet, and I believe him. But still. I've been blindly relying on him for all this time and it turns out he's maybe a complete psychopath.

And then we tried to break out of this compound and got caught. So here I sit, locked up. The woman who runs the place took Bazooka away, told the men to put him with the livestock that they'll cull before the blast, and had the nerve to scold me for my foolishness like I was some kind of unruly child. She told me how they want me safe, how they're giving me a home and a purpose, and how they can't let my pig-headedness result in my death on the road. It was okay if I didn't see it their way. They were still going to help me.

I'm sick to death of people telling me what I should want, what I need. After a lifetime of hearing this from every adult I know, I'm ready to move on. I want to decide things for myself and not be beholden to anyone who thinks they know better just because they're older.

So here I am. No vehicle. No slightly untrustworthy helper imp. No escape plan.

No hope.

It's over. This is rock bottom, not a single card left to play. I finally did a bunch of brave stuff—really impulsive shit, Em—and it didn't work out any better than being a coward ever did.

What was even the point?

I'm so sorry I didn't get to you. I really tried.

Love, Lou.

****

I spent the next two days pacing the small room I'd been locked in, my nights hunched over in a ball of despair. The room was somewhere on the first floor, with only a single tiny window. From it, I could see the smokehouse and part of the barn. The door was old but sturdy, solid wood, and bolted from the outside. I'd spent portions of the first day trying to either pound it down or pick it open, but neither had worked.

Thankfully, I had my notebooks and my pack. Writing to Emmett was an escape of sorts, although it also brought my failure to the forefront. I had thirty-one days left to find Emmett, and I was stuck in this stupid ranch house, losing time I couldn't afford, with no prospects and no plan.

And even if I had a plan, if I got myself from Idaho to Bend, another three hundred miles, Bend was still only where I *thought* my brother might be. Getting there might take a few days, depending on what type of vehicle I could find—I'd be willing to even accept a bicycle at this point. And then, what? Maybe a week or two to find Emmett? If he was even still in Bend. If he was still alive. If he hadn't moved on to somewhere else and forgotten to tell me about it.

I thunked my head down on the pillow and threw both arms over my eyes, feeling hot tears slide down the sides of my face and soak my hair. It was impossible. Absolutely impossible. What an idiot I was, thinking I could do this.

I turned to face the wall beside me, my body shaking as I let a bit of the devastation I was feeling out. I tried to at least sob quietly. I didn't want to give anyone the satisfaction of knowing they'd broken me.

The deadbolt turned with a clunk, and I scrambled up into a sitting position, facing the door head on. Whoever was coming, I wanted to see them first, while being as far away from easy reach as possible.

The door swung open and Ivy entered, carrying a tray. I hadn't seen her since they'd locked me up. I'd wondered if she would show up.

"Oh yay," I said flatly. "It's you."

Ivy looked upset. "Lou, I'm so sorry. I didn't mean for this to happen to you."

I snorted. "Oh really? From what I understand, Ma sent you and your brother out on a recruiting trip, looking for fertile young girls to strong arm into your survival cult."

Her face hardened. "That isn't true."

"It is. I overheard Ma and another man talking about it, right before I tried to get out of here." I pointed a finger at her. "Don't even try to tell me you weren't in on it! You were the bait, right? Go befriend the girl who's all alone, ease her into the group?"

"I wasn't," she insisted, setting down the tray on the small dresser with shaking hands. "I swear! Dan told me to go see if you needed help. If he had his own reasons for that, I didn't know about them. You have to believe me."

Fat fucking chance. I didn't have to do anything. Still, her eyes were sincere, and she looked genuinely distressed. Who knew?

"Where's my goose?"

She looked around, confused. "I—I don't know. He's not in here with you?"

"Ma told someone to take him to the cull barn. If he's dead…"

"I'll see if I can find out," she said, reaching a hand toward me. I shifted away. "I'm so sorry, Lou. I don't want you to be locked up like this. I was hoping you'd choose to stay, but only because it would be nice to have a friend around."

"I'm not your friend."

She looked down. "Anyway, try to eat something. Ma will let you out pretty soon here, I'm sure, and there's no point in going on a hunger strike. Okay? I'll try to find out about Bazooka and I'll visit you later."

My face froze into a sneer. "Don't do me any favors."

She turned and left, saying nothing further.

****

I spent most of the next day pacing, worrying myself raw about Bazooka. What had they done to him? How could they just take him from me? Would Ivy be able to find anything out? If they'd hurt him, if they'd carved him up into *foie gras* or something, I was going to have to make an exception to my lifelong objection to violence.

I didn't see Ivy again until the next evening, when she brought me another tray of food. This time her eyes were red, and she'd clearly been pulling on her hair—her curls stuck out in every direction. I didn't ask about it. She wasn't my friend.

She put the tray down and then stood there, uncertain. "You were right about Dan." She stuffed her fists into her pockets and took a deep breath before the words spilled out. "He was trying to find girls to join the compound. He said they do it every time they're out. He says we don't have enough potential mothers, and how we need to have lots of babies after the blast clears."

I sniffed. "What else are your brother and his friends doing when they're out? Ma said they gather supplies from deserted ranches and farms around here. But how do you know they're really deserted? Are they raiding? Killing people?"

She tried to be tough, I could see it, but then her eyes met mine and her shoulders slumped. "I don't know," she admitted. "I honestly don't. I mean, I don't think Dan would do that, but…"

Hope bloomed in me. She honestly seemed horrified about what was going on. Maybe she was telling me the truth and would help me.

"Ivy, you know this isn't right." I scooted to the edge of the bed, closer to her. "Do you want to be stuck in an underground bunker with a bunch of people who see you as breeding stock? Who hurt and maybe even kill other people to steal their belongings?"

"No," she snapped, sitting down next to the bed like a puppet whose strings had been cut. "Of course I don't. But what can I do? This is my family!"

"My family is problematic too, believe me. I get it. You don't *have* to stay with them, and leaving doesn't mean you don't care about them." I leaned forward and laid a hand on her shoulder. "Help me get out of here. Come with me. We can both leave for Oregon. We can make it!"

She looked up. "And then what? The comet is still coming! At least here I have a chance to live. What happens when we get to Oregon?" Her eyes got even wider. "Lou, I'm only eighteen. I don't want to die!"

"I don't either. But there's no guarantee that you'll make it, even here. All kinds of things could go wrong. At least with me, you'll be free to make your own decisions."

She stared at me like I was speaking another language, and I kept quiet, letting my words sink in.

"What do you want me to do?" she finally asked.

"Could you maybe leave the door unlocked when you leave? I'll wait until everyone is asleep and then late tonight I'll find a way out."

"And what about me?"

"Meet me at two a.m. out behind the garage. We'll try to start up one of the ATVs and make it across the mountains."

She stood and shook her head. "I don't know, Lou. I don't know if I can run away. But I'll help. It's the least I could do after getting you into this."

I grabbed her arm. "Please come with me, Ivy. You don't belong here."

She crushed me to her in a hug. "I can't, Lou. I'm so sorry. This is my family, and I don't want to leave them, even if they're awful."

I couldn't argue with her. I understood. I could only leave my parents behind because I was running toward something, or someone. Another part of my family, a piece of my heart. If it weren't for Emmett, I would undoubtedly have stayed put, church camp and all. No one wanted to face the end alone.

"But I'll help you get out," she continued. "I'll make it look like I've locked it, but leave it open. You need to go tonight, though."

"Thank you. I'm sorry I blamed you for this. I believe you."

She hugged me again. "I hope you find your brother, Lou." She turned to go, then turned back. "I couldn't find out anything about your goose, Lou. I'm sorry. I got out to the barn, but I didn't see him anywhere."

I wanted to break down again at the news; I wanted to throw something at the walls, slam the tray against the glass in the window until it broke, scream. With my only real friend left behind, a missing brother, and a family I'd abandoned, Bazooka and Falthaom were literally the only friends I had left to lose. I wrapped my arms around my stomach and gulped down the tears that wanted to emerge. If Bazooka was dead, I could mourn him later. I couldn't afford any more time lost right now, no matter how much my insides felt like a giant bruise. I had to focus on getting out of here.

Ivy nodded once and was gone. The key rasped in the lock, and I listened as she turned it part way, then returned it to its original position. The usual thump of the deadbolt sliding into place did not occur. Smart girl. To anyone watching, it would look like she'd locked me in for the night. I could see from my side of the door that she hadn't engaged the bolt; the crack of light between the door and the frame was unbroken.

"I'm sorry, Bazooka," I whispered, looking around the room and wishing I could do something, anything, to make him appear.

Finally, holding onto to my plan, I turned to the tray and ate as much as I could. No telling when I'd get another hot meal again. Then I spent the next few hours fully dressed, packed and listening hard to the silence of the surrounding house. I couldn't afford to rush this. I'd only get one chance.

Just when everyone had finally gone to bed, something hit the window with a faint clatter. I ignored it. With my luck, it was a gigantic doom-ranch cockroach or a poisonous, pre-apocalyptic night snake that could climb in through windows and kill you with its spit.

Then it happened again. I froze, every cell in my body straining to hear more, figure out what the danger was and react.

And again.

Clearly, someone was throwing something at the window, trying to get my attention. I took a deep breath and tiptoed over, trying to peek around the curtains without being seen.

As my eyes adjusted to the darkness, I saw the outline of a large bird perched on a nearby railing. When it saw me, it flapped my way.

Bazooka! Bazooka was alive!

I opened the sash, and he somehow crammed his body through the tiny opening and tolerated my hug. When I put him down, he spat something heavy out, wrapped in fabric. It landed on my lap with a familiar metallic jangling sound.

"Bazooka!" I whispered. "I thought you were dead!"

"Yeah, yeah. Forgive me yet for the whole brownie evening?"

I hugged him again. "You're forgiven. Oh my god, I'm glad to see you."

I filled him in on my conversations with Ivy. How she might help me. How the door was secretly unlocked.

"Well, that's a stroke of good luck," he said, "since it means I won't have to coach you through elementary lock picking. Anyway, open your present, princess." He gestured to the bundle on my lap.

I unwrapped the faded red bandanna and found—car keys?

"There's one thing both geese and imps have in common. You don't want to piss either of us off."

I laughed. "So what's the plan?"

"We get out of this building and make our way to the Jeep I stole the keys to. It's out by the front gate." He looked back. "You can drive a stick shift, right?"

"I grew up on a farm. Of course I can drive a stick."

He clucked quietly. "Good. Let's go."

My pulse pounded in my ears as I eased the door open, taking a long time to avoid any creaks or unnecessary noises. No one seemed to be around. The hallway was lit by a couple of small sconces on the walls, the back stairs looming dark at one end. I picked up my bag and Bazooka, and we crept for the stairs.

We made it down to the back door and slipped out without being noticed. As we paused in the shadows at the back of the house, I saw something strange. Every animal on the farm wandered the yard. Dozens of chickens, ducks, cows, horses... it hit me that this couldn't be an accident.

"Bazooka, did you let everyone out of the barn?"

He cackled. "I might have. Might become a grand tradition for us whenever we break out of a place. Free the animal kingdom before we go. We'll be like Robin Hood, but for barnyard beasts."

"They're going to wake everyone up," I said, biting the inside of my lip. "And how are we going to start a car and get past the guards? And won't they follow us?"

"I have a plan," Bazooka said. "And my friends here are part of it. Those with beaks punctured tires. Those with hooves kicked in headlights. And the entire crew is about to start a very loud ruckus in the north pasture. It'll be a great distraction."

Almost on cue, the yard exploded into commotion. The roosters crowed at full volume, even though it was hours before sunrise. In the back fields, the cows all lowed as one, and the pigs squealed like they were being slaughtered. Bulls started crashing against the fence line, over and over, the heavy thuds of their impact traveling clearly in the still night air. The horses neighed wildly, bucking like rodeo players. It was a mesmerizing, deafening din.

Bazooka pulled me to the shelter of the tall row of shrubs lining the driveway as lights flashed on in windows behind us. The shrubs hid us as people poured out, pulling on boots and jackets. At first it was only a few, but soon more and more joined in.

The clamor pulled their attention in the opposite direction from us, and Bazooka and I moved further down the driveway, then stopped under the shadow of a large tree.

"Hang on," he said, sounding pleased. "There's still one more—"

With a WHOOSH, the smokehouse out behind the barn lit up in flames.

"Oh my god, Bazooka, did you set a fire? Was anyone in there? You didn't kill anyone, did you?"

Bazooka huffed. "No, of course no one was in there.

That's why I set fire to the smokehouse instead of the barn. Not gonna take a chance on killing those nice ducks and their stupid chicken friends, am I? Sheesh. You give me no credit at all."

The bodies pouring out of the house were now running to the smokehouse, and muffled yells reached us about finding a hose, getting a bucket line going. Three men with guns ran by without ever noticing us.

"Those were the front gate guards," he said. "As I said, don't fuck around with a goose. Time to go."

We took off at a run for the Jeep, and between the fire and the animal breakout, no one noticed as we started the Jeep's engine, propped open the gates, and slipped away into the night.

****

We found the highway mostly through memory. Luckily it wasn't far, a couple of turns off the dirt road that led to the ranch. It was harder to figure out how to drive the Jeep. Even though I grew up driving farm machines and trucks, doing so on a dusty field going all of thirteen miles an hour was a vastly different experience than trying to manage the stick shift in a top-of-the-line Jeep while fleeing for your life.

Add in mountain roads and a complete lack of streetlights? Absolutely terrifying. I tried to white-knuckle it and not let Bazooka know how scared I was, but he could tell.

"Maybe hold the wheel in less of a death grip," he offered at one point. "And also, breathe once in a while."

I made a face and glanced over at him. "I'm getting the hang of it."

"I'm wishing I'd run away with a more competent driver," he muttered. Then his voice became a shout.

"CURVE!"

I swung the wheel, and we careened around a sharp turn, narrowly missing the guardrail that was the only thing keeping us from a fiery death in the valley below.

I pulled over to the side of the road and leaned my head on the steering wheel. Bazooka gave me a minute. In fact, he seemed distracted, peering around the Jeep and poking at various bits. "What're you doing?"

"I think maybe we should rip out the GPS and this radio," he said, pointing at it with a wing tip. "It looks custom and has that talky thing; they might be able to track us with it."

I felt my face turn pale. "Yep. Let's do it."

A few minutes later, between his sharp bill and a screwdriver I found in the back seat, we had pulled it out and dumped it on the side of the road, and the obviously souped-up antenna from the front hood too.

Then we poked around in the back to see what else might betray us or be valuable enough for them to come after. There wasn't a lot. An extra jerrycan of gasoline that we kept. A lock box made of steel that we dumped without opening. A couple of tarps piled in one corner. Bazooka kicked them and something rattled beneath.

I peeled back the tarp, and we stared, speechless, at three large rifles and boxes of ammunition.

"What should we do with those?" I asked.

"Dump them. Guns are a liability if you're not prepared to use them, and I'm one hundred percent sure you're not going to look convincing, pointing one of those at anyone."

I gingerly scooped the rifles out and carried them over to the side of the road, placing them in a neat and obvious pile. If they came after us, maybe they'd be satisfied just to get their valuables back and decide to leave us alone.

Finally, we pulled out Mari's maps and tried to trace where we were. It took a long time and a bit of aerial reconnaissance from Bazooka, but we finally pinpointed ourselves on the map and traced out a route to the Oregon border and beyond it to Bend.

"Looks like about five hours," I said. "At least this thing goes faster than the scooter."

"We've got about that until sunrise. Wanna make a straight run for it?"

I nodded. "I think that would be best. Let's go."

Chapter Twenty-Two

"*Welcome To Bend*," a small green sign proclaimed, lit dramatically by the early morning sun behind us as we headed west into town on Highway 20. After miles and miles of absolutely nothing—low mountains, flat plains of scrub brush, rocky ridges and deep, sudden canyons— I was happy to see signs of life again. All that emptiness felt a little too apocalyptic.

I drove through the outskirts, then took a turn toward the heart of town. I pulled into a parking space by a large river and killed the engine, then sat, trying to let it sink in.

We'd made it to the place I'd been trying to reach since we left home three weeks ago. My knees weakened with an overwhelming surge of relief, like Bend itself was going to sweep its metaphorical arms around me and keep me safe from now on. We'd made it. It was the biggest goal I'd ever achieved.

Beside me, Bazooka was still asleep on the leather seat, his head tucked under his wing.

I prodded him. "Bazooka. Wake up. We're here."

His head popped out, feathers mussed. "Already? I wasn't sleeping, just resting my eyes."

"Uh huh. For the last three hours."

"Oh, shut up." He looked around, taking in the river winding along to our right, and the broad expanse of green grass and trees in front of it. "We should think about abandoning the jeep and walk from here to wherever we're going. It could still have a tracker on it, and we don't want them to find it in the driveway of wherever we end up."

That seemed smart. I pulled everything I needed out of the vehicle and stuffed it into my carry bag, then took one last look around before opening the glove box and tossing the keys inside.

"Where to from here?" Bazooka asked.

"There's a shopping area a couple blocks back." A shopping area meant people, and people meant someone might know Emmett. "We might as well start there."

We walked back a few winding blocks, keeping the park and the river to our left, passing stately houses that rich families built to take in the river view from their front porches. It was quiet this early in the morning, peaceful. Birds squawked, and sunlight glinted off the water.

We passed a few houses that were boarded up or looked deserted, but there were still cars parked on the street, people out walking dogs, and even evidence of newspapers being delivered. It was the least disrupted town we'd seen on our journey. Could life in Bend be continuing almost like normal? What was this town's secret?

The river road curved into downtown proper where small businesses, mostly brick but some brightly colored, lined both sides of the street. An old theater stood with a colorful yellow tower announcing its name, its marquee empty of any current showings. We wandered through, gazing in shuttered shops, peering through windows, nodding hello to the occasional person we saw on the streets, then on a whim followed someone through a narrow alley to the next street over, and stopped, dumbfounded.

Bright orange cones blocked off traffic at either end of a long shopping area stretching for several blocks, and someone—or a group of someones—had painted the pavement here, end to end, in an endless row of colorful murals. Long rainbows arced down the street, surrounded by pine trees, stars, moons, even a giant picture in one intersection of the comet itself. Instead of a tail, people had painted long streams of words coming out of it—family, love, peace. *"Save the world." "Live every moment." "Life is still good." "I love you David." "Marry me Kacey."*

It was stunningly beautiful. We stepped into the intersection and walked around the comet, reading and admiring.

"You want to add something, hon?" a voice called out from the corner across from us.

I looked up and found a woman, middle-aged, sitting behind a card table on the sidewalk. She'd tied her cropped, graying hair back with a turquoise scarf, and her brown skin shone in the early morning light. In front of her, buckets held paintbrushes, squeeze bottles, and colored chalk. Behind her, a glass door opened into a small cafe. A painted sign in the window read *"Raven Cafe."*

I scooped up Bazooka and walked us over. "Hi, I'm Lou, and this is Bazooka."

"Nice to meet you." She swept out a hand to greet me. I shook it. "Belinda. Welcome to Bend. I see you've found our public art project."

"What is this?"

"Our hopes, dreams, and fears writ large on the

pavement of life. All are welcome to contribute, no talent necessary." She looked at me, eyes narrowed. "You seem like a chalk type. Would you like to add something?"

The question made me feel strangely shy. "I wouldn't know what to make."

"Anything that means something to you. A picture, a quote, a word. It doesn't have to be great art, just something from the heart."

She held out a bucket of colorful chalk to me, and after a moment's hesitation, I took it.

"Add something anywhere you like; the murals go on for blocks. When you're finished, please put the chalk back on the table, hon," she said. "And come join me in the diner if you'd like to chat. I'll be in there all morning."

Bazooka and I wandered down the block, looking at the amazing variety of paintings and drawings people had made—everything from mountain ranges to ghosts, human and animal faces, lava flows… it was gorgeous. Here and there, someone had written a poem or an entire letter on the street, and reading them felt almost like eavesdropping on a private conversation.

"Gimme some chalk," Bazooka said, hovering over a stretch of sidewalk. "Black please."

What was he going to do? One of his old tricks at the petting zoo had been to draw simple shapes with a marker, so I suppose it wasn't too far of a stretch to think he might use his higher imp functions to produce a work of art. He popped the chalk in his bill and started making scratchy marks on the ground, then looked askance at me and spat it out.

"Don't watch! I'm creating, here. Find your own

spot."

I picked a few colors of my own and drew, just simple hearts at first, but then inspiration hit. I found a more open stretch and started drawing everything that meant something to me. Our farm, with the green rolling hills of Iowa behind it. A few of the animals. I drew small figures for my parents and Maggie. I drew the sun and the moon, the trees I'd seen in the mountains in Wyoming, a glowing blue river like the one we'd crossed in Nebraska. And finally, taking the polaroid from my pocket for reference, I drew Emmett's face as large as I could.

When I'd finished, I surrounded the whole thing in a heart, and wrote around it.

"Emmett, it's Lou. Are you here? I've come to find you."

I stood back to look over my work, surprised to notice that I'd filled enough pavement to occupy half the storefront behind us.

Bazooka had wandered over a few times, spitting out one chalk and taking another. I went to see what he'd been working on and found him nestled quietly on a bench, his artistic urge spent.

I turned to his work and found a strange, dark stick figure. Parts of it looked like a bird—there was a suggestion of wings. I could make out a long, spiky tail that bent several times at 90-degree angles, culminating in a point. The figure had a short, squat body with four limbs and the suggestion of bright yellow eyes. And... were those horns?

Whatever it was, it was angular and odd, and despite the roughness of the technique, it communicated a feeling to me. And that feeling was recognition.

"Bazooka, is this you? I mean, is this what you really look like?"

Bazooka ruffled his feathers nonchalantly. "It's a poor likeness. It's impossible to do this without arms. But yes. That's me."

"It's very good! Man, if you'd been able to draw like that back at the petting zoo, we would've been millionaires."

He cocked his head at me. "I believe your avian friend here was more proficient at drawing squiggly lines. He's more of an abstract artist." He stood and stretched. "Do you still have money? Let's go get some breakfast, like the lady suggested."

****

Belinda greeted us, ushering us into a small café. There didn't seem to be any customers at this hour. A man behind the counter smiled as we entered. He looked like her: warm, burnished skin, graying hair, a face creased from many years of life.

"I'm so glad you came!" she announced. "This is my brother, Jonah. Jonah, this is Lou. And her goose, Bazooka, you said? Is that right?"

"That's right." I shook Jonah's hand. "Thanks for inviting us in."

"Did you get your message out?" At my shocked look, she raised a hand. "Oh no, don't worry. I'm not reading your mind or anything. I get flashes. And the flash about you said that you had something you needed to put out into the world with my chalk."

She sat back down at the booth and waved me in next to her. Jonah brought over a coffee pot and filled the two cups that were already sitting on the table between us.

"Would your goose like anything?" he asked. "I'm not sure what a goose would want from a diner."

"Hrm. Do you have oatmeal? He really likes that." Bazooka bobbed his head in excitement as I looked down at him. "I have money. I can pay."

"I can do that," Jonah said. "We'd offer you a menu, but we're out of most things on it, now that the trucks don't run very often. Lots of eggs, though. You like eggs?" I nodded and Jonah headed off to the kitchen to rattle pans and bowls.

We sipped our coffee as Belinda told me about herself. Born and raised in Bend, she and Jonah had been running the diner for the last twenty years. In light of the incoming comet, they'd decided to keep it open.

"People still need a warm cup of coffee and a place to go, you know?" she said. "Oh, we've had a little trouble around here. Some people ransacked a few of the grocery stores and most of the outdoor equipment places were long since emptied. But overall, it hasn't been too bad. Mostly people leaving."

"Did lots of people leave? I saw some boarded-up houses."

Belinda thought. "My guess is maybe a quarter of the town went off to reunite with family or check off their bucket lists or whatever. But mostly, trouble's bypassed us. We're pretty far out of the way for strangers looking to cause mayhem."

It was true. I'd noticed it on the maps back when I was planning this journey. Bend was hours away from any other big city, way more than an easy, one-day round trip from most places. There was an entire mountain range between Bend and the main highway that ran all the way down the West coast to Mexico, and the largest east-west interstate was hours away to the north.

"Your town is in good shape," I said. "We've been traveling all the way from Iowa. Most of the places we've been through have been deserted or half destroyed."

Jonah came and laid two plates in front of us, each with a steaming pile of scrambled eggs and two pieces of toast. He sat a pot of jam near us. "No point in saving up the jam stores," he said with a wink, then he headed back toward the counter and the newspaper he'd been perusing earlier.

"That's a long trip, hon," Belinda said. "Just the two of you? All that way?"

I took a huge bite of my toast and chewed slowly, trying to decide how much to tell. My judgment on trusting people had been way off on this trip so far. I glanced over to the counter, where Bazooka perched precariously on a stool, guzzling down a bowl of hot oatmeal with an expression of immense bliss on his face.

"Sorry if this is insulting, but we've had some weird experiences lately," I blurted out. "You guys aren't, like, in a cult, are you? Or drugging us to sell us to a mob?"

Jonah laughed. Belinda shook her head. "I promise you, this is just a diner. No ulterior motives."

Looking at their faces, I suddenly realized something: this place felt quiet, safe, in a way that meant something. My hesitations melted away.

I grinned. And so I told her, not only about the trip, but about home, about my family and the farm, the animals I'd cared for and freed, about Emmett leaving and finding his letters all these years later. How my parents' priorities and mine had split irrevocably. How I'd stolen the scooter and left. And I told her about the people we'd met along the way: Luke, Mari, Michael, Christina and Max, Ivy and Dan. I even told her about kissing Maggie and being distracted by Ivy's hand in mine in ways I didn't fully understand.

When I finished, I grabbed a napkin and dabbed at my eyes. Why was I crying again? I did nothing but cry these days. Belinda laid a hand on my arm and simply kept listening.

"And so, here I am, finally. Looking for my brother. This is the last place he wrote me from, around Christmas last year." I looked up, hopeful. "Do you know him? Emmett Compton? You must know everyone."

Belinda turned to her brother. "Do we know an Emmett?" Jonah lifted his head, considering, then shook it. I slumped. "I don't think so. But Bend's pretty big. Don't you worry. If he's here, we'll help you find him. Just because he's never been to our diner doesn't mean he's not here at all."

"I don't even know where to start."

"Well, you could put up signs in grocery stores and the library and the post office. I'm pretty sure the old copy place left a couple machines in good working order when they quit. Do you have a picture?"

"I do!" I pulled the polaroid out of my pocket and laid it on the table in front of her.

She smoothed it out and examined it. "Okay, we can work with this. But finish your breakfast and let's get you settled in. There are empty apartments all over town, and I might have the keys to one or two."

****

Belinda was as good as her word. She owned several small apartments around town, and many of her renters had left for their families or hometowns. After breakfast, she grabbed a big keyring from behind the counter and led us to a rafting tour shop, now shuttered, and around back to a staircase that rose to the top floor of the structure. The apartment at the top of the stairs was perfect for one person—a small kitchen, a living room with a foldout couch, and a bathroom.

"It's perfect," I said, overcome. "How much do I owe you?"

Belinda shrugged. "How much do you have, hon?"

I pulled out my roll of bills and counted. "About three hundred."

"Let's say, twenty a week. Is that good?" She waved away the objections she could see forming on my face. "It's not like I'm making anything with it empty, but it's also not nothing, so you don't feel like a charity case. And it'll help me buy eggs from some people who could use the money."

I peeled out a pile of twenties and handed them to her. "There's a month. Is that okay?"

She nodded and folded it away in her front pocket. "Oh! I forgot to show you. Follow me." She clattered down the stairs into the backyard, where a ten-speed bike sat propped up against the garage. "This belongs to Laney, who owns the rafting company. She left for California a couple weeks ago. Anyway, I know she wouldn't mind if you use it."

I threw myself at Belinda in an enormous hug. "You're amazing. Thank you so much."

She hugged back. "I'll leave you to get settled. But you stop by the diner if you have anything you need, you hear?"

I nodded.

"You'll have to let go of me, though," she added.

****

I swear, I've never been more filled with hope than that first day in Bend. The journey was over. We'd arrived, found a town that seemed free of rioting and looters, and left our hearts and secrets on the pavements in swipes of chalky pigment. We'd met people who, as far as I could tell, were actually kind. And we had a roof over our head, a bed to sleep in, and all our limbs, fully intact. It felt almost miraculous.

We toured the town that first day, me on the bike and Bazooka flapping along overhead, getting the lay of the land. I knew finding Emmett wouldn't be as simple as just riding around, but a part of me hoped Bend would work magic and we'd literally run into him, crossing the street somewhere. We didn't, but by the end of the day, we knew our way around better.

I made signs at the copy shop and found a small market where we bought strange-looking sprouted bread and cokes and a few other things to augment my all-peanut butter diet.

When I went to bed that night, with Bazooka snoring away in a laundry basket next to me, my body vibrated with hope.

Twenty-eight days left. We were about to find Emmett. I could feel it.

****

Three days later, it was getting harder to keep my chin up. It was September 13th, barely over three weeks left, and there was no sign of Emmett anywhere. Bend was big. Much bigger than I'd thought. We'd found the apartment from the return address on his letters, but no one lived there now and the neighbors didn't know him.

We stapled up hundreds of signs, on telephone poles, on bulletin boards, on the front of every grocery store, outside schools, and at the entrance to every park we could find. Still, it seemed like such a long shot that he might see them.

The only good news was that no one from the Idaho compound had shown up, and the Jeep was still right where we'd left it on the bank of the river. I'd almost stopped checking behind me or jumping every time a vehicle approached. Apparently, my nascent life as a car thief would not be the end of me.

Aside from that, I'd had no luck at all. No one here had heard of Emmett. He didn't seem to have ever been here. He didn't have a library card, or a post office box, or anything.

How could that be? I had at least four letters from him, spaced months apart, all postmarked from Bend, Oregon. Maybe it was time to study them, to look for anything I'd missed.

An hour later, I was hurrying over to the diner to talk to Belinda.

"Lou!" she said, happy as always to see me. There were a few people drinking coffee at a table in the back, but otherwise it was quiet. She put down the rag she was using to wipe the counter. "How are you?"

"The farmer's market!" I blurted out. "Does it still happen? Where? When?"

Belinda chuckled. "Okay, honey, you need to take a breath and maybe sit down for a second. Did you run here?"

"No. Well maybe." I took a deep breath and sat on one of the counter stools, accepting the cup of coffee Belinda poured.

"Now, hon, what's this about the farmer's market?" she asked, as I took a grateful sip.

"Emmett mentioned it in his letters from here. That he went to it and met someone special there."

"And you're thinking he might still hang around there?"

I tried to hold on to the feeling. I knew it was unlikely. "Well, he might. Or someone there might know him. Do they still have it?"

"There were a couple of different farmers' markets. Jonah, do they still run the farmer's market on Wednesdays, down by the river walk?"

Jonah looked up from his crossword. "They do! It's a lot smaller, but a few growers still come, and some artists."

"What day is it today?" I asked.

"Tuesday."

"So, it's tomorrow?"

"Two to six, like always."

I took a sip of my coffee and thought hard. "He's going to be there. He has to be there. Nothing else has worked!"

Belinda nodded. "I've seen your signs. Give them a chance, honey. They've only been up a couple of days."

I put down my cup as sudden inspiration struck. "Belinda, can I borrow the chalk from your art table for a couple hours?"

Chapter Twenty-Three

Interlude: Bazooka

To be honest, I wasn't sure we'd ever actually reach Bend, but now that we're here, I'm not sure what all the fuss was about. It doesn't seem like a destination that's worth everything Lou has put herself through since we left Iowa. It's nothing more than another mid-sized, western-looking mountain town. Yes, it's more intact than some of the other places we've been, but that doesn't make it special. It's not like it's Rome in the 4th century, or Damascus in the 7th.

But I digress.

Now that we are temporarily out of danger, I've had some time to think. I set out on this trip hoping to learn enough about humans to know whether they are worth saving. I thought it would be a simple exercise, a series of checks in a ledger, and all I'd have to do is weigh one against the other. And yet, somehow, every stop has made the whole thing more complicated.

What is it about humanity that makes it so hard to get a handle on them? Lou and I have seen so many permutations of how people are reacting to the comet's arrival. Worship, fear, disbelief, paranoia, tribalism, altruism. But above all else, utterly reckless and foolish levels of hope.

What do any of them have to be hopeful about? It has no basis in reality. None. And yet, despite the negative encounters we've had—the military with their roadblocks and guns, the rapist at the rest stop, the doomsday prophets with their fervor—most of the people we've met, even those overwhelmed with their coming fate, have tried to help Lou. A teenager on her ridiculous death-wish of a mission to cross the country on a tiny, underpowered scooter. To find someone who might not even be alive.

And even the people who tried to stop her did so, at least partly, out of some misguided sense of care. Even Ma, Dan, and Ivy. They had their own vision of what humans should do to prepare, for sure, but they seemed to genuinely want to save Lou from what they saw as a terrible death alone in the wild. Even bad humans, the ones we had to get away from, view themselves as the keepers of collective hopes and dreams, the ones who would save themselves and each other. Why? Why do they persist in their heroics in the face of almost certain death?

I don't understand them, what drives them, what makes them try so hard. And I don't like not understanding. I thought humans were simpler than this.

To find out that they aren't? To be surprised by them at every turn?

Well, isn't that just a kick in the ass.

I'm beginning to feel bad for the lot of them. Not that I do that, of course. Feel bad for humans. I have a strong personal policy of non-compassion for most of them. But I'm tempted to make an exception in this case.

It all seems like such a fucking waste. Throwing away this whole planet and everything on it, just to teach me a lesson? Who thinks like that? Even if demons detest humans, what about the billions and billions of other life forms that live here?

Show me another planet with twenty quadrillion cooperating ants, for fuck's sake.

Show me somewhere else with whales that sing so loud they can be heard a thousand kilometers away.

Where there exists a single aspen tree whose forty-three thousand offshoots cover a hundred acres and react as one being to every breath of shivering wind.

Where there is life from the top of Mt. Everest to the bottom of the Mariana Trench, inside volcanoes, in caves sealed from the sun for millions of years.

Destroy all this to get back at me for cheating at croquet?

If I said it before, I'll repeat it now: Demons are fucking bastards, and they care about no one. And although I said earlier that I wasn't sure humanity is worth saving, I'm beginning to wonder if the question even matters. I may have been asking the wrong question all along.

What if the important question isn't "should I try to find a way out of this mess for the sake of the humans" but "should I try to save them simply because the demons who did this were wrong?"

It's a much easier question to answer.

Chapter Twenty-Four

September 12, 2024
Dear Emmett,
I'm in Bend. Can you believe it? Despite my last letter, which I wrote in the depths of despair, we somehow got away—with help, of course, from a girl at the compound named Ivy, and from Bazooka—and stole a jeep and drove. All night. Through the mountains.

Let me tell you, that was one of the most terrifying drives of my life. You may remember from a few letters ago that I got my driver's license maybe two months ago. Let's just say I haven't had enough practice yet, and mountain roads are a few skill levels above me. It was probably good that it was night, so I couldn't see how close to death we were most of the time.

But by mid-morning we were here. And you were so right about this place. It's magical. The enormous river winding through town, all the gigantic trees and mountains everywhere you look, and how good the air smells. I completely understand why you might have settled down here. The people are friendly, and you were right about another thing: we've been here twelve hours and I've met approximately five hundred dogs. It's a place I could fall in love with.

I realized that last week was the sixth anniversary of the day you left home. That seems like a sign. In my heart, I know you're here. I keep thinking I'll run into you somewhere, like maybe you live next door—how would I know? Maybe I'll run into you at Belinda's when I go in for breakfast, or on the sidewalk outside the diner. But I feel the strangest pull, like this is it. You're like a moon, pulling me into your gravitational orbit.

Tomorrow, I'll go looking for you again.

Love, Lou

****

I ran home, bucket of chalk in hand, and grabbed the bike. Bazooka was chowing down on something in the backyard. Probably ants. So gross. I rang the bicycle bell at him.

"Bazooka, c'mon, we have work to do."

He looked up. "Where're we going?"

"To the alley where the farmer's market will be tomorrow. Time for more art."

He looked with obvious longing at the backyard bugs, but flapped along gamely enough. The long, brick-paved alley where the market would be was lined with goose-necked street lamps and nestled between the river and the back of the shopping district. I looked around, trying to envision how it would look tomorrow full of vendors, then launched my plan of attack.

Bazooka waddled into the center of the street. "So, what are we doing?"

"Leaving messages," I said, picking up a bright purple chalk.

****

An hour later, I stood back to admire my work.

All the way down the middle of the alley, embellished with attention-grabbing stars and whirls, were my messages. At all the entrances and exits, and around nearby crosswalks, where people would walk

247

toward the market, in huge block letters. On the paths from the nearby river walk and the park behind the alley. On the sides of a few buildings in the area, wherever I could find a blank spot.

"Emmett C. It's Lou. I'm Here."

"Emmett Compton. See Belinda At The Raven Diner."

"If Anyone Knows Emmett Compton, See Belinda At The Diner."

"That should do it," Bazooka said.

It would, wouldn't it? It had to. He had to be here. I didn't want to even think about what I'd do if he wasn't.

****

Sleep was beyond me. I tossed and turned, wondering what would happen the next day. I imagined the scenario playing out in so many ways. Would Emmett be there, and would he be glad to see me? I hadn't heard from him in six years, not since the day he left home. What if his letters were putting a finer gloss on things, and his feelings for me were more complicated? What if there was anger and blame hiding among all the rest of it? What if he wasn't pleased to find himself saddled with his seventeen-year-old sister a few weeks before the end of the world?

And the almost unthinkable—what if he wasn't there at all?

I fell asleep around five a.m., and I woke hours later to the trumpeting of an extremely helpful goose in my ear. There's a reason no manufacturer in the world has ever put a goose call as an option on an alarm clock. It is not a pleasant way to wake up.

When I picked myself up off the floor, I checked the time. It was late enough that the market vendors had undoubtedly already started setting up. Shit shit shit. I meant to be there early, to watch each person arrive and unload, and to hopefully pick Emmett out of the fray before he even saw me.

With my stomach suddenly twisted into knots, I threw on my only clean outfit, scrubbed my face, then tried to tame my rust-colored hair into a semi-presentable braid. Would Emmett even recognize me when he saw me? I'd changed a lot between eleven and seventeen. I inspected myself in the mirror and saw enough landmarks that should be familiar to him. My ridiculous freckles. The gap between my front teeth. My gangly frame.

I'd know him on sight. I hoped he'd know me.

September had a fresh bite to it. I dragged my sweater closer around me as we set out, Bazooka easily keeping pace, and soon we perched on the edge of the riverside park, staring across the street toward the market, which was slowly getting underway. By the number of empty spaces, I guessed that only about half of the vendors had shown up, but there were a handful of customers wandering around with baskets and bags.

"Go get 'em," Bazooka said, before he wandered off to frighten away some ducks that were floating nearby. I leaned the bike against a tree and took a deep breath. Time to head into the fray.

But first, I stopped to tie my shoe. I retied it again. Then I stood up and fidgeted with the bike, checking and rechecking the kickstand. Then I stood there, swallowing hard, feeling like my legs wouldn't move no matter how much I told them to.

Bazooka circled down from the sky and came to a skidding stop near me. "What's wrong with you? Why are you out here instead of in there?"

I wrapped my arms around myself. "Because I'm terrified."

"Of?"

"Of everything. What if he's there? What if he doesn't know me? What if he's not glad to see me?" I took a gulping breath. "And even worse, what if he's not there?"

Bazooka hissed. "What am I, your cheerleader? Don't be stupid. There are other markets. There's a chance he doesn't come every single week. You still have time." He leaned in and snapped at my ankle viciously. "Now pull yourself together. I did not drag you across the entire country and two mountain ranges, only to have you chicken out now."

I swore and pulled my ankle out of striking range, and then laughed. "Thanks, Bazooka. Perfect day for someone to act like a drill sergeant."

"I'm not acting," he said, circling in for another ankle attack. "Let's go, or the next one draws blood."

I hopped away. "Okay, okay, I'm going!"

****

Pointless. Worthless. Hopeless.

It was worse than I'd imagined. Emmett wasn't there. I visited every booth. No one had ever heard of him. No one recognized his picture from the flyers I showed around. Not even a flicker of recognition. It was a complete and total bust.

I sank onto a bench at the far end of the market and buried my head in my knees. Even Bazooka knew better than to cheer me up. He flapped away, off on some mission of his own, and I gave in to the gathering tears.

Bend was a dead end. What on Earth was I going to

do now? I'd traveled almost two thousand miles, committed actual crimes, left everyone I cared about. All for what? To end my days here? Alone in the high desert of Oregon, with no one at all who cared for me and no time or energy left to even try to get back home?

Let the comet come. Let it do its worst. I was done.

A quiet footstep broke through my misery, and I looked up. A man who I hadn't seen before stood there. Not Emmett, my brain pointed out. I told it to shut up. I was already painfully aware of that.

"Hi," the man said. "I'm Marcus. Can I join you?"

"Sure, why not?" I muttered, wiping my eyes. I shoved over and made room. He sat.

"Want to talk? You seem like you're not okay."

I looked him over, instinctive caution warring with my curiosity. I liked his voice; it was friendly without being pushy, and his concern seemed genuine. Late twenties, I guessed, with olive skin, warm and appealing eyes, and a dark beard and mustache he kept close-trimmed. His hands were dirty, and he wore a baseball cap and a blue hoodie with the word "Purple Sage Farms" emblazoned over his chest. He sat, hands clasped together on his knees, watching me closely. I trusted him.

"I'm so far from okay, there's not even a word for it," I said. "I'm a mess. My life is basically over. I threw everything away—my home, my friends, my family—to come out here on a stupid, unreasonable quest that's come to a dead end. It's finished. Failed."

A fresh sob broke out, and he handed me a tissue. I mopped my face off as best as I could.

"Are you Lou?" he asked. "The one who left the messages all over the street and sidewalks?"

I grimaced. "You saw that, huh? Fat lot of good it

did me."

He didn't say anything, and something in his silence made my heart speed up, and the blood pounded in my ears as a sudden intuition hit me. This man knew something. I took a deep, dizzying breath.

"Oh my god. Do you... do you know Emmett?"

Marcus leaned forward, resting his arms on his knees. "I do. But there's something you need to know, Lou."

My surroundings spun. I clasped onto the seat of the bench with both hands and spoke as clearly as I could. "You. Know. Emmett?"

"Lou," he said. "Breathe in. That's good. Breathe out. Okay. Do that a couple more times."

I did as he said, still feeling like the bench might tilt me off as sparks popped at the edges of my vision. After a few more breaths, my symptoms eased. When I was sure I wasn't going to pass out, I focused on Marcus again.

"Where is he? Will you take me to him, please?"

"I will," Marcus said. "But you need to know. Emmett isn't Emmett anymore. He doesn't go by that name. That's why most people here don't know who you're talking about."

"I don't care what name he goes by! Whatever he wants to be called, I'll call him that. It's fine by me. Please, can we go see him?"

"Lou, listen," he said, and the serious tone stopped me short. I looked him in the eyes and waited. "Emmett goes by Emily now."

I blinked. "What?"

"Emmett lives as a woman now. She's a woman. Emily. We're together. Emily is my partner."

I stared.

"We saw your signs just now—we got here late. But she's pretty shaken up and wanted me to come see how you'd react before meeting you. And honestly, that's important to me, too. Em's been through enough, you know? I need to know how much damage control I'm going to have to do."

I caught the unspoken bit. Em had been through enough pain from us, from my family. My parents. Marcus meant that if I was going to be a dick about this, I could just head right back to Iowa. I flushed with shame for my family, for all the things they'd done to him—her. For all the years of love lost, for the wound Emily had undoubtedly been carrying for the last six years.

I straightened my shoulders.

I was not part of that. I would never be a part of it.

"I—I'm surprised, I'll admit. But… I… I don't care! I don't care if Em is living as a Martian! I just…" The tears that had stopped from shock started flowing again. "I want to see him. Her. I came all this way to see Em before the world ends. Because I need him. Her." I grimaced. "Sorry, this might take me a while."

Marcus watched me for a moment longer, then nodded, satisfied. He stood and held out a hand to me. "Well then, Lou. Want to come meet your sister?"

I stood and took his hand, my heart pounding.

****

Marcus led me to a small blue tent on the far end of the alley, a spot that I was pretty sure had been empty earlier when I'd gone around. One person was unloading crates of flowers and greens from a small van, and another was unfurling an enormous banner in the front: Purple Sage Farms.

Neither of them looked up as we approached.

"Emily," Marcus said, looking at the figure who had their head buried in the van. "Lou's here. She wants to meet you."

I wiped my eyes with the back of a sleeve and tried to look less like a mess. The woman straightened up from the van and turned, her face pale and drawn, and our eyes met.

She looked like any of another dozen women in the market, other than the expression of fear on her face. Grubby, hot, wearing worn jeans and a fleece jacket, with a blue bandanna holding back hair that waved down to her shoulders. I squinted, trying to see it. Was that Em? My Em? After a second, the familiar touchpoints leaped out. Her hair was the same rust-color as mine. That long nose. The green eyes. The high cheekbones my mother had always bemoaned being wasted on her boy instead of her daughter.

"Em?" All my brain functions had ceased. I couldn't get out another word. I stood there, trying to figure out what to do with my hands, like I was inhabiting a human body for the first time. Maybe this was how Falthaom felt inside his goose suit.

"Lou?" she said, taking a step forward and then stopping. "I can't believe you're here. Are you... is this okay?" She stopped, looking unsure.

The idea of Em asking me if her existence was okay with me hurt like a punch, but I understood why she was asking. I'd been a literal child the last time she'd seen me, and she'd had six years of wondering why I never wrote back to her. God only knows what she had come up with.

I nodded vehemently. "Is it okay with me that you're

here, and that you're alive and well and apparently happy and have friends and, oh, maybe you dress a little differently now and have a slightly different name?" I huffed. "Of course it is."

Something in her face shifted, like a weight had lifted off. "Oh my God, Lou. I've really missed you." She took off her heavy canvas gloves and walked over to me. "Can I hug you?"

I nodded, and she wrapped her arms around me tightly, and I stood there, letting myself be crushed. She stepped back and looked at me, noting my tear-filled and probably slightly crazy looking eyes. "Come with me. You look like you need to sit down."

I followed, mute, as Em led me to a stack of crates away from the bustle of the market and got me seated on one, then plopped down across from me on another, so close that our knees were almost touching.

"Are you okay?" Em asked. "Lou, why are you here? How did you find me? I thought—" She fell silent, leaving the last thought unfinished.

I made my brain engage with some effort and took a deep breath. "I—I came to find you. I've always wanted to find you. I had no idea where you were."

"But I wrote to you—"

"Mom hid the letters from me. I didn't know you'd ever tried to contact me until a few weeks ago when I found them, in the old cookie jar in the basement."

Em reeled back as if she'd taken a punch, then put her head in her hand before looking up at me. "I guess I shouldn't be surprised by that. So, you thought I'd walked off and never thought about you again?"

I shrugged. "Kind of. But I guess you must've felt the same when you never heard back."

We both silently sat with that concept for a moment.

"Are they—are they still alive?" Emily asked. "Are you here because something happened to them?"

I made a face. "No, no, they're fine. I mean—" I gestured at the world "—as fine as anyone is right now. They're still back in Iowa. They abandoned the farm to go live in a camp at the church. We were packing, and then I found your letters."

Em smiled wryly and gestured at herself. "Not exactly what you expected to find, I guess?"

I shook my head. "It doesn't matter. I found you, Emmett."

"I go by Emily now," Em said gently, but her face betrayed a level of guardedness. I mumbled a quick but sincere apology. "Or Em. I started transitioning when I was twenty-one, and now I live exclusively as a woman. Always felt like I was one, underneath. Mom and Dad didn't tell you about that, I guess?"

"They *knew*?"

"It's the main reason they told me to leave," Emmett said. "It wasn't just me liking a boy. I'd journaled about feeling confused about my identity and feeling like a girl inside. And I had some women's clothes they found in my dresser. Dad took one look, declared it the work of the devil, and that was that."

"So, does that make you my sister?"

"I guess. Is that okay?"

I looked at the woman in front of me. Emmett? Emmett was now Emily. Em was shaped like I remembered—tall and slim, narrow hips, long legs, pointy shoulders. Her face was like Emmett's but softer somehow, with slightly rounder cheeks and more fullness in the mouth, and instead of the spiky reddish-brown hair I remembered, Em had grown her hair out to shoulder length. It looked good on her.

But the eyes—I'd know those eyes anywhere. Emily's eyes were the same: warm, green, shining with concern. With love. I'd know that look anywhere.

I swallowed down my initial fear of anything that differed from how I'd imagined it, and reached for the burning core underneath it. This was my brother—my sister, now—the person I'd been yearning to find for the last six years. It didn't matter what the outside looked like. The world was ending, and I knew with an unshakeable certainty: it didn't matter at all.

Wordlessly, I threw myself into Emily's arms and all but knocked her over with a hug. Em leaned back for a fraction of a second, surprised, but then wrapped her arms around me as tightly as she could, lifting me off the ground.

"Of course it's okay," I said. "It's you. It's you."

Bazooka chose that moment to fly in for a terrible landing, skidding through the straw that was scattered around our feet. Em leaped back, startled, then looked at me as I laughed.

"This is Bazooka. From our farm."

Em gaped at me. "You can't be serious. You brought a goose?"

"Well," I said, feeling either tears or laughter building up inside me. "It's a really, really long story."

"Marcus," Em called.

Marcus's head popped around the back side of the booth. "Yeah, love?"

Love? Love? It suddenly hit me. Marcus. Was Marcus the person Em had told me about in her letters? The person he'd—she'd—met at the farmer's market? I

257

made a mental note to ask as soon as I could fit it in.

"We—" Em stopped and took a breath. "Lou and I are gonna go have some tea."

"No problem."

Em grabbed a thermos out of the van, took my hand in hers, and together we walked from the market down toward the water.

Chapter Twenty-Five

September 17, 2024
Dear Maggie,
I've never written you a letter before, mostly because we've never really been apart since I met you in third grade. But I was thinking about you today, and I decided that maybe what has worked all these years with Em—sitting down to pretend I'm having a conversation with him I can't really have—will work with you, too.

So, anyway, here's the REALLY BIG NEWS.
Are you ready?
I found Em, Maggie! Can you believe it? Em was in Bend, where the last letter came from. It's like a miracle. You probably knew this right from the start, but I really never thought we'd make it, deep down. All my confidence was surface level.

But we did, and I'm getting to know Em again in a whole new way—parts of it have been surprising, and sometimes awkward, but Em is still Em, if that makes any sense. We're still family. I'm so, so glad I came.

You wouldn't believe what a crazy trip it's been, right from the off. In every place we've stopped— Nebraska, Wyoming, Idaho—we've met people running the full gamut of emotional reactions to Comet Lucinda.

A couple people didn't even think the comet was real, or that it's not going to be as bad as we've been told. A few others were using Lucinda as an excuse to do bad things to each other, like it's a free pass for evil. It's like the approaching end has stripped away all the layers of padding on a person, making them more of who they really are, underneath.

Has it done that to you? It has for me. Comet Lucinda and this road trip have turned me into someone much braver than I ever realized I could be. Things that sound like movie scripts have happened to us. The military, a cult, lots and lots of guns. So many daring escapes. I ended up stealing a jeep and driving through the Cascade mountains to get to Oregon.

Yes, really. I stole a car! I've committed actual crimes. You'd have been so proud of me. It's like I've lived more in the last three weeks than I did for the entire previous year.

Now, impact day is looming—less than three weeks away—and it doesn't look like we're going to get back to Iowa before it happens. I suppose you already knew that, too. It's dangerous, but that's not the main reason. Em has a very cute significant other out here. They have a life together, and a farm, and a bunch of people they care about. So, of course, they don't want to leave to drive back to a place where they're not even welcome.

I can't blame Em. I always knew we probably weren't returning. So I'm staying here on the farm with Em and Marcus to see what happens on impact day. But I'll be thinking about you on that last day, and wishing I could hold your hand when it happens.

I wish I could tell you how much your friendship has meant to me all these years. No matter what happened or how weird I was acting or how much I didn't fit in, you were always there for me, and I couldn't have survived without you. I hope I helped you even a fraction of the same amount.

I don't know what our kiss meant, there at the end, but it doesn't matter. It's another beautiful moment in a long friendship, and I really just want to thank you for being my best friend, Maggie. Every day I think about you, and I miss you so much.

I hope you're not too scared. I love you. Goodbye.

Love, Lou

****

"So first off," I said, playing with the paper cup of tea Em poured for me as we sat on a bench close to the river's edge, "there's something you need to know about the goose."

Bazooka squawked loudly. "She means to say I can talk. Hiya Em, I've heard so much about you. Too much, really. She never shuts up about you."

Emily looked dumbfounded. "What in the hell…"

"Exactly right," Bazooka said.

"Emily, meet Falthaom the Repulsive. Falthaom, meet Emily. You can call him Bazooka, though. it's the goose's name." I made hand gestures between them; Em's eyes grew wide. "Falthaom is an imp."

"Like, a demon?"

"No!" I shouted, trying to stop Bazooka from going into his usual rage. "He's not a demon; he's something older, an imp. It's kind of like a primeval nature spirit." I looked at Bazooka, who studied me. "Did I get that right?"

"Close enough for the way you humans understand things," Bazooka said, then stopped suddenly to spear a bug that was walking by and gurgle it down, bill up.

"Lou…" Em looked frightened. "Am I—are you—are we hallucinating?"

I shook my head. "No, although I understand why you'd ask that. Falthaom was stuck in Bazooka as a punishment, after… after a game he was playing with some demons went wrong."

"As in, I cheated and won, which is what all talented players do, but my opponents got unreasonably bent out of shape about it," Bazooka added.

"And what, you discovered him? In your goose?"

"Pretty much. He's been helping me, Em. He made one tank of gas last the whole way from Davenport to Jackson, Wyoming. And he saved me from a guy at a rest stop that wanted to hurt me. And, well, there was the thing with the soldiers."

Emily looked like she wanted to sit down, hard— except she was already seated. She took a deep breath. "I think you better tell me as much of this story as you can. Start from the beginning, please?"

****

An hour later, I'd filled Emily in on most of what had happened on our trip. The only thing I left out was Falthaom's responsibility for the comet's path. Given how difficult I'd found that to accept, it seemed like a lot to dump on Emily right at the start. I was already worried that she'd think I was crazy from the parts of the story I'd left in. Plus, I wanted her to like Bazooka, or at least tolerate him, and there was no guarantee she would if she knew he was the guilty party in our current predicament.

When I finished, we both sat in silence, sipping the last of our tea and staring out at the empty street. We were a few blocks down from Belinda's diner, but the murals continued here. I traced a few of them with my eyes, following the loops and whorls of what looked like ocean waves while I waited for Em to speak.

"I can't believe you went through all that, Lou," she said, finally. "It's—it's a lot. And all by yourself! You could've—anything could've happened to you. All that to get here? To me?"

"Yeah."

"Why?"

I leaned in and laid a hand on Em's wrist, feeling the delicate bones jutting out there, fragile. "Because you're my family and I've missed you so damn much. I always assumed I'd find you once I graduated and left home. But that timeline got shortened, so it had to be now. I couldn't face the end of things without seeing you again."

Em swallowed heavily. "I've never stopped thinking about you either, Lou. It just… it hasn't been easy being cast out. I've imagined all kinds of things over the years. That they'd get you thinking like them." I swallowed as Em's voice broke, her eyes cast down. "That you'd wind up thinking who I am is wrong."

"Em—all this happened to you because of *me*! Because *I* spilled your secret when Mom pried. This is all my fault, all of it." My voice broke, too, and I took a second to get control of myself. "You should hate me. Not the other way around."

It was Em's turn to look shocked. "Lou, no. Absolutely not. You were a kid. I should never have put that on you." She ran a hand over her face. "Have you been blaming yourself for it all these years?"

I shrugged and found I couldn't look at her. "Maybe."

"Well, you need to stop." Em wrapped an arm around my shoulder and pulled me in. "It wasn't your fault. It would've come out anyway because I was running wild back then, experimenting with all kinds of things with no sense of the potential consequences. Trying to get away from who I really am. Having to face Mom and Dad. And even if I'd been good at covering my tracks, I would've had to own up to things eventually. The outcome was always going to be me leaving the family, in one form or another."

Could that be true? It had a certain ring of truth to it. I leaned against Em, suddenly exhausted. There was so much more to say, but I couldn't find the words to say any of it right now. The adrenaline of the day evaporated from my system as quickly as it arrived, and suddenly, I wanted nothing more than to sleep.

Here. With Em. Finally.

Maybe now I could rest.

****

We took the van back to Marcus's farm, and Em settled me into a spare room where I took a long, much needed nap. Bazooka wasn't interested—he headed outside to investigate the farm and probably eat anything that wasn't fastened down. I made a mental note to check on him soon, then I fell deeply unconscious.

When I woke, I took a better look at the surrounding room. It was small, but lovely. I lay on an old brass bed with embroidered linens, and across from me standing tall was an old-fashioned, dark wood dresser with one of those mirrors that swivels up and down and a lace cloth laid across the top of it. From the window, I could see out toward a fenced field that seemed to be devoted to growing flowers. I picked out what looked like dahlias, in all colors and sizes, and sunflowers as well, towering over everything around them.

The smell of something cooking—maybe spaghetti

sauce—and the clatter of pans and conversation broke my reverie, and I realized I was starving. Had I eaten today? Not really. I'd woken up so late and made a mad dash for the market before thinking of it.

I came out of my room feeling almost shy, like this couldn't possibly be real. Like I was intruding on someone else's special place. I hovered in the doorway to the kitchen, watching Marcus and Em cooking together in a casual intimacy you couldn't fake—passing each other things without needing to ask, sharing a casual touch as one passed behind the other. They looked happy and in tune with each other.

It wasn't until Marcus held up a spoon coated in sauce for Em to try that they both saw me.

"Lou!" Em said, with a genuine smile that took my anxiety down a notch. "Come in. Sit down. Dinner's almost ready."

They set the table for eight, and soon enough, other people began arriving: a few farm workers, and two of the tenants who lived with them. I tried to keep names straight through a blur of introductions, but after a while I lost track and grinned at being introduced as "Em's kid sister" and shook hands wherever offered. People dished out food and poured wine from a big jug, and we all set in to steaming heaps of pasta.

"Lou, did you really ride a Vespa halfway across the country to get here?" one woman with striking cobalt-blue hair said, putting down her fork to smile at me.

I concentrated on what I'd kept of the introductions. She was one of the tenants and also worked on the farm. She and her partner, a skinny man with heavy black-framed glasses who sat beside her, lived in one of the small cottages on the back acreage. Her name was something odd. Sparky? Sparkle? I couldn't remember.

"Em's old scooter, yeah. It did really well until it didn't. It died in Wyoming and was laid to rest in Idaho. We went the rest of the way in a Jeep."

"How'd you know how to drive it?" her partner asked, the light from the candles flickering off his glasses.

"Em taught me when I was little," I said. "She and Luke—her friend—took me out in the fields one day and showed me the basics. After that I rode it once in a while. Took a bit to remember how it all worked, but I had a thousand miles to work the kinks out before it died."

"That's a long way," one of the farm workers, a tough-looking woman with buzz-cut hair, said. Her speckled, peeling face had that look of someone who's been out in the sun since birth, chiseled by wind and rain like some kind of modern day sphinx. "You must've really wanted to get here."

I looked at Em. "I really, really did."

Em raised a jelly jar full of dark wine. "A toast. To my intrepid little sister, who begged, borrowed, and stole her way across the country to end up at our door."

"To Lou," everyone echoed.

****

After dinner, I helped Em clean up, and then joined a few of the others in the living room, where Marcus and two others were chatting near the fire, crackling in the grate. Large bookcases framed both sides of the mantel, and I studied their contents. Books were always my escape from any awkward social situations, and my earlier shyness had returned stronger than ever.

"Help yourself to anything you want to read," Marcus said, as he came up to fuss at the fire beside me with an iron poker. The logs hissed and sparked as he redistributed them. "Are you a big reader?"

"Oh yeah." I scanned the shelves. There seemed to be two main categories: technical stuff—lots of books on agriculture and vegetable farming and pruning and such, and mysteries. "Are these yours?"

"Most of them," Marcus said. "Em brought some of them when she moved in."

"How long ago was that?"

Marcus put down the poker. "We met two years ago, so it must've been about a year back when she moved in."

"You met at the farmer's market, right?" I asked. He looked surprised. "Em mentioned it in one of her letters. She didn't say your name, just said she'd met someone special."

He smiled. "Yeah. Took some time to feel each other out, but when it's right, it's right. I always heard that you just know, and to be honest, I always thought it was the kind of bullshit that smug, happy couples say. But it turns out it's true."

I laughed, then tried to sort through more of the hundreds of questions that were crowding my mind. "How'd you come to have a farm like this when you're so young?"

"Ah, good question." He beckoned to me. "Come here. I want to show you something."

I followed him to the other side of the room where an old, framed black-and-white photo hung on the wall. He gestured at it and I leaned in, seeing the farmhouse, and the barn behind it, stark and crisp, and on the porch two people, standing proud.

"My grandparents," he said, at my questioning look.

"They built this place, farmed it for years. After they died, my parents weren't interested in running the place, but they knew I was. They leased it out for a few years until I got out of college and was ready to make a go of it here."

"That's so cool," I said. "Did you change a lot of things when you took over?"

"A bit," he said. "Switched to all organic farming methods, updated and expanded on the orchards. Added the flower side of the operation, which has been a nice money maker since."

"It's really beautiful here," I said, meaning it with all my heart. "Thank you for letting me come to stay. I know you weren't expecting to have a teenager hanging around."

His eyes met mine and I could see the kindness in him. He smiled softly. "I'm glad you're here, Lou. Em really needs this." He looked around the room at the other people lounging around, reading, talking. "And as you can see, we're a community, anyway. Always room for one more."

He squeezed my shoulder, then headed back off to finish seeing to the fire.

I selected a mystery that looked interesting and settled myself in an unclaimed chair, close enough to hear what was going on and feel some warmth from the fire, but also far enough away that I could be quiet and not take part in the conversation. I opened the book but was only pretending to read. Instead, my mind played back over my earlier conversation with Emily, where she'd told me I couldn't hold myself accountable for her problems anymore.

Setting down the burden of guilt I'd been

shouldering for almost half my life was harder than I'd expected. I'd thought it would be an enormous relief, hearing Em say it was never my fault, that I'd walk away miraculously lighter, cured. But the guilt had carved out a shape inside of me, its edges dense and hard, and it didn't want to let go. Instead, it fought me, clinging on by tooth and nail, whispering to me that Marcus and Em were just being nice, that they didn't really want me here, and that everyone still thought it was my fault.

I lay in bed that night, in my comfortable room on Purple Sage Farm, staring at the ceiling and feeling out the edges of that hole my guilt used to occupy. like probing the spot a lost tooth left behind. It felt tender, throbbing faintly, with a memory of blood and pain. Like it still wanted something from me.

It was going to take me a while to get all the remnants out. To flush it clean. To really accept absolution.

But I was going to try really hard.

Chapter Twenty-Six

September 15, 2024
Dear Mari,
I wanted to tell you, even just in my head, that I found Em. Who is now Emily. She said you already knew. I remember you saying what I found might surprise me. I didn't know what you meant then, but I do now. Thank you for trying to prepare me, and for keeping Em's secret. It was a surprise, for sure, but in the end I'm fine with it. More than fine: I'm happy she has found herself. I'm learning to get all my pronouns right after a lifetime of thinking of her as a "him", but Em is as patient as ever and I'm figuring it out.

I'm so glad that we got here. It's amazing to get to know her again, and meet new people who care about Em.

After we left you, both Bazooka and I had moments when we regretted not taking you up on your invitation to stay. The trip was rough, but we got to Bend about eight days later, and five days after that we found Em, and now we're all together. Me and Em and her partner, Marcus, who's great. They live on an organic farm outside Bend and it's gorgeous there. They spend their days trying to feed the people left in town, gathering produce and eggs up from the farm and selling them or giving them away for free at the town market. I help.

It's not a bad way to spend the end. Helping people,

loving my new family, and thinking about the people I've left behind.

A year ago, at school, the guidance counselor started asking me what I wanted to do with my life, and I didn't really have an answer. The future seemed so unimaginable then, so blurry and far off. What's funny is that now that there's not going to be a future, I suddenly find it so much easier to imagine what I might have done with my life if I'd had the chance. Every day, I wake up with another idea. I could be a scholar, researching fascinating old books at a university somewhere. I could be a vet, fixing horses and sheep and dogs. I could be a marine biologist and spend my day with whales and seals.

But the thing that comes to me the most lately is partly based on you. I think I would've liked to be a librarian someday. Maybe in another life.

Thank you for loving and helping Em when he needed it, and for helping me and Bazooka, too.

Love, Lou

****

"Wake up, Lou," Emily said, knocking on my partly open bedroom door. "It's flower day."

I shook myself awake. All week, I'd been trying to fold myself into life on the farm, helping in the barn and fields with the rest of the crew, but I'd especially been looking forward to this. Every Monday and Tuesday, they harvested everything for the weekly market— vegetables, flowers, herbs. Emily oversaw most of the flower operation, picking half-blooming flowers in the early morning to put in a cooler, then making bouquets the next day. It appealed to my artistic side, playing with all those colorful blooms.

271

I threw on my clothes, washed my face quickly, and headed out to the kitchen where Em was waiting. She pushed a lidded cup of coffee and a biscuit into my hands and headed for the backdoor.

I stuffed the biscuit into my mouth as we made our way to the field. It was early, past dawn, but not by much. Em had already gotten things set up—there was a large pull-cart waiting full of clean buckets full of cool water, and sharp clippers and wipes.

Emily showed me what to do, hurrying through a set of dahlias, cutting long stems in clusters and putting them into a bucket, sorted by color. "Leave the ones that are already past their prime. You want the ones like this—" she gestured at a blossom whose petals were partly furled in on themselves "—that are just opening."

I got to work on the next row over, and we passed a companionable hour cutting, running full buckets back to a shed where a large, electric cooler would keep the flowers fresh for the next two days. I lost myself in the rhythm and color of it—bright tangerine, eggplant purple, deep burgundy, and crisp white. Flowers of all shapes and types, grouped by size into their own containers.

We took a break when the temperature rose, and Em plopped down on the ground outside the shed to take a long sip from her travel mug. I sat down beside her and drank my coffee—cooler now, but still good.

"So," Em said, "you must have a lot of questions. Ask me some, if you'd like."

She was perceptive. I'd been thinking a lot the last few days about how much I didn't know about Em's life, about all the things we'd both missed. I felt welcomed into her life, but completely frustrated by how much we still had to learn about each other and how short our time was to do so. It was so unfair. We needed time, the one thing that we couldn't get more of.

"How come you kept moving around so much after you left?" I finally said.

Em pondered for a minute. "I guess partly because I didn't know where I wanted to end up, other than needing something different from Iowa. I liked some places I lived—Friend and Jackson were pretty great, at least for a while—but then suddenly, no matter where I was, a place would feel wrong and I'd get this itch to move on."

I took another sip and listened.

"The best way I can describe it," Em said after a moment, "is that for a long time I thought the places I lived were wrong in some way, but it turns out that what was wrong was me."

"What does that mean?"

Em waved a hand at herself. "I needed to become who I really am. Emily, not Emmett. You know? Once I did, then suddenly it felt a lot easier to find a place I wanted to stay."

I didn't fully understand, but I wanted to. The things Emily had been through over the last six years were so foreign to me; I knew I would need a while to reflect on it all.

"When did you transition?" I asked. "Is that too nosey?"

Em smiled. "No, of course not. Let's see. I started experimenting with being Emily while I was in Jackson, but mostly just in private. After I left there to wander around northern California, I started being Emily full-time. That was about six months before I ended up here, so I'd had some time to adjust before I met Marcus."

I considered that for a minute. "Did it feel good?"

"It was such a relief," she said, sagging dramatically against the wall behind her. "Like I'd always been pretending until then, and now I could be real. Which is terrifying, sometimes but also fantastic."

That made sense to me. I'd felt like a fake for a lot of the last six years, going along with my parents' beliefs out of the fear that they might turn on me too, saying next to nothing about what I really thought about what they'd done to Em when my heart was burning with shame and rage. Running away had given me that same sense of being the person I really was for the first time, of not having to hide a part of myself.

It wasn't the same, but it felt like a bridge to help me understand.

"And then you met Marcus? So, he never knew you as Emmett?"

Em nodded. "Yeah. I told him, of course, almost right away, which was another terrifying moment. He was great about it. We tried to go slow; I'm still figuring a lot out. But I love him."

I tipped my head to the side and smiled at her. "He loves you, too. He said that he knew you were right for him, right away."

She grinned. "The feeling is mutual."

I fidgeted with my cup for a second, then took a deep breath. "Did I tell you I kissed a girl right before I left Iowa?"

Em raised an eyebrow, her green eyes on mine, silently letting me continue.

"It was really great," I admitted. "Definitely something I'd like to do again. With her, I mean. If I can get back. So that'll be a fun one for Mom and Dad to deal with if we survive the impact. My new life of crime, my possible gayness. They're gonna freak."

Em sighed, then said, quietly, "Well, that's on them." She grinned again. "But if it helps, I think my scooter stealing, car thief, runaway little sister who might be gay has turned out to be pretty damn cool."

I laughed. "That's good. I'm really glad."

She looked up, clocking how high the sun was in the sky. "We should get back to work. We need to finish up before it gets too hot, or all the flowers will wilt."

She reached down and held out a hand to help me get up off the ground, and I took it, then followed her back into the rainbow of color that was all around us.

****

After we put the flowers away and cleaned the buckets, I found Bazooka waiting for us outside the shed.

"Hello Bazooka," Em said. She still seemed a little guarded around him, but that was probably a more normal reaction to finding yourself speaking to an imp than mine had been. Most people would probably be a little hesitant, less inclined than me to pop the goose and whoever was possessing him on the back of a scooter and run away from home after knowing them for barely a week.

"Em." Bazooka inclined his head. "Been eating the bugs off your roses all morning. Very nice crop you're raising out there." He burped. "Juicy."

"Glad you think so," Em said, "but the roses are the actual crop, not the bugs."

Bazooka cackled. "Well, rethink that. It's like an avian spa here. Fresh worms everywhere, more grain than you could ever eat. You could charge a fortune for admittance."

Em laughed, then her face turned serious. "So Bazooka. What happens to you after all this?" She waved at the sky. "You know, when the comet hits."

Bazooka fluttered his wings and looked at Em, consideringly. "Well, if you're asking if I'll die, the answer is no." He stretched his neck taller. "As long as I wait until impact, the real me will survive."

"What does that mean?" I was still fuzzy on some of the rules.

Bazooka sighed dramatically, sounding put upon. "Didn't I tell you this on brownie night? There are rules to this prison. I can't off myself: if I do, I'll migrate into some other nearby animal body. Still imprisoned. Otherwise, don't you think I would've walked in front of a truck the second I found myself here? It's not that simple."

"I—I didn't know that," I said.

"The whole point is for me to be stuck here and have to watch the comet land," he snapped. "I'm the witness. After that, the goose is toast, but I am back to normal. As far as I know."

"So, you'll have a different form, then?" Em asked.

"Yeah. More vaporous. I can take a solid form if I want to, but I don't have to. When I'm resting, I'm a lot more like…" He stopped for a second, frowning. "Like smoke."

I blinked, interested. This hadn't come up before.

"So, can you do anything?" Em asked, voice serious. "I mean, Lou told me you can't stop the comet, but can you do anything to protect anyone? Can you save Lou?"

"Just Lou?" Bazooka said, eyes glittering. "Not you and your cute little boyfriend and all your friends?"

Em frowned. "Could you do all of that?"

Bazooka plopped down in the dirt. "No," he admitted. "Probably not."

"So save Lou, then. Can you?"

"I don't know," Bazooka said. "My powers are limited, but possibly."

I cleared my throat, and they both looked at me. "What's the point of that, though? The world would still be a big molten rock, right? And I don't want to be the last living person on Earth."

Bazooka shrugged. Em looked at me, then back at the goose.

"I suppose you're right," she said. "It was just a stray idea. I'd like it, knowing you were going to survive. Be nice to know someone was still here after we're all gone."

Bazooka said nothing, but his eyes lingered on me.

****

We sat down for a smaller meal late that evening, the three of us. Dark greens from the farm mixed with some edible flower buds and goat's cheese to make a peppery salad. Someone had baked bread. We tore steaming hunks off it, eating it with our fingers.

"I'll leave you two to it," Marcus said as the meal ended. "I need to go do the books for the month." He leaned over to drop a tender kiss to the top of Em's head and headed to his office near the back of the house.

I sat fiddling with my fork as I finished a slice of pie.

"So, what are you guys doing? You know, about the comet. Anything?"

Emily put down the dishtowel she'd been wiping the table with and sat. "Like what, Lou?" she asked, her voice gentle. "There's not much we can do."

"Did you ever think about running away somewhere? Trying to find a shelter?"

Emily looked thoughtful. "Yeah, we talked about it at first. But there wasn't enough time to build a shelter of our own and stock it with all the supplies we would need to last a couple of years, and it didn't seem super likely that we were going to get a bunk anywhere else. Small-time flower farming queer couples aren't real high on the government's list of people to save."

I balled up my napkin. "Well, that sucks."

"Yeah. But in the end, the only solution we saw was to stay on the farm and make the most of the time we have here. We decided to take care of our tenants and keep doing the things we do: caring for the plants and helping make sure the people left in town don't starve before the end."

"That's why you still do the markets?"

Em nodded. "Yeah. The trucks mostly stopped running weeks ago. If it weren't for the farms still operating, things would get pretty tight around here. This is our community, you know? I feel like this town welcomed me when I needed a home."

The people of Bend welcomed her when everyone else had rejected her. Suddenly, those waves of nausea and remorse hit me again, curling my toes. Whether Em blamed me, the guilt and shame of my family pressed down on me like a boulder. I stared at the table in front of me, feeling the breath seep out of me like a punctured balloon.

"Oh!" I said, struck by something I'd forgotten. "I wrote you letters!"

"You did?"

"Oh my God, so many letters. Over a hundred,

actually." I looked down, unable to account for the sudden wave of shyness that had overcome me.

"I wish I could have read them."

I looked up. "Well, you can. I brought them with me."

"You didn't!"

"Absolutely did."

Em's face was a wonder. "You brought both a goose and all the letters you wrote me? What are you, a magician? Do you have a really deep, magical pocket somewhere?"

"Saddlebags," I said. "They're in my room. You want them?"

Em's first attempt to get words out failed. Then she scrubbed a hand over her face and tried again. "Yes," she said, her voice half-choked. "Yes, please. I very much want them. Can I please have them?"

I pushed back my chair and ran to my room to dig out the notebooks. And then I deposited the unruly pile in front of Emily and fled to my room.

****

I jolted awake the next morning in a panic. I'd forgotten that some of my letters were less-than-nice. There were at least three where I'd been angry at Em for abandoning me. There was one I clearly remembered where I'd berated my then brother for not taking me along, using pretty awful names to express my point. What was I thinking, leaving the pile with Em? What if she was upset?

I checked the clock. Almost noon. Great. I'd done something awful, and overslept on the final, busiest day before the market. And with only two weeks left before impact, sleeping in felt like an inexcusable loss of time with Em.

The kitchen was empty. I grabbed a cup of cold coffee from the pot and headed for the barn, my heart in my throat.

Bazooka was sitting on the back steps, looking peaceful. "There you are. I was wondering if they'd poisoned you or something."

I blushed. "It seems I'm low on sleep. I can't stop drifting off."

"Makes sense. You've either been a prisoner or been camping in less than ideal circumstances for the last few weeks. It hasn't exactly been restful."

I huffed. That was the truth. I looked around, observing Marcus and a couple others out in the fields. No sign of Em. "What do you think of it here?"

Bazooka fluttered his wings and then smoothed them back down. "It's a good place, well-managed. Lots of land. There's an actual pond in the back, although it's full of ducks. I had a brawl with a couple of them last night and now I've got squatting rights to the easternmost end."

"Please tell me you didn't kill anyone."

He gave me a look. "Like I'm going to go to all that bother for a duck. No, I just intimidated them. I'm roughly twice their size, and I'm way meaner. Anyway, Em's cool and Marcus is a good guy. He's been passing me worms when he finds them."

"That's good. Know where Em is?"

He pointed his long neck at the blue wooden barn behind the field. "In there, I think." He pulled a sour face. "Chickens. Ugh. Remind me not to go in there again. They're so bitchy."

I laughed. "Thanks, Bazooka."

****

I found Em alone in the barn, a basket of blue-green eggs at her side. She sat on the floor, three chickens on her lap while a dozen others scrabbled around on the barn floor, looking for feed.

"They sure like you," I said, joining Em on the floor.

She looked up and grinned. "Meet my biggest fans—Roxie, Mixie, and Pixie. They're special friends of mine."

I leaned in and ruffled their feathers. They ignored me and continued in their single-minded devotion to Em. I knew chickens. I understood.

"Hey, so." I stopped, trying to find the words. "I know my letters were kind of all over the place. Emotionally, I mean. I hope you weren't—"

Em raised her head and looked at me. "Your letters were amazing, Lou. I can't tell you how much reading them meant to me. I don't even know where to start with all the things I feel about them."

I forced a fake laugh. "Like irritated?"

"No. Like sad I missed all that. But also like I was getting to see who you were during the last six years." Em swallowed. "It makes me really sad, but also really happy, all at the same time. Does that make any sense?"

"Yeah." Did it ever. My throat tightened up. "We lost a lot of time."

"You know I wanted to come back for you like a million times, right?" she said, not looking at me.

I followed her gaze out to the hills around us and let that one sink in until words came. "I'm not a kid anymore, Em. I know you were eighteen, and you weren't ready to raise a kid."

Emily laughed, but the sound was a little strangled.

"I wasn't really in any shape to take care of you, that's true. I could hardly take care of myself. But I'm not sure it was better to leave you there, filled with all those feelings, and with no one to help." She curled forward, cupping her arms around her knees, and fidgeted a little. "I should've tried harder. I should've found a way to get in touch with you that Mom and Dad couldn't intercept, except I didn't know if they were keeping you from writing or if you didn't want to hear from me. It was all so confusing—"

I bumped shoulders with Em, cutting her off. "Now who's doing the guilt thing?"

She took a deep breath and settled back against the wall. "Ha. You got me there, Lou."

"We're a mess," I said, keeping my voice light.

"Must be genetic. Corn fields, earnestness, and guilt, born and bred."

I laughed.

Em reached over and took my hand. "Whatever insanity made you decide to run away on a scooter and drive two thousand miles during the biggest disaster in the planet's history, I'm so glad you did. Even if we don't get much time together. I'm very glad you're here."

****

I enjoyed market day more than I expected. The sky was blue, it was sunny, and it was familiar work, piling vegetables into baskets in ways that made them look appealing, ringing up customers like I had at the petting zoo, sorting eggs into boxes. We were busy for the first hour, but when it slowed down, I took a break to go check in with Belinda.

Chimes tinkled as I pushed open the door of the cafe,

and Belinda and Jonah looked up from something in the newspaper they were examining together.

"Lou!" Belinda said, her face lit up by her smile. She waved me over to a stool at the counter. "Are you okay, honey? I've been wondering what happened to you!"

"I'm sorry," I said as I sat down. "I didn't mean to disappear."

"I hope it means you found what you were looking for?"

If my face could crack from the force of a smile, it would've. "I did! I found him. Her."

Belinda grabbed the coffeepot and two cups. "Now this sounds like even more of a story," she said as she poured. "Please tell me everything."

I pulled the cup of coffee into my hand, more to enjoy the warm feeling of the ceramic cup against my skin, and started at the beginning.

****

"Did you find her?" Em asked when I got back.

I smiled. "Yeah. Let her know I haven't been kidnapped and that I'm staying at the farm. I mentioned earlier that I might have a cult after me, actually. I think she was a little worried."

Em laughed. "Okay, good. I'd like to meet her. You seem close."

I mulled that over. A few months ago, I would've called myself guarded to a fault, too afraid to let anyone know me; no one in Iowa except Maggie really knew my secrets. And now? Now I seemed to meet people—Ivy, Mari, Belinda, even Marcus—and immediately bare my soul to them, even if they were nearly strangers. Had I lost my inhibitions entirely with the looming end of the world, or was there something more to it? Maybe the ticking clock made it easier to override the bullshit small talk and gossip and really connect with people. Or maybe I'd been waiting all these years to meet people I could tell the truth to. About myself, about Em, about everything I couldn't share at home.

Maybe the new me was just more willing to be open than I'd ever realized.

Maybe I was brave.

Chapter Twenty-Seven

September 26, 2024
Dear Mom and Dad,
I know you won't get this letter. I'm not going to even pretend I can send it. There's no point—there are only twelve days left. But writing has become a habit, and today I realized that maybe my last letter needed to be to you.

It feels right, somehow.

I made it to Bend, where Em is. I am NOT going to tell you about all the things that happened to me on the way. You might have a heart attack before the comet even arrives. But I made it here, eventually, and I'm safe.

And I did it, Mom. Dad. I found Em.

But I'm getting ahead of myself.

Do you have any idea how much I missed Emmett after he left? Whatever you thought of his choices and his lifestyle, he was my first friend, my first playmate, the person I looked up to more than anyone in the world. Do you know how it destroyed me when you sent him away? Do you know how that hit me? I felt so many things—devastated, lonely, furious. Terrified you'd do the same to me. Nothing ever felt completely safe again.

But I also want to tell you I know you aren't cartoon villains, and that whatever I think of your reasoning, you were trying to do what you thought was right. And that I left because I had to do this, not because I hate you. I disagree with some of your choices and a lot of your beliefs, but I know you love me and you've always tried to do right by me. And if I've learned anything lately, it's that love is complicated. Messy. Convoluted. And that I love you too.

Em has grown into an amazing person, even with all that happened. I'm spending the last days on the farm Em co-owns with their partner now. We're talking a lot about the years we missed. It's really nice to get to know each other again, as scared as we both are about what's coming.

I hope you make it through the comet. I hope we all do. If we survive and I can, I'll try to get back to you, at least for a visit. But my guess is that this is goodbye.

Thank you for my life.

Love, Lou.

****

Back at the farm a few nights later, Marcus lit a fire in an old oil drum, and we sat out around it with the entire group, cooking hotdogs over the fire and even roasting a large bag of marshmallows someone found. There weren't any graham crackers or chocolate to make them into smores, but they were still sticky and golden and delicious. One tenant brought out an old guitar and played softly, and laughter and conversation filled the air.

As the evening quieted down, people drifted away, until it was just Marcus, Em, and me. And Bazooka, of course. He'd been doing a good job of not revealing his identity to anyone except the three of us.

I looked over at Marcus and Em, their hands entwined and their faces blanketed in the flicker of golden light. The goodness of the moment suddenly hurt like a cracked rib as the countdown rang out in my head. Nine days. Nine days. Nine days. I squeezed my eyes shut, and the firelight played on my lids, awash in both the pain and a sudden, burning fury that made my fists curl and my shoulders go rigid. It wasn't fair! How could I get this back and then lose it so soon?

"I can't believe this is all ending," I cried. "How are you both okay with this?"

Marcus looked up at me from his seat by the fire. "We're not okay. But we can't stop it or change it, we can't escape it, and we don't have the resources to build some kind of underground survival complex like your friends in Idaho."

"Not my friends."

He made a gesture of acknowledgment. "So, Em and I decided that only leaves us with one real course of action."

"Keep living our lives," Em said, reaching out and taking Marcus's hand. The firelight lit her face in strange angles, making her look so familiar and so entirely foreign at the same time. I watched the play of light and shadow, mesmerized and broken. "All we can do is tend to the things we love. And grieve, but mostly make the time we have left meaningful, if we can."

Marcus's face did this complicated dance of emotion, landing on a smile of such love and loss that my heart nearly broke at the sight. "Would we want more time together? Of course. But this is what we have. We got the last two years, loving each other, running this farm." He squeezed Em's hand. "It's not enough. It could never be enough. But also, it's everything."

Bazooka had to spoil the moment; it was like a social imperative. He stood from his spot where he'd been dozing by the fire and glared at all of us. "So what, you're going to sit here? Like lambs to the slaughter? You're not going to even try to find a fucking cave or a hole in the ground or even a basement or anything?" He turned and honked angrily at the sky. "I should've left you in Idaho, Lou. At least then you'd have had a damn chance."

He stalked off into the night and we all stared after him.

"Your goose has a potty mouth," Marcus observed.

"You haven't heard the half of it," I said. I heaved myself up off the ground and shrugged apologetically. "Excuse me. I better make sure he's not off setting fire to anything."

****

It wasn't hard to find him. A pissed off goose who's making no effort to conceal his agitation cuts quite a path through a field. I could hear him batting aside grasses and honking aggressively from a mile away.

He stopped dead, obviously aware I was behind him. "Go away."

"Bazooka... Falthaom... are you okay?"

He turned on me and flung his neck out straight, his posture somehow accusatory. "No, I'm not okay. This stupid body is fucking fond of you and now so am I. It's like a virus or something. I can't seem to shake it off anymore. You're going to die? And you're okay with that?"

I wrapped my arms around myself. "No, of course I'm not okay with that. I'm terrified. But it's not like I have much of a choice."

"Ivy and Dan are going to live. You would've too if you stayed."

"Ivy and Dan are going to live for a *while*," I said. "Who knows what they're going to find when they come out of that bunker, though? It might be worse for them, in the end."

Bazooka flapped his wings and took a step closer. "I'm not going to die, you know. I mean, the goose will, but I'll still be alive afterward, and I still have a bit of my powers. I might—" He stopped. "No, never mind."

"You might what? Tell me!"

"I can't save everyone. But I might be able to save you," Bazooka said, his voice low and urgent. "I could summon enough power to protect you from whatever is coming, I think. I could keep you alive, help you get somewhere safe after."

I turned to stare at the outline of the distant hills against the moonlit sky, trying to land on a feeling. It was getting harder and harder not to think about what was coming now that I'd found Emily, Em, my brother-now-sister and still the person I loved most in the world. Now that impact day was so much closer, I was aware, like a subtle web of electricity, of every single person I currently or had ever loved, sprinkled across the planet. My parents, sitting in a tent in the churchyard at home, missing me, praying for the end to be kind. Maggie and her family. The teachers who had been kind to me when no one else was. My aunts and uncles and cousins scattered around the Midwest. An old friend from kindergarten who'd moved away. Mari in her library. Michael in his visitor's booth. Christina and Max in Jackson at their endless, hopeful party. Even Ivy. Everyone. They shone like little pinpricks of light in my mind, and I felt like, if I concentrated enough, I could bring them here with nothing more than the power of my love.

Less than two weeks left. While I could stuff the feelings under before, now I was waking up at least once a night with my vision full of flames, a visceral terror squeezing every muscle and turning my limbs to stone. I'd lay in bed and gasp raggedly until the feeling eased up. It was coming so soon. Obliterating all these pinpricks of love. Obliterating me.

And to find out I might not have to be burned to ash by the impending comet strike?

It was tempting. It was so, so tempting.

"But—what about Em?"

"I don't know, maybe. But I couldn't make it much bigger."

Adding Em to the mix? I stuffed down an impulsive "yes, please." The two of us, together, surviving, trying to make it in whatever came next? I could see it playing out like a movie. Like some grim, smoke-infested version of those books we used to read about the little girl who lived in a dugout on the prairie. I wouldn't need anyone else if I had Em, would I?

The problem hit me quickly. We weren't individuals. We were interconnected with the people who loved us, who we loved. To save only me left my web of friends and family behind. Saving only me and Em left Marcus, which Em would never accept. Cramming in Marcus and making it a three-person family left behind everyone Marcus cared about. There was no way to make the safety net big enough to make the decision less impossible.

I took a deep breath, cherishing for one more second the idea that it didn't all have to end in two measly weeks—and then I let it all out in a whoosh.

"I can't do it," I whispered. "I just can't. There are too many people I love that I'd be leaving behind. And that Em would leave behind."

Bazooka spread his bill at me threateningly. "If this is about how you don't deserve this, because everything in the fucking world is your fucking fault—"

"It isn't," I said. "Not anymore. It's just that I love Em, and I won't leave her. And she loves Marcus, and she won't leave him."

"You won't save yourself because of love?"

I nodded, and I felt the tears leak.

"If this is love, it's making you miserable!" he howled. "Look at you, you're weeping!"

I avoided the urge to wipe the tears away, and faced him squarely, letting him see the humanity as it left its tracks running down my cheeks.

"You wanted to know what it means to be human," I said. "And this is it. This right here. It means we aren't solitary creatures. It means we're worth more together than we are apart. It means that sometimes, in some circumstances, the love we feel for each other, for our families and loved ones, matters more than our own individual ambitions."

"If I could only get out of this idiotic body for five minutes," he said, but then he turned away to peck at the grass without finishing the sentence. I sat as the sun continued to slip behind the hills, but he never turned around to re-engage, and for some reason, the angle of his tail feathers made me think he would have wept if he knew how.

****

We sat in silence on opposite sides of the backyard. I was mulling over the whole situation, the offer Bazooka made, about how much it sucked to have to refuse it, and about his last partial thought. If he could get out of his body, he could what? Fix things?

Nine days. A little more than a week. The terror was slowly turning my blood to frozen slush. I could barely move at the thought of it. Whatever I'd said, I absolutely didn't want to die.

A sudden flash of an idea hit me, but it curdled my stomach so much that I almost couldn't bring myself to say it out loud. I forced the words out despite the buzzing in my head. "Bazooka. Wait. What did they say about your body?"

He didn't turn around, but his neck perked up and I could tell he was interested. "What did who say?"

"The demon who stuck you here, in my goose."

"That I was stuck here until the comet kills the goose. And that I can't do anything deliberate to free myself."

I swallowed, more and more sure that my horrifying idea might have merit. I wasn't sure I wanted it to. "Did they say that exactly? Like word for word?

He turned around, head cocked, clearly unsure what I'm getting at. "I… think so."

"Did they say *you* can't free yourself or that no one can free you?"

Bazooka's eyes gleamed; he was catching on. "Are you thinking—"

The person I used to be, the sheltered teenager who knew nothing of the world, howled as I said it. The new me, all too aware of the compromises the world forces upon people, spat it out. "That maybe someone else can free you? Without you hopping into the next available body? Maybe they didn't think of that one?"

"You're right! It could work. We don't know for certain, but it's worth a try. Kill me. Let's find out."

I jumped to my feet. It was too much. I wanted to take it all back, wipe it all away. "Wait. Wait a second. I'm not going to up and murder you at the drop of a hat like that."

"I mean, I know this stupid bird's a friend of yours and all that, but one goose versus the fate of all humanity? This should be easy math," Bazooka said, a dangerous glitter in his eye. "Even for a someone like you."

Someone like me? Someone from a small town, with a conservative upbringing? Someone recovering from a frightening childhood half spent wondering if my parents would throw me out someday? Someone who made terrible mistakes? The possibilities were so vast that I couldn't refuse to ask. "What does that mean, exactly?"

Bazooka sat his fluffy body down in a huff. "Someone kind," he spat out. "Someone who would never hurt a fly if you didn't have to. Or a goose."

That was not what I expected. "What's happened to you, Falthaom the Repulsive?" I whispered, not trusting my voice. "You could've said so many horrible things right there. A month ago you would've."

"Yeah, yeah," he sighed. "Kick an imp when he's down, why don't you? I've gone soft. Five weeks with you and I've lost my edge."

I nodded. "I won't tell anyone."

"I appreciate that."

I blinked hard, trying to clear my vision as tears ran down my cheeks. "I don't want Bazooka to die. But if he has to, how could we do it without hurting him?"

"Fast twist to the neck is the usual method, but that

might be too much to ask," Bazooka replied. "Someone could run me over. It'd be quick, and you don't have to be the one to do it."

I shook my head. "No, too painful, and he'd be aware of it, wouldn't he? I'd rather he didn't know. Can we, like, do it while he's asleep?"

"You mean can I hypnotize him or something? Trust me, aside from the infuriating waves of affection, the biological goose isn't super aware of what's going on most of the time. He's mostly asleep down inside some corner of his soul."

"Could I… could I talk to him?"

"What, you want to explain? I can't relinquish complete control of this body."

I stared back. "But you could ease up, right? Let him through?"

He flopped his neck flat on the ground in defeat. "You're impossible."

I smiled lopsidedly, relief at a possible solution grappling with the idea of deliberately killing my goose. I'd never killed anything. It felt impossible.

He closed his eyes, and a second later I could feel it—the change from imp to goose. Bazooka blinked his eyes open, looked at me, and squawked in curiosity.

"Bazooka? Is that you, sweetie?"

Bazooka the goose—and only the goose—bobbed and waddled his way over to me, and climbed heavily into my lap. He pecked softly at my head and hair, then nuzzled and wrapped his long neck over my shoulder like he used to, and I wrapped my arms around him and hugged him, eyes closed, tears leaking out of the corner of my eyes, running into his thick feathers.

We sat like that, rocking gently, for several minutes,

while I tried to explain. How much I loved him. What had happened over the last few weeks. Where we were now, and what we needed to do. How sorry I was to lose him. Of course, he didn't understand; there was no way he could. But I know he understood the hugs, the warmth and affection that had always been between us. And he understood when I pulled out a handful of corn, always his favorite treat, and scratched his back as he gobbled it down, kernel by kernel.

"Okay, Falthaom," I said, wiping my eyes. "You can come back."

The goose shivered and then straightened up into a different posture that meant that Falthaom had resumed control of higher brain functions. When his head turned toward me, I knew who I was speaking to.

"Yes, I'm crying," I snapped. "Don't pick on me about it. Sentimental sap, remember?"

He clucked deep in his throat and carefully stepped free. "Well," he said, "shall we?"

I wiped my eyes. "I'm going to go get everything we need. I'll be right back."

****

In the bathroom, I rummaged through Em's medicine cabinet until I found the sleeping pills she'd mentioned earlier in the week, then I went out to find her. She was at the kitchen sink, scrubbing marshmallow goo off the metal rods we'd roasted them on. When I approached, she turned, dishrag in hand, and smiled.

I shoved the bottle at her. "Can I have a handful of these?" She looked up, alarmed. "They're not for me! Really! Bazooka needs them. He—he's sick. You can come observe."

Em looked horrified. "Wait, what? You're putting

295

him down? Why?"

I took a deep breath and spewed out the tale as best as I could.

"…and so we figured it out," I concluded, tears overflowing again. "We have to kill the goose to let him out, and then he can try to do something about the comet."

"Why do we think your imp is going to stop a giant rock?"

"Well," I said, "he put it there to begin with. And he's got an idea. And literally, it's our only shot at this point."

"And do we trust him?"

I did. Falthaom the Repulsive might have been snarky and cruel from time to time. He might have been tempted to leave me. And he might not always be the most pleasant company in the world, but the fact of the matter was that Falthaom, while in the body of my goose, had never deserted me, despite multiple opportunities. He didn't have to see me safely all the way across the country, but he did. And if he said he was going to help now, I genuinely believed him.

"I do," I said. "He's our last chance. Will you help me?"

She looked down at the prescription bottle in her hand, reading the label carefully, then looked around the kitchen. "I will. But not like this. There's no way of telling what sleeping pills will do to a goose. It might not be the most humane approach, if it even works. It might make him super hyper or give him a heart attack or kidney damage or something, but not kill him."

"Then what should we do?"

"Like Dad taught me to do with the chickens at

home. We break his neck. It's the easiest and most painless way."

I cried harder. "I can't do that, Em. I just can't."

She stood and wrapped me in a hug and I breathed in the soft, warm smell of her flannel shirt and felt the familiar bones of her shoulder. Em. My family. My home.

"I know." She squeezed me tighter, her head leaning into mine. "I'll do it."

****

It was quick. Falthaom made a joke of blessing Em with absolution before it happened, which I think made everyone except him uncomfortable. And then he tucked himself into Em's side without complaint.

"Goodbye," I said. I closed my eyes, and there was a quiet crack, and then it was over.

Chapter Twenty-Eight

Interlude: Bazooka

Fine.

So you want me to learn about humanity?

You want me to understand them?

Here's what I understand.

Humans are impossible to fully understand. They're idiots with the sense of literal children. They love each other and they hate each other. They do terrible things to other people, and yet they'll lay down their lives for a loved one at the most unexpected times. They will insult you, mock you, berate you, and then wrap you in a warm blanket when you're cold and make you soup. They cry at the slightest thing, snap at each other when they mean to be kind, and they couldn't read their own emotions clearly if the gods gave them a handbook.

They're absolutely infuriating.

They're insanely wonderful.

And gods be damned, I don't want them all to die.

Chapter Twenty-Nine

Interlude: Bazooka

Freedom feels as good as I remembered. The only reason it doesn't overwhelm me, that I don't lose myself in the immediate bliss of the sensation, is that I knew it was coming, that feathery idiot's death. If my discorporation had been a surprise, I don't think I could have stopped myself from veering off like a pinball, wildly ricocheting off mountain and valley, ocean floor to upper stratosphere.

But no. I have a purpose, and for once in my life, it's a fucking noble one. This is a unique feeling for me, and I intend to savor it. I suspect it will be some time before I can feel noble again. The chance to make a huge, symbolic sacrifice doesn't come often to my kind.

In the deep, frosty night, I unfurl all the parts of my being into the surrounding darkness, enjoying one long, luxurious stretch before I propel myself up and out. Through the flight lanes that are now mostly empty, and even further into the stratosphere, until I break through the delicate edge of the Earth's atmosphere and into the vast chill beyond.

I can't feel the cold, not really, but the transition makes me want to shiver. I look around slowly, clocking the moon, the nearby planets, a satellite or two—and then I catch sight of it.

The comet.

It's closer than I realized, easily visible, although it's partly an illusion—it's so unimaginably huge that it's further away than it looks. Even so, with so little time until impact, I'm really splitting hairs. I zoom in for a closer look, and float there, stunned, a tiny speck of black smoke against a mind-bending colossus. It's stunningly, phenomenally beautiful—and believe me, I've seen nearly everything. I've never seen a comet so big or so luminous this close before. Is it made of diamond? Why does it shimmer like that? Its long glowing tails—one blue, one white—trail out behind it like a forked tongue. Of course there's no noise, but my mind helpfully supplies the sound effects—a fizzing, sparkle-pop hum with harmonic overtones.

Beneath the wonder and awe, I'm aware of another recognition—that it's definitely too big and too fast for me to move directly. I may have stretched the truth to the breaking point several times with Lou, but never about that. I can't vaporize it. I can't fling it away with brute strength.

I follow its trajectory with my eyes, calculating, and confirm that it's true what the Earthers are saying. It's on a direct impact course, probably going to hit somewhere in Mexico. Whatever the continent did to piss off the original Pangaean gods, it must have been something truly dire, because it seems unfair to have the new existential threat hit in nearly the same place as the dinosaur-killer did. Not that it really matters. It's large enough and close enough that it's going to do an extreme amount of damage. It will undoubtedly wipe Lou and her friends out on impact, and I wouldn't put big money on any of the ordinary, non-bunkered humans making it very far beyond the next year.

Well, that can't be. Now that I'm free, it's time for me to do what I do best. Which is cheat death, kick ass, and win.

I look around for the best and closest item of the appropriate shape. What to choose? I'm tempted to use a bunch of the satellites belonging to that idiot billionaire who's actively trying to destroy the world with his self-driving cars and faulty communications networks, but in the end, I reject them as not heavy enough to make the impact I need. The idea of using the moon makes me grin, but losing its gravitational field would destroy the Earth in a whole new way, so I give up on that one. Same for any of the smaller planets, even though I've always had a grudge against Pluto.

Back to the asteroid belt, then. Sorting through them is like trying to find the perfect rock for skipping across water; it must be exactly the right shape, the right size, made of the right material to not shatter from the force of my shot. I'm picky about this. I take a while to find exactly the right one.

There. There it is. The perfect contours for what I have in mind. A good quantity of metal—mostly iron—to give it heft, plus some significant ice crystals to vaporize in the heat of impact and give everything some extra oomph. It's jagged on one end, to help it punch into the comet's surface. It's perfect.

And now? I just need a lever.

Something like a croquet mallet.

Perfect.

****

It unfolds in slow motion.

A dull, misshapen rock, not that big, shoots across the sky, heading straight for the heart of the gleaming, diamond-hued monster lumbering its way toward Earth.

As it gets closer, it's practically swallowed by the gargantuan size of the colossus in front of it, but if you squint, and you're not distracted by the Earth beyond it, you can still make it out. See? Right there. It tumbles end over end and hits with an explosion of force that belies its small size.

Right there. In the center.

Right in one of the major seams of ice that are holding this giant accumulation of nickel and iron and ice together.

The resulting blast is brighter than the moon, brighter than the stars winking millions of miles away in the background, brighter than all the planets.

I drift, spellbound, waiting for the dust to clear, waiting to see. Did it work? Did I save them? Will they live?

Chapter Thirty

On Earth, it's touted as a miracle. Somehow, the comet, which broke all orbital models right from the start, collided with another object in space, vaporizing a large portion of it and turning the rest into much smaller pieces, with wildly differing trajectories. They call it a debris cloud. We can already see some pieces streaking by the Earth in the night sky like a meteor shower. Most of them are on a trajectory to miss the Earth entirely.

The Earth isn't totally off the hook—some of Lucinda's pieces are still on an impact course, but they're much, much smaller. Survivable, surely. It's too early to tell where they're all going to land. There will undoubtedly be impacts, wildfire, maybe flooding. But, the scientists say, it won't be a planet-killing event. Most of us will survive.

Around the world, celebrations break out and feverish work gets underway. Frenzied scientists pound out models of what objects will hit where, what size they are, what we can do. People emerge from their hidey-holes like mole people, blinking wide-eyed into a sun they hadn't expected to see again. Others refuse to come out, still terrified, unable to accept that heralded disaster might be averted.

There's an undercurrent of sorrow to the celebrations. Despite our miraculous save, so much has already been lost. Around the world, people wonder—

how do we go on from here? Many people abandoned their homes, their jobs, their lifelong beliefs, even their loved ones. Governments, banking systems, higher education, and social safety nets have disintegrated. Many people died in violence, in suicide, or from long-term medical conditions that no longer seemed worth fighting.

Relationships were shored up, torn down, formed, and lost as we saw through the illusions we'd built over the years and glimpsed each other as we really were, the drives that moved us when it truly mattered. It's hard to pretend, after something like this, that we're the people we were before. We're newly hatched, blinking at the sky like baby goslings, our primary feathers not yet grown in to give us the gift of flight.

Nothing will ever be the same.

One thing everyone agrees on—the people of planet Earth have a lot of work to do, to mend what we can mend, to move on in a new way.

****

The remaining members of the Bend town council throw a gigantic party in Drake Park the night it's confirmed: "Comet Lucinda is dead. Long Live Meteor Shower Lucinda." It's a crazy, brilliant night—it seems like half the remaining residents of Bend are in attendance, and someone, somewhere, has found an old stash of sparklers left over from some old Fourth of July celebration. Kids run around clutching them and people are laughing and crying and hugging one another with abandon. As much as it feels like a party at the end of the world, I think we're all aware that it's also something else entirely. A party to mark the beginning of something.

A new world, one we hadn't expected. Torn from oblivion by a hair's breadth.

As the streaks of brilliant light dash across the sky in fits and start, as the people watching gasp in a combination of admiration and fear at the pyrotechnics, what I know, deep down, is this: Falthaom is still out there.

After going through so much together, it's like I can feel him. We're connected by a cosmic string. I know he's still there, helping to clean up the mess. Late that night, I'm almost convinced that if I listen closely, on the right frequency, I can hear him, carefully lining up his shot, chalking his proverbial pool cue, and cackling like the demented imp he is as he nudges one piece after another out of disaster's way.

In future years, scientists will gather satellite imagery, review the films and snapshots and recordings made in these last days. The scientists will slowly puzzle over the data of Comet Lucinda, trying to determine why its behavior at the last moments broke all known laws of planetary motion and orbital mechanics. Why it behaved like it was being buffeted around with intent, rather than breaking up randomly and engulfing the Earth in its debris cloud. And most importantly, certain subsets of scientists, the brethren of those who clipped microphones to NASA's Perseverance rover on Mars and recorded the Martian winds, the sisters of the researcher who converted wave forms from distant galaxies to audio to let humans hear the music of the stars—they'll debate behind locked doors and in secret chambers why the sound of Comet Lucinda is like nothing ever heard before, on Earth or in space.

It's the sound of a manic goose, honking with glee,

as it sets another rock hurtling off into the universe.
We're going to survive. I know it.
We've got Falthaom on our side.

A word about the author...

Megan Zalkan grew up in Ohio, and then went on her own life-changing road trip to gorgeous, rain-soaked Seattle, where she currently lives with her husband, daughter, and too many cats. She's been a technical writer, grant researcher, concert violinist, Reiki practitioner, and occupational therapist, and has an MA in Professional Writing from Carnegie Mellon. She loves to write humorous YA and adult fiction, always with a thread of magic running through, and she reads compulsively. The Last Road Trip is her first published work. http://www.meganzalkanwriter.com

Thank you for purchasing
this publication of The Wild Rose Press, Inc.

For questions or more information
contact us at
info@thewildrosepress.com.

The Wild Rose Press, Inc.
www.thewildrosepress.com